Marlborough Man

A Novel

Milda L. Leonard

DEDICATION

To my oldest son, who has always been my biggest supporter but swore he would never read this book.

Marlborough Man

Inspired by true events

CHAPTER 1
Sending out an SOS

Spring 2013

A shard of gray daylight sliced through the heavy drapery in Kaisa's hotel room. She extended her arms above her head and slid out of the desk chair to stretch her legs. Kaisa peeled back the layers to take a look from her 10th floor window. Down below, the road was quiet, aside from the sporadic whooshes of traffic. The streetlights were growing dim, and the sidewalks were virtually empty except for a jogger or two. *There is nothing better than a Sunday morning in a city. Even cities that never sleep take somewhat of a power nap in the early morning hours of a weekend, particularly on a Sunday.*

Kaisa looked forward to mornings like these, in whatever city she visited for business or pleasure. But she had an unusual history with this city and, despite that, long considered it to be her favorite place in the world.

She had arrived the night before, two days ahead of her conference, to dedicate a day to herself and enjoy the rare occurrence of freedom. She was staying at the Sheraton, not far from her old stomping ground. The landscape differed from when she was a college freshman decades earlier. Most of the city was unrecognizable, except for the protected historic landmarks. It had grown and morphed much like she had. One of the few semi-recognizable sites was her "beloved university." *Isn't that what he called it?* She smirked and shook her head.

Visiting her old school was on the list for today, but it was only 6 a.m. and her brain, like the sky, was still foggy. The heavy clouds were expected to dissipate later that morning, promising a clear day with little to no wind, a rarity for early April in Boston. Tired from working on her presentation for most of the night, Kaisa dove back into bed and closed her eyes, hoping to doze off for a few minutes but awoke to the sound of nearby church bells two hours later.

As if by impulse, Kaisa picked up her iPhone, checked her Gmail, Facebook, then pivoted to Twitter. Like the rest of society, she had come to rely on websites and apps to help navigate her life. Most of the time, she cursed modern technology, with everyone so obsessed with their phones, treating them like another appendage. But every once in a while, she wished she could have had access to all these digital accouterments back then.

But now, it was time to enjoy a little nostalgia and retrace old steps. She threw on her worn Northeastern sweatshirt and a pair of jeans. Maybe there was a newspaper in the lobby to help guide her itinerary, the old-fashioned way. When she opened her door, a complimentary Boston Globe lay at her feet as if she willed it there. Kaisa picked it up with a smile and went back into her room. *Reading the Sunday newspaper has become a lost art for some. Maybe that's why they were just giving this one away?*

Kaisa quickly scanned the front page for any major event or catastrophe. Finding nothing of the sort, she threw the remaining boring news aside and went straight for the Weekend section. She leafed through, considering the afternoon performance at the Boston Symphony, the food tasting at Faneuil Hall, along with other mainstream events and activities at unheard of places that must have emerged during her absence. *What I wouldn't give for a copy of the Boston Phoenix. I miss that rag with its listings for things like animation festivals and performance art.*

Next, she attempted the crossword but gave up after only being able to figure out three words. Kaisa was convinced Sunday newspaper crosswords were designed by a secret society of MENSA members and specifically intended for those with genius IQs or, at minimum, an ivy league education. To date, she had only met one person who could always finish them.

The Real Estate section was last, featuring luxury properties she could only dream of buying. There were plenty of those where she grew up, not that she ever saw the inside of one. Sometimes she would go to an open house pretending to be someone else, picturing herself in this new environment under entirely different circumstances. As she perused the listings, a prominently placed quarter-page ad with a familiar address brought her to an abrupt stop. *This isn't possible. Is it fate again?* she muttered. Her face flushed and that old nervous twinge in her stomach reemerged.

Priced at a "reasonable" $5.2 million, the studio apartment where she frequented so long ago was now part of a stunning converted single-family townhome with an Open House that afternoon. There was no way she was going to pass this up. But she couldn't go to that Open House in this outfit. Luckily, she had fancier work clothes in her suitcase that might help her blend in as a potential buyer.

But there were still a few hours to kill. She picked up an apple from the breakfast buffet and headed toward Northeastern. With her phone in hand and her earbuds in, a far cry from the cumbersome Walkman and headphones she used to carry everywhere, she selected a throwback playlist to transport her back in time. Her thoughts drifted to memories associated with each track, recreating scenes engraved in her soul.

She crossed Westland Avenue, around the corner from where she lived her freshman year. The old Stop & Shop that used to look like it barely passed the health code was now a beautiful Whole Foods Market with a five-story garage. The surrounding, dated, down-trodden neighborhood with affordable housing had received a much-needed facelift and had signs boasting studios for nearly $3000 a month. She marveled at the fact that she used to walk by herself through that area at night in blind faith and somehow always reached her destination unscathed.

Down the street was the infamous Hotel Hemenway. It was still standing, looking a lot fresher and more inviting. She turned the corner and proceeded down Hemenway Street, passing by 119 - her freshman year dorm - then continued toward the main campus. The apartment building, she lived in her sophomore year was reborn as a luxury high rise. It had skyrocketed along with the price of tuition. Given her financial circumstances back then, she could have never afforded it now.

A few steps away was the library, the one they finished building the year she graduated. She yanked on the heavy metal door, noting it was exceptionally quiet when she passed through. Most students were likely hungover or sleeping late except the young girl working behind the counter.

"Hi. Can you direct me to your periodicals section?" Kaisa asked.

"The what?" she said, crinkling one eye and raising an eyebrow.

"The magazines?"

"Yeah, whatever we have is over there next to the computers."

Kaisa found a People Magazine and settled in for some long-deserved time to herself. As she thumbed through the pages, she couldn't help recalling someone who spent plenty of time frequenting libraries, especially ones that were open all night. She flipped through to the empty crossword got up to make a copy and finished it in record time.

As her weather app predicted, it had turned into an ideal day. At noon, she returned to her hotel to change her clothes. This time she headed in the opposite direction toward Back Bay, picking out the old from the new – the foreign from the familiar. One of the newer features was a long, enclosed passageway that spanned across a good portion of her old route to work. How great would it have been on those bone-chilling days to avoid the wind, rain, or other nasty weather? Instead, she took many twists and turns around the Christian Science Center and the open-air shopping plaza that used to surround the Prudential Building. Sometimes she would cut through Saks Fifth Avenue to regain the feeling in her extremities before darting outside once again to get to Copley Place.

It appeared Copley Place, the upscale mall with its revolving retail stores, had transformed into an even more lavish shopping experience, barely a step down from Rodeo Drive. Even though she could afford to splurge a little now and then, she couldn't understand the need for a thousand-dollar designer handbag.

Thankfully, Au Bon Pain was still there on the lower level, but not her chicken tarragon sandwich. This cafe was her splurge when she was a poor college student; more than an hour's worth of pay, but a welcome switch from the university cafeteria, Cappy's cheesesteaks, or pizza. Much more than the menu had changed. Café tables were now filled with laptops or patrons engaged in deep face to Facetime conversations. She ordered the closest thing to her former favorite and chose a table opposite the window. Teems of people shuffled by on the sidewalk, but she only had one person in mind. He used to frequent the Copley trifecta: Place, Plaza, and Square, but mostly the indoor mall. She knew there would be little chance that she would ever see him again, but that didn't compel her to look any less intently at each passerby to try to pick him out from the crowd, wishing he would materialize.

Kaisa climbed the stairs up to the main level. The bookstore where she worked was no longer there, along with the three-story waterfall it was once nestled behind. It had gone by the wayside as many independent bookstores had in the digital age. She got on the escalator to ascend one more level recalling the sweet, inviting aroma of baked chocolate that used to waft down to greet her from another employer. It was on that level near that store where they met. Kaisa circled the area, retracing her steps and taking in the altered scenery, wishing that if she turned around, he would magically appear, like that winter day in 1987.

It was time to head to the Open House. The best way to get there was on the other side of the mall through the Westin Hotel. Its exit or entrance, depending on which direction she was going, still had a giant waterfall the entire length of the steep escalator. It reminded her of the tradition she had with her freshman year roommate. If they were going down the escalator on their way home from work, they would pull out whatever pennies they had and launch them in mid-descent into the flowing backdrop while making a wish. The rule was only to throw the penny if you were going down because wishes didn't work when pennies were thrown against gravity. Figuring she was heading in the right direction, it was an opportune time to pay tribute to the tradition. She reached into her sensible purse, pulled out a quarter, and launched it into the cascading flow with her eyes closed.

Kaisa arrived at 293 Marlborough Street, in a charming tree-lined neighborhood full of historic brownstones and spotted the Open House sign in front of its cobblestone walkway. She tried to disguise her awe as she entered the foyer of this beautiful, coveted five-story Back Bay townhome.

She picked up a listing sheet describing the property:

The home offers a generous floor plan and incredible architecture. The parlor level includes a welcoming sun-drenched reception room.

Indeed, it was nothing like the former entryway with dingy wallpaper and matted mauve carpeting. Kaisa was amazed that this brownstone, once a collection of unimpressive tiny studio apartment rentals, had reemerged as one of the most prime real estate locations in the city.

Starting at the top floor, Kaisa worked her way around the property. Every room was precisely decorated and perfectly staged. *It should be for the price tag.*

The second floor slapped her with an overwhelming sense of déjà vu. How ironic that her feeling was based on a French term. Kaisa glanced at the listing sheet:

The living room with a grand bay window and oversized fireplace presents an elegant setting for entertaining.

When she was there last, the setting hadn't been so elegant, but there was plenty of entertaining. That grand bay window was once the main focal point of Apartment 5. She recalled standing in front of its towering panes of glass, partially clothed, with his arms wrapped around her, the glow of the streetlights and the illuminated Prudential Building casting shadows on her once slender young frame.

"There's an amazing private roof deck with incredible views of Back Bay," said an agent boasting to a well-dressed prospective couple standing nearby.

How about that? It appears not all residents had access to the roof deck back then and had to seek them out elsewhere.

Oh no! An urgent rumble welled up in the pit of her stomach. Kaisa's eyes ricocheted around the room to make sure no one was looking as she discreetly ducked into the nearby bathroom. The once dark, drab bathroom with the rose-colored tub and tiles was bright, warm, and welcoming with a faint lavender scent. After taking a few deep breaths, she was grateful that the horrible sensation subsided. *This isn't the same place anymore.* He was long gone. But apparently, the thought of him hadn't lost its impact. He could still stir her insides even though she did not know if he was alive or dead.

She took a last look around the room. Compared to its current grandeur, it was a far cry from the highly intellectual crack den she knew with its dismal white paint, sheer curtains secured by butcher string, a lone futon mattress, and shelves and shelves of books. And don't forget the desk. The desk filled with his thesis' or theseses or whatever the plural was; papers intended for Harvard. This was his last known address. It had been 25 years since she last saw him and even longer since she had been at this quintessential residence. *1987. That was the year I got a crash course in everything. I had no idea what I was in for.*

Kaisa burst into her hotel room. She opened her laptop and entered what little facts or half-truths she knew about him into the search engine for at least the hundredth time. "I give up," she said under her breath as she pounded her fist.

Then it dawned on her. Facebook had community pages created by people looking for someone as a way of reaching out to the masses for help. Maybe she could harness the power of social media for answers that she hadn't been able to find on her own. Facebook was approaching two billion unique registered users with an audience dominated by her Generation-X demographic. She could cast quite a net. Social media was not an option back then. Hell, the internet didn't even exist.

That's how it was when she first fell in love with this city and with him. People could be more elusive, mysterious, and could easily disappear. Kaisa set up a new profile with the namesake Seeking Closure and created a 'Help Find Christopher Morton Community

Page.' Perhaps someone else had a similar encounter over this long period and was seeking the same sort of closure for something that wouldn't let them go. It was worth one last try.

CHAPTER 2
Open Your Heart to Me

Fall 1986

O ne chilly September morning, Kaisa and her parents left their pint-sized house in Westport, Connecticut, to make the three-hour trip to Boston. Kaisa felt like she was escaping into the night, departing from St. Charles Street at 5:30 a.m. in their pale blue 1978 Chevy Nova. As they drove along the highway, Kaisa rested her chin on her hand, watching the sun ascend over the horizon, taking it as a sign of a bright new beginning.

Her parents wanted her to go to a state college and live at home for the first two years to save money because that's all they could afford. But she had a tidy sum saved up over her short life and was willing to spend it all to get out of Westport and go away to school like almost all her classmates. It was Boston's majestic architecture and centuries of history that made her fall in love with the city when she did her college tours a year earlier.

Her father said: 'if you are going to go away to college, don't major in nothing.' But she was way ahead of him, deciding to enroll in the business program hoping Northeastern might help her secure the contacts that neither she nor her parents had.

"Don't worry Dad, someday, I'm going to be a successful executive in New York."

A majority of her classmates' fathers worked in New York City. These students were easily identified by brightly colored designer clothes with little alligators or horses on their chests. The fathers boarded the gray flannel express each morning to their esteemed high-level executive positions, while their stay-at-home mothers kept a strict diet of tennis, committees, and wine.

The only reason her parents could afford to live where they did was that they bought a tiny prefab two-bedroom house with a cracked foundation and no garage in 1961. The kitchen floor was so slanted that no one ever ate a level bowl of soup. Her parents had fled Eastern Europe as young teenagers with their families during World War II. They met and fell in love in a make-shift high school at a displacement camp. Neither went to college. When they reached 18 and were old enough to be assigned any type of work outside of the camp, life took over. Trying to measure up to the kids in her school was nothing compared to the hardships her parents faced at her age. For that, she was grateful.

"I think this is it," Kaisa said as she and her parents pulled up to 119 Hemenway. Her new home was not a traditional dorm but a converted white townhouse on University property. A smile spread wide across her face. "This is going to be awesome."

"I have to take a picture!" her mother exclaimed. She loved documenting every aspect of Kaisa's life and was ready with camera in hand to capture the moment.

Kaisa was assigned to the top floor. As luck would have it, the elevator had an impeccably timed out of order sign. She hoped someone had put it there as a joke, but it was accurate. She grabbed one handle and helped her dad drag a trunk full of items up four flights until she found her intended destination with a note saying: **Welcome to Suite 401.**

A bleach blonde with dark brown roots greeted her on the other side of the door. "Hi, I'm Mindy, I'm the Resident Assistant and one of your suitemates, and you are...?"

"Kaisa Blazielijus."

"Oh, that's how you pronounce your last name. Nice to meet you, and welcome to Northeastern. You are in Room A. There are three bedrooms in the suite, two are doubles, and my room is the single, and that's our bathroom. Take a look around. You are the first one here."

Mindy handed Kaisa a key to the suite and one for her room, which was the furthest from the door and the closest to the bathroom. The suite was way better than the other freshman dorms with the shared bathroom in the hallway. Kaisa peeked into her new space. It was a large, quiet room overlooking the fire escape at the back of the building, much larger than she expected and with more character than the mirror image cell blocks she had seen on her tour. She claimed the bottom bunk of the metal-framed bed and placed the new pink boombox her mother bought for her 18th birthday on top of the desk by the window. Kaisa unpacked her things while listening to her mixtape. She put away the clothes she had purchased at a discount to freshen up her wardrobe with what little money she had left after paying that first big tuition bill.

A few moments later, a thunder of suitcases echoed from the common area. She stretched her neck out to see who had arrived. There was a tall attractive brunette who resembled the actress Phoebe Cates and another girl barely five feet tall with dark shoulder-length hair and a boxy body. She was wearing a Bruce Springsteen concert shirt. *I'll bet she's from New Jersey.* Kaisa listened from her room as Mindy checked them in. The tall girl was named Heather, and the shorter girl was Jill, who was indeed from the Garden State. They were to share the other room in the suite.

It was getting close to noon, and Kaisa's new roommate still had not shown. Kaisa had looked her up in the hardcover bound freshman directory she received from the school along with a letter with her room and roommate assignment. Her name was Deborah McAllister, and she was from New York. She and Kaisa not only had similar features but were both enrolled in the business program. Over the summer, Kaisa had written her a letter to introduce herself, but she didn't respond.

"If you guys want to go to lunch, the dining hall is

open," Mindy called out from the common area. "Since it's move-in day, parents are welcome. I'd go, but I have to check in new students on the floor."

Kaisa overheard Jill and Heather decline Mindy's invitation and casually passed by their room. She proceeded to the dining hall with her parents. But she was too wound up and could barely eat a thing. Which, based on the food selection, wasn't a tragedy. After lunch, Kaisa said she pretty much had things covered, and her parents should probably go.

"Will you be okay?" her mom asked, giving her a hug.

"I'll be fine," she said, brushing away a tear from her eye. "I'll miss you."

"You can call me whenever you need anything," she replied, equally misty-eyed, before getting into the car.

"Don't go out with any losers," her dad added from the driver seat. "You seem to like them."

Kaisa smirked, shook her head, and ran back upstairs, where she found a new girl unpacking. "Hi, I'm Kaisa."

"Hi… Deborah," she said, barely looking up.

"Do you go by Debbie?"

"No, I prefer Deborah."

"I hope you are fine with the top bunk," Kaisa inquired.

"Sure, I'm like my dad. I can fall asleep anywhere."

She must have left him asleep somewhere because he didn't make the trip. Only her mother accompanied Deborah. Even dressed in casual clothes, she looked polished and professional with perfectly coiffed hair and freshly manicured nails. Deborah looked the opposite and nothing like her picture in the freshman directory. Her blonde hair was much longer with thick bangs, and her look had a bohemian vibe: a tie-dyed t-shirt, leather vest, and ripped bellbottom jeans.

"What are you majoring in," Kaisa asked as if she didn't already know.

"International Business," she declared dryly, eyeing her mother.

"I have to go now, Debbie," her mom announced.

Deborah winced.

"I have a client dinner tonight. He's only in town for a short time, and this was his only available day," she said before giving Deborah a quick peck on the cheek. "I'm off now."

A business meeting on a Saturday? Boy, she must be dedicated to her work.

After unloading the usual college provisions: clothes, toiletries, and books, Deborah opened a decent size box that included a couple of portraits, a giant tapestry, votives, and sticks of incense.

"Do you want me to help you hang these things?" Kaisa asked.

"No, I've got it. Here's a dorm-warming present for you," Deborah said, handing over a T-shirt. "My dad's a professional artist. He made this."

Kaisa held up the soft cotton T-shirt. It was dyed light

blue with a silkscreened illustration of a frog peering out of the pocket with another frog using its head as a step stool.

"Thanks, this is so cute! I feel bad I don't have anything to give you in return."

"That's okay. You can make it up to me eventually," she grinned.

That night, the streets were crowded and rowdy as classes weren't starting until Tuesday. Heather suggested kicking off their first night by going to Faneuil Hall for dinner, saying she was not ready to commit to the university cafeteria. Heather was from the area and knew her way around town. It sounded like a great idea. Given the quality of lunch or lack thereof, it was likely dinner would suck as well.

Faneuil Hall had an enormous food court as far as the eye could see. The girls shuffled through the narrow corridor and abundant crowds sampling whatever culinary delight was available for free. Everything Kaisa tasted was better than the next.

"Would you like to try a scallop wrapped in bacon?" one vendor offered.

"Sure, that sounds amazing," Kaisa replied, wolfing it down, before begging for another.

When they were full, they headed back to the Government Center T-stop. Faneuil Hall was lit up under a clear, navy-blue sky. The open-air market surrounding the main building was buzzing with energy from the crowds, the street performers, and the lingering symphony of savory and sweet smells. Kaisa took in the beauty and bustle of her new city, knowing for sure that she had made the right decision to attend school in Boston.

Back at Northeastern, the streets were still rumbling with students, no doubt celebrating their newfound freedom. In their short trek back to Hemenway street, they received two or three invitations from male students for one inaugural keg party or another.

"Hey, you girls want to come to a party at 115?" one gorgeous guy asked, carrying a case of beer.

Heather flirtatiously responded, "Someone already invited us. I think we are going to the same place."

"I hope we don't get in trouble," Kaisa said. "Mindy probably knows the R.A.'s there." But her concerns were immediately dismissed by the rest of the group.

"Don't worry about it. I've gone to a number of these parties and have heard that some R.A.'s actually buy the beer." Heather said.

"We'll check it out. I mean, it's right next door," Jill said.

While underage drinking parties were very much a part of a teen's social life in Kaisa's hometown, they were never a part of hers. Though, for her other roommates, this activity wasn't much different from their usual weekend.

Kaisa squeezed into the crowded, smoky dorm room and anchored herself into a secluded corner near the door. She watched as the other girls mingled. It wasn't long before Kaisa lost sight of Jill through the haze. When she returned, she was carrying a six-pack of Budweiser in her hand and four cups.

"This won't get us drunk, but it's a start," she said. "Let's blow this popsicle stand."

"Did anyone see you?" Kaisa asked, concerned yet impressed by Jill's bold resourcefulness.

"Chill. Don't worry about it," Jill said.

Just then, someone tapped Kaisa on the shoulder. "And where do you think you are going?" he slurred. "I've been wanting to talk to you."

Kaisa turned her head. "I was just leaving. I'm going back to my dorm now."

"Can I come along?" he asked.

Figures someone attractive finally takes an interest in me, and he's hammered. "I'm sorry, I'm tired. Maybe another time. Have a good night," she responded politely, not wanting to offend him.

Jill opened the door slowly to Suite 401 and popped her head in to see if Mindy was around. "Doesn't look like she's here."

The girls weren't sure if she would be cool with them drinking in the suite, mainly because she lived there too. They moved the party to Jill's room, just in case. Jill opened one of the beer cans and poured half of it into Kaisa's cup. "That's probably all you can handle."

Kaisa wondered if she could even handle that.

As the girls drank their stolen alcohol, they talked about high school, families, and their love lives. Everyone was in or associated with the popular crowd at home and had reached some degree of high school royalty. From a social and sexual perspective, it was becoming evident that the other girls were light years ahead of her. How was she ever going to compete against two former Homecoming Queens?

Deborah chimed in, saying she was in an exploration phase. She kept referring to her past boyfriends by their given names as if she were trying to max out the number of syllables. There was Anthony, Jonathan, and Roberto. No one was John or Bob, but apparently, one or more turned out to be 'dicks.' Despite that, Kaisa marveled at how nonchalantly Deborah spoke about her past encounters, emphasizing that 'the best way to get over someone is to get under someone else.'

For Kaisa, her lips were wired to her brain. She couldn't imagine how much more intense the feeling would be if it involved her vagina. After her first kiss with a boy she met on a summer program, she could not stop thinking about him. Why did intimacy mean so much more to her? Was there something wrong with her that she couldn't turn off these feelings?

"Kaisa, do you have a boyfriend?" Jill interrupted.

"No, I haven't had much luck or experience in that area." *More like none.* "How about you?" she said, quickly changing the subject.

Kaisa never had a boyfriend in high school and had only been on a few dates, mainly set up by her friends. Boys she did like, ended up liking someone else. She never went to either her junior or senior prom and was turned down by the guys she asked. Her 'best friend' Gina went with Kaisa's crush to both dances. Over the summer, Kaisa laid in her bedroom in a panic that no one would ever fall in love with her. Inside, she was still that chubby, buck-toothed ballerina in the first grade and designated guard on the elementary school playground who kept the boys away when her classmates played a game called "boys chase girls." Even though she had whittled down to a slender size six by age 15, the boys still kept away.

Hopefully, a romantic city like Boston would be the catalyst to finally find a mutual connection. If she was going to hang with this crowd, she would have a lot of catching up to do. But that drunk guy was probably not the place to start.

CHAPTER 3
Why Can't I Have You

T he first couple of months of school were tough – not only learning the new curriculum but trying to keep track of everyone's love life. Suite 401 became a revolving door of men for everyone except Kaisa. All the guys she was interested in, once again, relegated her to the friend zone.

Kaisa did meet someone outside a large lecture hall on the first day of school. She was standing with a swarm of at least 75 other students, waiting for the professor to unlock the door, when someone asked: 'Is this Intro to Communications?' She turned to see an average looking guy who was slightly shorter than her five foot five inches. Or maybe he was the same height since her boots had one-inch heels. "I hope so. Otherwise, I'm in the wrong place," she replied, half smiling.

"Hi, I'm Josh."

"Hi, I'm Kaisa."

"Are you in the business program? I thought I recognized you from freshman orientation."

"Yes, my concentration is marketing. How about yourself?"

"I'm studying accounting. Do you know what you would like to do someday?"

"Yes. My dream job would be to work for an advertising agency in New York City."

"Do you live in New York?" he asked.

"No, I live in Connecticut, but that's where a lot of people in my town work."

"Me too."

Josh asked if he could sit next to Kaisa after the lecture hall opened and after a few classes, he asked her out. She accepted even though she wasn't attracted to him, and he was the only sober one who had shown an interest.

On their first date, she suggested they go to Faneuil Hall to feast on scallops wrapped in bacon. But Josh said he was an Orthodox Jew and didn't eat shellfish or pork, so that was a double whammy. With each date, she tried to convince herself that she liked him as more than a friend. But when they kissed, it didn't stir any motion or emotion inside her.

In the meantime, Deborah spent most of her time pursuing artsy-looking guys. The more disheveled they were, the more she was attracted to them. Deborah told the girls about a guy she had seen a few times in the adjacent building's dining hall. He met her criteria of pseudo-intellectual hippie-type with long flowing hair. She called him "Ian" because she didn't know his real name.

One night, after a few shots of Cuervo, Deborah and Kaisa left to walk off the tequila as Deborah called out, "Ian? Ian?" down Hemenway Street. She eventually met up with him in the dining hall a few days after that and started seeing him from time to time. When Jill and Kaisa looked him up in the freshman directory, his student photo was of a clean-cut guy named Ira majoring in Computer Science. At least she was close on the name.

Before long, Deborah was on to someone else and was either staying over their place or bringing them back to the dorm. Their shared room became a parade of Patchouli oil-wearing, anti-antiperspirant, non-conformists. Every so often, one of Deborah's suitors from home would visit her over a weekend. Her guests became so frequent that Kaisa spent many a night sleeping on a cheap foam fold-out cushion, which she contributed to the common area décor so that Deborah could have privacy. She continued to be amazed at how casually Deborah approached her relationships, and when they ended, they didn't seem to faze her.

One of Deborah's attempted conquests lived directly below them with three other members of the crew team. The University must have intentionally put them together because they all had to get up at the same ungodly morning hour to practice. His name was Ransom, and a handsome Ransom he was. He was slightly outside of

Deborah's type, looking like Billy Idol, with short platinum blond hair, piercing blue eyes, and a tall, toned rower's body. Despite his stunning looks, he was an authentically nice guy. While Deborah tried to ensnare him, he turned her down because he belonged to someone on the girl's crew team, who everyone thought was well below his league.

The crew guys became friends with Kaisa's roommates and would make frequent visits to Suite 401 because, at the end of the day, or any part of the day, their suite was dirty, disgusting, and smelled foul. Throughout the fall, two of the other crew guys paired off with Jill and Heather. The remaining crew guy and Kaisa didn't have much to talk about, nor was there any chemistry.

The biggest event of the year for the crew team was the Head of the Charles regatta in October, the annual race on the Charles River. For most college students, the regatta was a giant drink fest, with hundreds of thousands of students lining the banks of the river teeming over on either side. The Northeastern Crew Team prevailed that day. To celebrate, Ransom invited the girls to a party at the team captain's off-campus apartment. Dave's parents had a townhouse close to Northeastern that they kept as an investment property and were letting him live there.

Dave looked like the preppy boys Kaisa grew up with and the properly groomed guys Deborah said she dated back in the city, or those she introduced to her mother. They were the only ones that her mother would approve of, which seemed highly hypocritical because she was married to an artist. Well, not for much longer. Kaisa had heard that Deborah's mother and father were splitting up. To add salt to the wound, her mother was now seeing some younger guy. That seemed to explain the evening dinners and possibly Deborah's behavior.

On all fronts, Dave did not match Deborah's current criteria. But they hit it off, and it wasn't long before he became a part of her rotation. She started to call him David, but he politely asked that she call him Dave like everyone else. He was the whole suite's favorite in terms of the guys she brought back. A clean-cut captain of the crew team and a sweetheart of a guy, he was approachable with a friendly smile that immediately warmed you inside. You could see that he genuinely cared for Deborah. He was almost too nice. Deborah seemed to overlook how kind and considerate he was and disregarded that her suitemates all liked and very much approved of him.

"Hey, I wanted to let you know, David's invited the Girls of 401 to his place for a casual gathering of friends tonight," Deborah said.

"I think that's code for a keg party," Jill confirmed.

It was a Thursday, and there were classes tomorrow. "I think I'm going to hang back. I still have one more chapter to read," Kaisa said.

"Come on, you do more studying than all of us combined. If anyone deserves a break, it's you."

Schoolwork was a secondary concern for the rest of her freshman roommates. It was standard practice for Deborah, Jill, and Heather to skip a class here or there. But Kaisa didn't miss one. She wasn't going to blow off classes that she paid for with her own money, which was running low.

Going to Northeastern was already a financial stretch for her, and her family and the college costs were piling up. She had to find steady part-time work soon to help pay for tuition and other incidentals. But so far, her efforts to find a job had been unsuccessful.

However, there was nothing she could do about that tonight. Besides, Jill was right, she was entitled to a little fun.

Kaisa and Jill set out for the party later that night, while Deborah was still getting ready.

"You can go ahead without me. I'll be right behind," she yelled from her room.

When they arrived at Dave's apartment, a stunning specimen of a man was greeting guests at the door.

"Hi, I'm Ben. I'm Dave's roommate. I don't think we've met?" he said softly, extending out his hand. He was somewhere around six-foot-two, with sandy blonde hair, pale blue eyes, and a lean and fit body.

God, he's beautiful. Kaisa stopped dead in her tracks as her tongue twisted into a knot. It was like the time she went to Canada with her mom. Her mother's friend had a gorgeous son around her age. Kaisa spent the entire visit not saying a word, figuring anything she would say would sound stupid.

Thankfully, Jill was there to help with the

introductions and carry the conversation. Ben was a philosophy major who did not fit the mold of a typical Northeastern student. Most students Kaisa had met had more practical majors like business, pharmacy, or engineering, whereas Ben looked like he was plucked out of a remote liberal arts college.

Kaisa stood in awe, smiling, nodding, and interjecting laughter at appropriate moments. Her attempts at eye contact with Ben were equally futile. She could barely hold his gaze for more than one second before shifting her glance down toward her shoes.

"Hey there, Benjamin," Deborah said, waltzing through the door, throwing her arm around him, and planting a kiss on his cheek.

Hmm, Benjamin, not Ben; three syllables no less. Benjamin did fit all of Deborah's checkboxes for a slightly disheveled, tall, handsome artsy-looking type. In her heart, Kaisa didn't think she had a prayer with a guy like Ben, but at least Deborah couldn't have him either because she was with Dave.

As the night went on, Benjamin spent a fair share of time with Deborah, refilling her drinks and engaging in extended existential discussion, more than likely wanting to provoke more than her thoughts. Whenever Deborah stepped away, Benjamin's eyes darted around the room, no doubt seeking her out. Poor Dave. He was such a trusting person who was oblivious to their flirtations while he played the proper host and made the rounds visiting the other guests, ensuring they were having a good time.

Kaisa clung to Jill for most of the night. Even though she had been to more keg parties in the last two months than in her four years of high school, she hadn't mastered the mingle and didn't feel comfortable on her own.

Eventually, she had enough beer, and most everyone else was paired off for the evening. There were a couple of guys who had come up and talked to her again through their drunken stupor. Jill advised not to bother with them because they were just horny and only looking to hook up with a warm body. Kaisa still considered it progress since no one even wanted her for that in high school.

As Don McLean's "American Pie" wafted through the sound system, whoever was left and coherent enough joined in the sing-along. Kaisa ambled toward the stereo to study a vast cassette collection in a large wooden bracket. The music was a mix of classical, jazz, obscure rock bands, and some more mainstream favorites. This was a collection Kaisa aspired to have. She loved taking the T after class sometimes to Tower Records to peruse the shelves, wishing she could afford what she wanted to buy.

"See anything you like?" Dave asked, standing nearby.

"Yeah, there's lots of good stuff here. Are these your tapes?"

"No, these belong to Benjamin."

One of her newly discovered favorite albums by R.E.M. stood out. Jill also had a copy, but the dub Kaisa had made on her pink boombox had a loud hissing noise and background chatter.

I could steal a little piece of him and think about him when I listen to it. Besides, it will give my music collection more credibility wedged between Air Supply and Barry Manilow. Maybe it will give him a reason to look for it. And with that, Kaisa slipped it into her purse.

Post-sing-along, Kaisa was itching to leave. There were only a few guests left. Kaisa scanned the room, having lost track of Deborah. Maybe she was downstairs already. Jill was in deep conversation with her own crew guy, who had his arm around her and clearly did not want her to leave. "Jill, sorry to interrupt, I'm going to head back. I'll see you later," she said.

As she descended the stairs, Kaisa caught a glimpse of Benjamin passionately kissing Deborah. There was no denying their lust for each other as it combusted through the window just outside the door. Kaisa stood for a moment and watched, wishing she was the one in his embrace. Kaisa knew it wouldn't be long before Deborah and Dave were history. Perhaps he was just too ordinary and stable for her. As she neared the landing, they parted at once, pretending to have a conversation.

"Are you heading back to the dorm, Deborah?" Kaisa asked as she exited the building.

"Not yet. I'm going to hang here a little while longer."

"I can try to hail you a cab," Benjamin offered.

"Sure, that would be nice."

About a week and a half later, Benjamin replaced Dave

in the rotation and began regularly appearing at the suite. Whenever he visited, Kaisa would sit and bask in his overall attractiveness, listening eagerly to him talk about any subject in his soft-spoken melodic growl.

Benjamin loved to challenge conventional ways of thinking and savored playing devil's advocate, which seemed appropriate for a philosophy major. Kaisa wasn't comfortable with her knowledge of current events, definitely not enough to offer a counterpoint or have a debate. Half the time, she couldn't follow his multi-faceted opinions and political ideologies, so she kept quiet for fear of sounding ignorant. As Kaisa got to know him, she became even more enamored. She fantasized about Benjamin, picturing them together, knowing full well a handsome intellectual like him would never be interested in her.

One afternoon, the downstairs buzzer rang at the suite.

"Who's there?" Kaisa asked.

"Benjamin."

Kaisa buzzed him in. When he came to the door, he was wearing a tattered jean jacket and was holding an eclectic but beautiful bouquet of wildflowers.

"Is Deborah here?" he asked.

"Yes, she's in our room napping. Is she expecting you?"

"No, but if you don't mind, I think I'll see if I can wake 'Sleeping Beauty' and bring her back to life," he said as he sauntered past her on his way to Deborah.

Kaisa stormed into Jill's room. "How is it she can find Prince Charming or several, and I can't? I don't think I'm that ugly. I mean, Deborah and I could pass for sisters!" Kaisa wailed. "Why is finding a boyfriend that I'm attracted to so hard for me? The guys I've met since school started, whom I like, don't want me."

"First of all, you're not ugly. Second, what about Josh from your communications class?" she asked. "He was nice."

"Yeah, but I towered over him when I wore anything more than flats. When I fooled around with him, and he was on top of me, it felt like I was making out with a little boy. I'd prefer a more experienced man or at least someone who looks like one."

"Was he at least good in bed?"

"We didn't go that far, and I wouldn't know," Kaisa muttered.

"Are you a virgin?" Jill asked, trying to mask a slight grin.

"Yeah, but so was he, not that he didn't try to convince me once or twice into changing our status. Honestly, it hasn't been that hard to hold on to. I never had any opportunity at home. Anyway, I didn't want to waste my first time on him. When it finally happens for me, I think one of us should know what we're doing."

Kaisa had long pictured her first time as a perfect sexual symphony of two people madly in love, complete with a romantic soundtrack playing in the background.

Benjamin fit the mold of an ideal candidate. Sadly, it was apparent that his mind and no doubt other parts of his body were focusing on someone else.

Kaisa returned to the common area to find the door to her bedroom slightly ajar. She could hear Deborah and Benjamin exchanging kisses and softly whispering. *How come I can't land someone like that?*

In December, the girls planned a small celebration before winter break. Earlier in the week, Jill found a tiny Charlie Brown Christmas tree outside of Star Market. A tree was a fire hazard and, according to the dorm by-laws, was forbidden. Mindy let the girls live on the edge if they promised to turn off the little white lights when they left the suite.

Kaisa was enjoying some precious and infrequent alone time in front of the mini tree while the girls were out getting last minute gifts. At home, as soon as her parents went out, she would put on an album and pretend she was in a music video, belting out her favorite hits. But living with four other girls meant this incidence was rare. The common area had no windows, which was perfect. She pulled out a small cassette suitcase from under her bed, selected Benjamin's R.E.M tape and inserted it into the boombox, then cranked the volume to an acceptable decibel. "Feathers hit the ground before the weight can leave the air," she sang along, swaying back and forth.

"BZZZ," went the intercom.

Who could that be? Kaisa let out a grunt and lowered the

volume. "Hi, who's there?"

"Benjamin."

Benjamin hadn't called or been around the dorm in a good couple of weeks.

"Um, Deborah is not here. She's at work right now."

"I know. Can I come up? I was hoping to talk to you."

Why does he want to talk to me? Has he realized I am the one for him? Yeah right. I wish! She waited outside the door in anticipation. "So, what's up?" she asked after he climbed the last step.

"I'm glad you're here," he said. "Are you alone?"

"Yeah, the other girls are out shopping. It's just me," she said, holding the heavy door open for him.

"Do you mind if we go to your room?"

"Sure," Kaisa said, leading the way and hiding a hopeful smile.

"Are you listening to R.E.M.?" he asked. "That's a great album."

"One of my new favorites." Kaisa nodded. "So, what brings you here. I haven't seen you in a while."

"Yeah, things with Deborah and me are a little rough right now," he said, sitting on her bottom bunk.

Kaisa's breath grew short. "Really?" Maybe things were fizzling out?

"I'd like to get her something for Christmas and, since you are her roommate, I thought you might have a better idea of what she would like."

Her heart sank. *Par for the course. Who was I kidding?* Kaisa sighed and shook her head. She had no idea what Deborah might like as she spent most of her time chatting with Jill and Mindy.

She scanned their bedroom, wanting to suggest something Deborah wouldn't care for, but decided to take the high road. "I'm not 100 percent sure. I mean, she uses this perfume," she suggested, picking up a small, nearly empty bottle of Pavlova 1922 from Deborah's dresser.

"Yeah, that is a great idea, thanks. Hey, do you mind if I borrow your R.E.M. cassette sometime so I could make a dub? Mine is missing. I haven't seen it since the party."

"Sure, no problem, you might as well take it now while you're here?" Kaisa grumbled, ejecting the tape from the boombox, and handing it to him.

"Well, I've got to go. Have a nice break."

"You too," she said. Kaisa wasn't excited about the upcoming winter break except for Christmas at home with her family and time away from schoolwork. It meant three months had flown by, and not much had changed since she had arrived in the fall. There was still no true love and no part-time job. However, Deborah had been able to find both a few times over. Everything came so easily to her.

A couple of hours later, the girls returned.

"I brought home some leftover cookies from work for our party," Deborah said.

Kaisa informed Deborah that Benjamin had paid a visit, but she barely acknowledged it.

Later, the girls had their 401 Christmas. The base of the tiny tree was overflowing with 25 small packages because all five girls got a present for each other. Some were thoughtful, some were gag gifts, but all were anonymous.

Kaisa received a pair of turquoise satin underwear with a lace butterfly connecting the panty in the front. The To/From card said to wear it for that special someone. Along with that, Kaisa got a cassette of Madonna's "Like a Virgin" album.

"We knew you liked Madonna and didn't have that tape," Jill said.

But there was more to it as all her gifts had a similar theme. She thanked them, wondering how long the panties would be collecting dust in her drawer.

Deborah received a little wind-up VW bug car and a toy crab plushie. Deborah grimaced when she opened the gifts. She tried to laugh them off, but it was apparent that she was visibly embarrassed.

Kaisa didn't get it. Even though she asked Jill and Mindy later, they said it was an inside joke and refused to explain its significance.

CHAPTER 4
Don't Get Me Wrong

Winter 1987

K aisa was on her way back to the dorm after her last class following her first week back at school. The January sky was a raw, overcast gray. The miserable weather was not helping her mood or her attitude.

During winter break, Kaisa spent most of her time at home bored or watching T.V. Her friends thought she would be home longer, like them (or so they said), and were busy with other things. One of those nights, she called Josh. Even though they weren't dating anymore, she was under the impression they had agreed to remain friends. As he only lived about thirty miles away, she figured the phone bill wouldn't be too high.

"Hi, is Josh there?" she asked with a polite ascending pitch in her voice.

"Who is speaking?" said an older woman, no doubt his mother.

"This is Kaisa. I know Josh from school."

"Josh, do you know a Kaisa?" she called out, sounding confused.

Kaisa could hear Josh yelling in the background, saying he would get the phone in another room.

"How did you get this number?" he demanded after picking up the line.

"I called information."

"Don't ever call me here!" he said in a harsh whisper.

"Why?"

"Because my mom only wants me associating with Jewish girls. She wouldn't be pleased if she knew about you, much less that I dated a Catholic."

Wow. The one guy who seemed into her at one time, and his parents didn't even know she existed. "I guess you can use those condoms you bought for us with some Jewish girl," she barked before slamming the phone into its cradle. *What a rebel, he wanted to lose his virginity to a 'shiksa.'* She was glad she had saved herself for someone else.

Kaisa returned to the dorm and carelessly threw her backpack on the floor. She turned on the T.V. and changed the channel to her soap opera, 'General Hospital.' She had been watching that show every weekday afternoon since age 11 when her mother went back to work, and she became a latch-key kid. It was her escape from reality. Boy, did she need that escape today. Even though it was blatantly fiction, the characters' lives were far more interesting and exciting than hers.

But today, the weekend cliffhanger wasn't holding her interest as usual. Despite the unpleasantly chilly afternoon, Kaisa decided to abandon the TV to escape her reality with a walk to Copley Place. She could check again to see if anyone was hiring. She hated living on the funds her parents sent each month, knowing it was extra money they didn't have to spend. Every time a $100 check arrived, she felt guilty. Her mother said she didn't mind because Kaisa was working hard and getting good grades. That was the only area in which she was accomplishing her goals.

Kaisa bundled up in her black and white houndstooth acrylic blend coat, securing the top button just under her chin. She planned out a route that would offer the most protection from the weather. After a few steps on the busy street, the icy wind sliced her nose and cheeks with its malicious gusts. Against the dreary backdrop, the bare tree limbs looked like outstretched claws trying to scratch through the clouds in search of warmth as well.

She crossed over Symphony Road, scrunching her neck and burying her face deep into her coat to protect her inner ears from throbbing. As she approached the Christian Science Center, the usual overflowing 15-acre reflecting pool had been drained for the winter. *I guess any sort of reflection will have to be postponed until Spring,* she giggled to herself. Kaisa darted to the semi-open mall area around the Prudential Building. She weaved through the covered passageways until she reached the heated glass overpass at the entrance of Copley Place.

Once inside, she surveyed the premium stores,

mentally checking off those she had already approached for a job. She applied at a few more and followed up with those who already had her application. As a reward for her productivity, she ascended the escalator towards Mrs. Fields Cookies. If she couldn't work there, like Deborah, she could still eat there. Mrs. Fields was surrounded by a fancy food court on the top mezzanine, along with a fine dining restaurant and a bunch of other gourmet places that were out of her price range. Just inside the cookie store was an exceptionally cute guy working the cash register.

Kaisa quickly changed her mind and passed on a cookie. *I don't need the calories anyway.* She circled the food court and was about to get on the escalator to go back down when she heard a soft-spoken manly voice behind her.

"Excuse me, do you know how to get to Symphony Road?"

She rolled her eyes. *Who asks for street directions in the middle of a mall? Well, maybe they are new to the area too.* She turned around to witness a gorgeous man, at least six-foot three-inches tall, with dirty blonde-hair and cyan eyes, all with flecks of gold. His hypnotic gaze pulled her in. He didn't look like a typical college boy, aside from the backpack slung over his shoulder, but more like a cross between William Hurt, Sting, and Benjamin. Kaisa's heart picked up speed. *He must be directing his question at someone else? This man couldn't be trying to engage me.* But there was no one else nearby.

"I live across the street from there," she replied with

her insides fluttering. "If you go down the escalator and turn left," she said, glancing down at her left hand with her thumb and pointer finger extended as a reference, "you'll see the exit by—"

"Do you go to school in Boston?" he interrupted.

"Yes, I go to Northeastern."

"What year?"

"Freshman. How about yourself?"

"I'm a graduate student at Harvard Divinity School."

Ding! Ding! Ding! Bells went off in her head like hitting a casino jackpot. *Oh my God, stunningly gorgeous AND goes to Harvard.* Kaisa could not fathom that someone like him would even stop to look at her, much less talk to her. She was sure this would be a brief run-in, and she should savor it for as long as possible. But their conversation continued without pause, as he flawlessly segued from one subject to another.

They discussed Northeastern's generic design versus the aesthetics of Harvard's campus. Appreciating the intellectual challenge, she did her best to impress him with her opinions, observations, and five-dollar words. It was such a welcome change from the conversations with most guys at Northeastern, which usually began with 'you can't believe how drunk I got last weekend!'

"Northeastern's architecture leaves a lot to be desired," Kaisa stated. "It is one of the 'fugliest' campuses in all of Boston. The quad is basically surrounded by three identical square concrete buildings that look more like they belong to a prison. But it is in the middle of the city so the topography doesn't really lend itself to rolling hills."

He jumped in. "Well, yes, but Harvard is in the middle of a busy city area in Cambridge, and yet it has this regality about it with its beautifully crafted buildings."

"Yeah, but I'm sure the endowment is much bigger there than at Northeastern," Kaisa countered. "Had I been in charge, I would have at least hired a better architect and landscape designer."

He went silent for a moment. "Don't take this the wrong way, but you don't seem the Northeastern type."

Kaisa scrunched her face and gave him a puzzled look.

"I mean, you're intelligent," he said.

What was he alluding to? Did he think all Northeastern students were stupid? Did he think she was an underachiever? Or that she was selling herself short? Kaisa retorted, "I know most people think of Northeastern as a commuter school, which doesn't set the bar very high on student admissions. But I chose to go there for the five-year co-op program so I could help pay for college and because I fell in love with Boston."

"I'm sorry if you took my compliment the wrong way," he stated apologetically as he reached out his hand. "I'm Christopher Morton."

"Kaisa Blazielijus," she replied as she took his hand in hers. His warm touch radiated up her arm like a shockwave.

"Nice to meet you," he said.

She was surprised he didn't ask her to repeat her last name. Most people she met, including all her teachers, had something to say about it, like: 'Wow, that was a mouthful!' or 'Can you say that again?' But he didn't seem to notice.

"Would you like to get a hot chocolate with me?" he asked.

"Sure. That would be great." Kaisa closely trailed Christopher as they passed all the available options in the mall. *Maybe he knows a cute place nearby?* They exited onto the street through the Westin's revolving door.

The sun had penetrated through the cloud cover and was casting an orange haze on the late afternoon. Her dreary day had changed costumes in more ways than one. Christopher continued walking toward Boylston Street, passing numerous cafes and restaurants, then kept on going past Newbury, which had the same. Against her better judgment, she continued to follow him, rationalizing that she was still out in the open and enjoying this out of the ordinary experience with this intriguing man. This was hardly an everyday occurrence.

A few yards ahead was a sign for Commonwealth Avenue – a wider two-way street lined with naked trees. But there was nothing there but residential properties.

"Let me show you my neighborhood," he said, as they carefully navigated the ice-encrusted cobblestones that crunched beneath their feet.

It was clear their destination wouldn't be in public. One block further, they arrived at his red front door at 293

Marlborough Street. She stood at the foot of the steps pondering if it was wise to enter. How could she resist this man of her dreams? The practical lobe in her brain was screaming: Are you crazy? You just met this guy like 15-20 minutes ago. He could be a psycho! But her romantic and adventurous side reassured: Don't worry, you'll be fine. Plus, it's still daylight. Curiosity overruled caution as she stepped inside.

He led her upstairs to a studio apartment on the second floor. There were no dead bodies in plain view, so that was comforting. It smelled musty, somewhere between damp laundry and an old library. The décor was minimalistic with a lone white futon mattress in the corner, a desk with a chair, a soft recliner, and seven long horizontal shelves of books. The coolest feature was the bay window veiled with dusty off-white sheer drapes, literally hanging on by a thread.

He threw his coat over a pile of clothes on the floor. "I'm sorry my apartment is in such a bedraggled state," he said.

Kaisa didn't think it was that bad, aside from a few unwashed dishes in the sink and the towering stacks of papers on his desk.

"My cleaning lady comes on Saturdays."

"You have a cleaning lady?"

He smiled, "No, I'm just kidding. I can barely afford rent. You can put your coat over there," he said, pointing to the closet.

"Where are you from?" she asked, detecting a touch of a southern accent.

"Oh, um, Nashville, Tennessee," he replied while putting on a kettle in his kitchenette.

"Have you lived in Boston long?"

"Yes, a little while."

Kaisa couldn't help fixating on the front door, which he had left open, questioning if she made the right choice to join him inside.

"If you are wondering, I left it that way on purpose so you would feel more comfortable. You can leave at any time."

Was he possibly a Southern gentleman as well?

He pointed to the mattress and asked her to sit down while he chose the chair across from her. They talked more about his current course load and lightly touched on hers.

"Wow, you have so many books!"

"This is a result of years and years of searching. When I was 18, I had no idea what I wanted to study. In the end, I chose Archaeology because I had to pick something. You're 18? 19?" he questioned.

"Eighteen," she confirmed.

"I'm not much older than you; I'm 26."

Kaisa automatically did some mental math regarding their age difference. Even though she was attracted to older men, he was a little older than she expected. He looked like he could be slightly more mature than that, but then everyone who wasn't a student looked like they were in their 40's. "When is your birthday?" she asked.

"March," he said.

"What day?"

"If we still know each other, then I'll tell you."

The kettle sounded its shrill whistle. He got up to prepare the hot chocolate then handed the steaming cup to Kaisa. She took a sip and feigned a smile.

"Does it taste all right?"

If you like watered-down chocolate grit. I guess that's why you're supposed to use milk with Nestle's Quik. "Yeah, it's fine," she said. Her anxiety was rising, and her stomach was already doing backflips, which wasn't helping. Kaisa wriggled her jaw to release the tension while letting out slow deep breaths.

Christopher seemed to sense her uneasiness and joined her on the mattress. "Are you familiar with any relaxation techniques practiced in Buddhist and Eastern Cultures?"

"I don't know. Maybe." Kaisa said.

"Do you know what shiatsu is?" he asked.

Sure, I'm about to shiatsu all over myself.

"It's a type of massage," he continued. "Eastern cultures see this as a relaxation method, as opposed to Western culture, which believes touching only has sexual implications."

He shifted his tall frame behind her and swept her hair to one side. His warm exhale on the back of her neck sent a tingle down her spine. She shuddered as his fingertips connected with her shoulders. "You're extremely tense."

Applying slight pressure on every tight muscle, Christopher progressively kneaded his way down her back. "You have nothing to worry about. I'm not going to do anything you don't want to do," he soothed. "As I said before, you can leave whenever you want. But I do wish you would stay."

Kaisa's mind and body were still at odds. Part of her wanted to give in to the pleasure of his touch, while part of her was struggling with her physical symptoms, wondering what could be next.

"Why don't you just lie back and relax," he said, putting a pillow behind her head. He laid down beside her and took her slightly quivering hand in his as he examined her long, slender fingers. "Do you know what body type you are?"

Kaisa took a deep breath. "I read something recently in Cosmopolitan about the best diet for your body type. Do you mean like ectomorph or endomorph?"

"Yes, exactly," he said, sounding surprised and possibly impressed by her response. "I was right; you are much too smart for Northeastern." He pulled her close and whispered something inaudible in her ear, then his lips grazed her cheek, and he kissed her once, then again. She closed her eyes to let her other senses take over, feeling his warm breath on her face. Christopher toyed with Kaisa hovering his lips slightly above hers, barely touching them, which fueled her hunger for more. With his mouth pressed firmly against her lips, he parted them with his tongue, plunging it inside. Kaisa jolted back and pushed her hands against his chest.

"You don't like to kiss with your tongue?"

"It's not that I don't like it. I just haven't done it... much," she added. *More like, not at all.*

"Here, let's try it again. This time you do it."

Following his lead, she tangled her tongue with his, exploring this new sensation and finding it kind of fun. Kaisa couldn't believe she was making out with this gorgeous guy she just met, at his place, no less. It didn't seem real. She definitely wasn't expecting anything like this to happen when she left her dorm that afternoon. Christopher's grip tightened as he ground his stiff bulge against her pubic bone while another hand grabbed the zipper of her pants. *Is this heading where I think it is? Is this my cue to leave? For God's sake, I'm wearing Garfield the cat underwear!*

"Sweetheart, where are you going?" he said softly as Kaisa wriggled away.

Despite savoring being in the presence of this intoxicating man, she could not ignore the voice in her head. "I'm sorry I have to stop you here," she said.

Christopher pouted. "We were having a fun time. What about being spontaneous and going with the moment? I didn't know when I woke up today that I would meet a hot girl at Copley, but I'm enjoying the fact that I did right now. Why don't we explore where this goes?"

"I don't have or am on any birth control," Kaisa exclaimed.

"Don't worry; I wasn't planning on having intercourse with you."

While she was certain his sentiment was supposed to put her at ease, in a way, she was kind of insulted. Go figure. "I'm glad; I'm not ready for that yet. I'm waiting for the right time and the right person. I hope you can respect that."

Christopher paused for a moment. "Are you a virgin?" he asked.

"Yes," she admitted.

He turned away, but she could see a glimpse of an asymmetrical smile on his profile.

"How about oral sex? Have you done that?"

"No!"

"Do you touch yourself?"

Kaisa's face flushed. This was getting way too personal. "I can't say that I have."

"So, you've never had an orgasm?"

"Yes, I think I did."

"You got it by being fingered by a boyfriend?"

"Yes, I had one last semester."

"An orgasm or a boyfriend?"

Kaisa smirked. "Both, but we broke up. He was a virgin too. Can we not talk about this anymore?"

"I'm not sure how you have been able to resist having sex with anyone yet. It must be difficult for an intelligent and attractive girl, like yourself, you must get lots of offers."

Kaisa didn't want to admit that couldn't have been further from the truth.

"At the very least, you owe it to yourself to explore your own body. How else will you learn what you like and what turns you on? You shouldn't feel self-conscious or ashamed about it. Now look what you have done to me," he said, coyly pointing to his erection. "Sweetheart, I know you don't have any experience in this area, but could I ask you to put your mouth on me? I'll walk you through it. It's only skin; there's nothing gross about it."

The extent of her blow job knowledge was Phoebe Cates sucking on a carrot in "Fast Times at Ridgemont High." Sucking off a man was supposed to be a great way to keep him coming back for more, or so she had heard from her roommates. But Kaisa wasn't in any hurry to give it a try. Anyway, it didn't seem right to give in so soon, although a couple of the girls had said they went a lot farther with some guys they had just met. *If I don't, he'll find someone else, and I'll never see him again. But, if I don't, it could leave something for him to shoot for next time. Maybe that wasn't the right choice of words.* "I can't," she said, despite his further pleas.

"So, you can't be persuaded?" he teased. "You should be more open-minded. A person who cannot be influenced, and veer off course, might as well be an inanimate rock."

"You majored in Archeology; you're supposed to like rocks," she replied.

Christopher put his sweater over his face. "I don't think I can come up with a response to that one. Can I try something else with you, then?"

Kaisa nodded.

He lifted her shirt and traced his fingers along her torso and laid her back down. Then he withdrew his fully erect penis and placed it in his hand. She didn't resist as he pleasured himself, feeling it was the least she could do without going too far.

He came on her midriff with a satisfied sigh. "Better there than in there," he said, pointing to her vagina. Christopher got up to get some paper towels while Kaisa remained on her back, dumbfounded with some strange man's ejaculate on her abdomen.

Within a few moments, his phone rang. "Hello. Oh, hi," he said, in a haunting whisper. He took the phone into the bathroom and locked the door. Kaisa laid back quietly and listened but couldn't make out anything he said.

She turned her head toward the giant bay window. The sun that had broken through the overcast sky was setting, and it was getting darker by the minute. On the other side of the mattress on the floor was a Pretenders tape. Chrissie Hynde's mouth was open with a look of ecstasy as if someone were stimulating her out of the frame below her guitar. *Did Christopher buy this tape because of the music, or was he drawn to her expression?* This cassette could be a great souvenir in case this was the last time she saw him.

The bathroom door unlatched. "That was Julie; she

was my best friend in college. She's in town, and I'm supposed to meet up with her for dinner, and I've been having so much fun with you, I almost forgot!"

Kaisa surmised this was her final curtain call. "Well, I had an interesting afternoon, but I should go now," she said.

"I'd like to get to know you better. Can I see you again?"

Kaisa perked up at once.

"You're probably very busy so, you won't have time for me," he said humbly.

Kaisa assured him with what little confidence she could muster, "I may be able to squeeze you in here and there."

He gave her a pen and a scrap of paper to write down her number. "By the way, do you have a couple of dollars on you? I'm out of tokens and don't have time to go to the ATM."

Really? She had five dollars with her but needed every cent. "I'm sorry, I intentionally didn't bring any money to Copley Place to keep me from buying anything."

"That's okay; I'll walk with you for a bit if you'd like."

"Sure, I would like that," she said.

He escorted her out of the apartment and latched his arm around hers. Kaisa walked proudly arm in arm with Christopher for a couple of blocks until they reached the Prudential Building.

"I had a nice time with you," Christopher said.

Kaisa nodded in agreement. "So what body type am I? You never said."

"Oh, you're an ectomorph. I look forward to exploring more of you next time. I'll call you soon." He leaned in and gave her a soft kiss goodbye, then walked off in the opposite direction.

Kaisa was on such a high; she ran home through the dimly lit streets that bordered her dorm. When she got back, she flung the suite door open, still overflowing with excitement and emotion, but no one was there to tell of her adventure.

When her roommates returned from dinner about a half-hour later, Kaisa could barely contain herself. "I think I met the man of my dreams this afternoon."

Everyone, including Jill's friends who were visiting from New Jersey, wanted to know more.

Kaisa began, "Let's call it: NORTHEASTERN MEETS HARVARD AT COPLEY." She described the entire course of events, taking care to omit specific X-rated details.

"I can't believe you went to his apartment. You could have been raped or killed." Jill scolded.

Deborah had a different perspective. "I don't think it's that big of a deal, you can usually sense when something doesn't feel right, but I'm glad it worked out for you. As much as I would like my own room, I wouldn't want you to be slaughtered."

"Thanks," Kaisa said, smiling proudly, thinking about her handsome conquest.

Later that night, when Kaisa was putting away the pink sweater she wore that day, she lifted it to her nose and smelled the sweet remnant of his cologne. Kaisa swore that, though the scent would eventually wash away, she would remember that intriguing, intellectual 26-year-old Harvard man, who, like some deity out of the sky, walked into her life one day when she needed cheering up the most. Maybe things were finally turning around for her. School was good, and now perhaps there was the promise of some sort of love life. But she didn't want to jinx it. *If I can only get Christopher to fall in love with me, life would be perfect.*

CHAPTER 5
The Deeper You Get the Sweeter the Pain

K aisa woke up the next morning, questioning if yesterday's encounter had actually happened. If he never called her again, though she desperately hoped he would, she would be satisfied that she didn't compromise herself that much and stayed true to her beliefs. In retrospect, she realized that going to a man's apartment twenty minutes after meeting him and engaging in sexual activity was not the smartest thing. But that's also what made it so exciting.

Three days later, a call came in at one in the afternoon. Jill picked up the phone. Kaisa could hear her saying casually, "let me check and see if she's here," hoping the call was for her. Jill knocked on Kaisa's door, covered the receiver, and mouthed, "I think it's 'the man of your dreams,'" she mocked.

Kaisa beamed. He did call as he promised. She jumped

up from her desk and grabbed the phone in disbelief. The last three days without hearing or seeing him seemed like an eternity.

"Hi, it's Chris. How are you?"

"I'm good," she replied. But ecstatic was more like it.

"If you're available, I would like to see you tonight around 7:30 after I study for my exam."

"Sure, where do you want to go?" she asked, trying to contain her excitement.

"I'm not sure yet. I wanted to see if you would be available. I'll call you later, okay?"

"That's fine. I'll talk to you soon."

Around 5 p.m., Kaisa was on the phone with her mother when she heard the call waiting signal's click. "Hold on, Mom; I have another call."

"Kaisa?" His breathy voice instantly released the butterflies in her stomach. "I finished a little earlier than I expected. Can we meet up in about 20 minutes?"

Kaisa was far from date-ready, wearing her Northeastern sweatshirt, sweatpants, and no makeup. "Wait one second. I have someone on the other line," she said. She clicked back onto her mom's call and asked if she could call her later. "Okay, I'm back. I was wondering where we were going to go?"

"Do you know that café near the top of Newbury Street? The one with the little bonsai trees in the window."

"You mean the Trident Booksellers Café?" Kaisa was familiar with it as it was only a few steps from Tower Records. She had recently discovered this spot and instantly fell in love with its atmosphere, artistic vibe, not to mention its delicious cappuccinos.

"That's the one," he said.

"I can meet you there."

Deborah and Jill were standing nearby and started waving her down, mouthing, "you have to have him come pick you up!"

"Hold on, please," she said, covering the receiver. "No, the suite is a mess, and I'd be embarrassed to invite him over."

"We'll all help out and clean. We want to meet him!" Jill hissed.

Kaisa didn't care if he came to the dorm but wanted to appease her roommates' concerns. Her guess was they were merely curious and wanted to see whom she had defined as 'the man of her dreams.' *I'm not sure what they're worried about. I already survived the first encounter.*

She pitched the idea to Christopher. "Can you come pick me up here?"

He quickly fired back. "Really? Why?"

"Isn't that proper protocol for a first date?"

"We technically already had our first date," he said.

It was apparent from Christopher's tone that he thought it was a big inconvenience. Kaisa wanted to abandon the suggestion, but the girls kept coaching her from the sidelines, telling her to stand her ground. Finally, after promising she would make it worth his while, Kaisa was able to persuade him to come to the dorm.

The girls helped straighten up the common area while she got ready. The bedrooms were still pigsties but could be hidden behind closed doors. When they finished cleaning the common area, they argued about the best way to set the ambiance. Kaisa wanted to have classical music playing when he arrived. Deborah and Jill said that was over the top, so Mindy suggested Steve Winwood. Immediately after they inserted the cassette into the common area boombox, the downstairs buzzer went off. As Kaisa opened the door to go downstairs, Jill blocked her path.

"You don't want to look overly anxious. I'll go down and get him."

"Sure, what the hell do I know?" Kaisa said under her breath.

A few minutes later, Jill came back upstairs, accompanied by no one.

"What happened. Where did he go?" Kaisa worried.

"He said he didn't want to come up and asked if I could just send you down," she said, curling her lip.

"I'm just going to go, all right? Bye," Kaisa said in a huff throwing on her coat and grabbing her purse.

"No, wait here a minute. The rest of us are going to dinner anyway; we'll walk down with you," Jill insisted.

Kaisa waited anxiously pacing around the common area as Deborah, Jill, and Mindy put on their coats and shoes, got their purses, and then invited Heather to come along. It felt like ages. She worried Christopher might give up and leave because she was taking so long. Instead, they found him standing in the vestibule, his back facing the door, trying to be inconspicuous. He seemed agitated, uncomfortable, and not interested in meeting Kaisa's roommates. They respected his body language and didn't push for introductions yet scanned him up and down as they exited in single file.

"Hey. Thanks for coming by," Kaisa said.

"Look, I'm not into the whole dorm scene. I don't appreciate your friends evaluating me," he said coldly when he and Kaisa were finally alone.

"They just wanted to meet you. It wasn't my idea to invite you over," she said, putting her hand gently on his arm.

But he wouldn't shut up. "You don't need their approval. You're a smart girl who should be able to determine whether or not you want to see me because of your point of view. I don't know why girls need to be so nosy. Guys aren't like that."

What the hell? Is he kidding me? Why was she being reprimanded for her roommates' concerns? She did not need a lecture, nor did she do anything to deserve it. Kaisa contemplated leaving him there and following her roommates to dinner. Instead, she calmly suggested, "I wish you would just drop this, please."

"Okay, well, just so you know, this is the last time I'm coming here."

He led her up Hemenway Street toward Massachusetts Avenue. Hemenway Street got a little sketchy past the pharmacy on the corner attached to a turn-of-the-century residential hotel. Its stone exterior was drab and worn from decades of neglect. She gripped Christopher's hand. The block's top section was ominous with burned-out streetlights and questionable alleyways reserved for the occasional hooker or drug deal, or that's what the crew guys had said. Even in daylight, it was usually empty, and Kaisa avoided walking that far up alone. It was a shame because she had also overheard there was a good pizza joint there.

When they reached the intersection at the top of the street, to Kaisa's surprise, there was Tower Records. She didn't realize it was so close to her dorm. She knew how to get to her new favorite destinations via Mass Transit but was still learning how to get from point A to B on foot.

"You look confused," he said, then laughed and joked that she didn't know her way around Back Bay.

"I'm a bit geographically dyslexic. Boston's streets are not as easy to follow. They are not numbered like midtown Manhattan for example," she exclaimed but felt more like saying, 'Screw you, I stay mainly inside and study, I don't have time to wander around.'

"Back Bay's street names aren't completely random. The cross streets are alphabetical between here and the Boston Commons."

"Wow, I never noticed that," she said. "You learn something new every day."

"Oh, I have lots of things I can teach you," he said as he interlaced his fingers with hers and crossed over to the other side.

They arrived at the Trident Booksellers Café around the next corner. He opened the door for her. "Let's go inside; I want to sit down and talk with you about a few things."

Kaisa wasn't sure what he meant by that, but it didn't sound positive. They found an open table in the far corner of the café area. When a server came over, Christopher said he didn't want anything. Kaisa felt guilty using a café table intended for paying customers and ordered a cappuccino for herself.

"I've been thinking about the potential of our friendship. I thought a lot about it after you left the other day and kept wondering if I should call you again," Christopher said.

Kaisa held her breath and braced herself for a letdown. *Oh well, it was nice knowing you, too.*

"I had a great time with you that afternoon, and I think you did too. I would like to continue to see you if you are interested?"

She let out a sigh of relief and gave Christopher a slight grin while she burst on the inside. *Yay! He wants to pursue this further!*

"I find myself very attracted to you and sense that you might be attracted to me too. But just so you know, I'm not looking to get involved with someone or have a serious relationship right now. I would like to pursue our new friendship but in a more casual way. I think we could have a lot of fun."

Kaisa rested her chin on her hand, mainly to keep her jaw from dropping as she digested his proposal. She was surprised by how forthcoming he was in terms of what he wanted from their future encounters, clearly defining how they would spend their time together. She listened intently to his speech, as it went on and on, sounding as if it might have been rehearsed. His monologue took into consideration a few factors, including their differing ages, life experiences, but most of all, how they could mutually please each other.

"I'm wondering if you could handle something like that?" he asked.

She stirred her decapitated cappuccino several times. No doubt, with his looks, intellect, and charm, he could replace her in a heartbeat. If she agreed to his non-negotiable terms, this was what she was going to have to do to hold on to him. This potential friendship with this older, far more experienced man was akin to the stages of their respective educations. In other words, like a freshman signing up for a graduate class. She hadn't filled any sexual prerequisites yet. Well, she had enrolled in a short introductory seminar with Josh, but he was pretty pathetic. Maybe this course was going to be too advanced. What if she couldn't keep up at his level? But, despite all her qualms, she still had a burning desire to take this elective. Kaisa nodded, still wavering on her decision. "I would like to try. I may be young, but I'm mature for my age, and I think I can manage it."

"Are you sure?"

Her life thus far had been uneventful and dull, and her love life almost non-existent. She firmly believed their exchanges would be anything but that.

"Yes, I would like to continue seeing you," she said, thinking she could manage this thrill-ride for at least one more night.

"That's great. I was hoping for that," Christopher said with a sigh and a grin.

Kaisa's stomach grumbled. According to her watch, it was about 7:30 p.m. She hadn't eaten much that day and still hadn't eaten dinner

Christopher helped himself to a few sips of her coffee then gulped down the rest. "I didn't bring any cash. I hope you don't mind covering your cappuccino?" he said.

She was surprised he didn't offer to pick up this small tab, especially after she just took a giant leap of faith. Kaisa paid for the coffee and left the change as a tip. "Where are we going next?" she asked as they left the café, hoping he would say a restaurant.

"We're going to my place," he said.

A tingling chill streamed down Kaisa's spine, followed by goosebumps. *Maybe I am getting in over my head?*

Christopher's apartment was not too far away. As they walked down Newbury Street, Kaisa remembered she had an old pack of cigarettes and matches in her purse. She pulled out a Marlboro Light, put it in her mouth, and lit it. Perhaps she could curb her hunger with a smoke.

"Wow, I would have never pictured you as a smoker. You shouldn't do that, sweetheart. It's bad for you." He slowly reached for the cigarette and carefully pulled it from her lips. He inhaled one long drag before throwing it on the sidewalk and stomping on it.

That night, Christopher's apartment was dim, with just a small black desk light. He removed her coat and hung it on a hook on his closet door. While his back was facing her, Kaisa sprinted to his desk chair and sat down.

"I'm working on a paper on Christian Ethics and wanted to read some of it to you if you don't mind."

"Sure."

After a few minutes of listening, Kaisa started to zone out. She wasn't sure if her head was spinning due to malnourishment or the long prose of his paper. Every word was no less than four syllables long. She didn't think this man could possibly bore her, but he was doing an excellent job. Maybe the subject matter was too advanced, or maybe he was trying to put her into some hypnotic trance. Was this some sort of intellectual foreplay? But she kept smiling and feigning interest, worrying about what might be next on his docket.

"What do you think?" he asked.

"It's good, but I think the prose are a bit gratuitous," she said, using her best SAT vocabulary. You can get your message across without tangling up the reader in one gargantuan word after another."

"I probably lost you because the paper is over your head," he said, evidently not appreciating her criticism.

"It seems I need to teach you a thing or two." He threw the papers to the side and scooped her up. Grabbing both sides of her sweater, he lifted her toward his face and kissed her with a passionate force. Kaisa parted her lips to welcome his tongue as he moaned in approval.

He guided her in a synchronized step toward the bay window, which framed the glowing phallic Prudential Building. Their eyes met in the window's reflection, with the dim light of his apartment serving as a backdrop against the night sky. She watched as his hand disappeared underneath her sweater, feeling his warm touch as he caressed her young skin.

"Come over here with me," he said, taking her hand. He led her to the mattress and laid her down. His fingers unzipped and slowly lowered her pants, revealing the turquoise butterfly underwear she received as a gift from her roommates, which she wore, just in case. "Aren't you a sexy little thing," he said, pulling off her panties, leaving them hanging on one ankle. "You make me so hot." He removed his pants then collapsed on top of her. Kaisa could feel his hard bulge circling and pounding the vicinity of her pubic area through his boxers.

"Do you know the difference between a bump and a grind?" he asked.

"Um, not really," she said.

Christopher proceeded to educate Kaisa on the difference by demonstrating each move as he gyrated against her pelvis. He gave her one last kiss before descending his face toward her stomach and continuing further south. His fingers explored in and around her body, uncovering erogenous zones Kaisa didn't know she had.

"You are so tight," he said before plunging several more digits into her vagina. Kaisa twitched as one entered her anal orifice. It felt strangely satisfying but painful, causing her to squirm at every thrust. But that unpleasant feeling quickly changed to another foreign but incredibly erotic sensation. His tongue was pulsating rapidly against her clitoris in an almost machine-like rhythm. She laid back and closed her eyes to focus on his talents. His performance was nothing short of sensational. Of course, she had nothing to compare it to, but whatever he was doing felt amazing and was making her writhe in pleasure. In one explosive burst, he sent her to a place she had never been before. Her body quivered in response to her first taste of ecstasy. She was hooked.

"Did you like that?" he asked.

"Yesss," she echoed breathlessly, her heart still throbbing. "That was just. Wow!"

"How would you describe my technique?"

"A delightful... vibration," she said, disappointed in her response.

"That's the worst possible description!" he said.

"I'm sorry it's all I could think of. I'll come up with a great one for next time." *Provided there is a next time.*

Christopher straddled Kaisa across her chest. She had a feeling he was expecting something in return. But after that sexual favor, she didn't mind reciprocating. "Put your mouth on me," he ordered.

She accepted his penis and glided her lips up and down his erection, doing her best to remember that carrot in the cafeteria scene. It concerned her that he might be less than pleased with her amateur performance. "Try to take me further down your throat!" he said as he thrust deeper. She gagged a couple of times but kept going, doing anything in her power to maximize his pleasure and amplify his experience. "Oh, sweetheart, I can't believe this is your first time doing this," he praised. "I knew you'd be a natural."

Kaisa hoped he was close to finishing as she anticipated his release. By now, her jaw was aching, and she just wanted it to be over. Just then, Christopher extracted himself from her mouth.

"We should probably hold off on actual intercourse, but there's always butt-fucking," he said so delicately.

Kaisa didn't know what to say. She had committed to their arrangement at least for tonight and promised herself she would see it through. He walked bottomless to the bathroom and retrieved a bottle of Nivea lotion, then squeezed a drop into his hand. She instantly recognized the fragrance. *So that was his "cologne."*

He turned her onto her stomach. "Lift your ass high, like a cat stretch," he instructed. Kaisa acquiesced. With her head on a pillow and her face buried under her long hair, she worried about what anal sex would feel like but kept going, knowing it was a less risky option in terms of getting pregnant.

She arched her back, and through a veil of hair, caught sight of herself in the reflection of the rounded TV screen.

Kaisa stared at this slutty girl with her behind in the air and a man rolling his erection along the crevice of her backside, as if she were watching someone else.

He pierced his cock between her cheeks. Kaisa shrieked at the sharp stabbing pain, then let out an instant cry of protest. "Christopher, please stop!"

He resisted and kept pumping, whispering, "Oh, just a little more, it feels so good to be inside you."

She wriggled away just as he reached orgasm. "I guess I can't deal with this. This is too fast for me!" She jumped up and scurried to the bathroom to clean off the mess. After she finished, she remembered what her friend Gina had said about pre-seminal droplets. Apparently, it was possible to get pregnant, even if a man's penis doesn't enter the vagina. He was in the general area. She hoped the cloth she used to clean up didn't push them up further. That's all she needed.

When Kaisa returned from the bathroom, she put on her clothes, sending what she hoped was a clear signal that tonight's party was over. She laid down next to him and put her head on his chest. He put his arm around her and tickled her ankle with his foot.

"I guess we're done for tonight?" he proclaimed. "I'm sorry if I went too far for you."

Kaisa looked away and shrugged her shoulders.

"I really enjoyed our time together. I wish I could make you my sex slave, hang you in my closet, and take you out when the mood strikes," he chuckled.

"Well, life's not that easy," she said.

He leaned in, smiled, and kissed the scowl off her face. "Listen, I have to study, and I have some people coming over soon."

Kaisa could have sworn he'd said that he finished for today when he called her earlier. "Could you walk me home then?"

"It's only about 9 p.m. There should be plenty of cabs out there," he said.

"I spent most of what I had on that cappuccino. I don't have enough to get me home from here."

"Unfortunately, I don't have any cash on me either. I can't just leave as they are probably on their way."

"I don't think after what I just did that I'm asking for a lot from you to see that I get home safely."

They compromised on having him escort her to the bookseller's café. As they strolled up Marlborough Street, Christopher talked casually about the weather and the cascading pink clouds in the sky, while Kaisa brooded in silence with her hands in her pockets, in utter disbelief of what she had let him do to a virgin like her. Or was she a virgin anymore? Kaisa wasn't sure. She never expected the first time a man would enter her; it would be in that way.

"I just found five bucks in my jacket lining. Do you want that cab to take you the rest of the way?" Christopher said, offering to hail it down.

"Never mind. See you around," Kaisa said, stretching out her hand, expecting this to be a permanent goodbye.

Christopher gave her a perplexed look. "What do you

mean by that? I hope we can see each other again." He kissed her goodbye and said, "I'll call you."

Famous last words. She watched him turn and walk away.

The feeling of starvation had passed, but there was still a lingering ache of hunger. The dining hall had closed hours ago. After reaching the top of Hemenway Street and not seeing any questionable individuals lurking, she ran down the iffy stretch toward the pizza place. She sat on a wide bench facing the window devouring her large slice. *Why did I go so far so soon? Am I a slut? Is this too much for me? Will he ever call me again?*

Kaisa took one last look around for shady characters, then dashed back to her dorm.

Deborah and Jill were watching TV in the common room, munching on a family-size bag of potato chips.

"How did it go?" Deborah asked.

"Umm, it was different," Kaisa replied, too shell-shocked to talk.

"Did you smoke him?" Jill said jokingly using Mindy's reference for a blow job.

"What?" Kaisa said.

"Well, he was squatting over me with his genitals in my face, so I had NO other option," Kaisa snapped without thinking.

Jill pulled back and held up her hands, "I was just kidding."

Kaisa paused, "Yeah, so was I," she said with a false

smile. "I'll tell you more tomorrow. I have to study for a quiz. Hey, can I have a few of your chips? I'm still hungry."

"Sure, help yourself."

"Thanks," Kaisa said, grabbing a good handful.

"Didn't you just go out to dinner?" Deborah asked.

Kaisa pretended she didn't hear and walked into her room.

"What was that about?" she overheard Jill ask Deborah as Kaisa closed the bedroom door.

CHAPTER 6
Defenses Down with the Trust of a Child

I t had been three days since Kaisa heard from Christopher. With each passing day, the future of their "friendship" became more uncertain. Had he concluded that she wasn't worth his time? If not, did she have the mettle to continue? The events of their last encounter kept repeating in her head, making her question if she made the right choices or if she said or did something wrong. Kaisa had documented their previous two meetings in a notebook because she could barely believe what happened herself. She hoped that expressing her emotions on paper would help her figure out what to do next. Along with her journal entries, she had penned several drafts of a letter, trying to sound as sophisticated and Harvard-esque as possible, in case she decided against moving forward:

Dear Christopher:

I've been analyzing and evaluating our present arrangement. I'm not sure how I feel about being a sex slave, as you so call it. I find you to be an interesting and fascinating individual who is not only physically but intellectually stimulating. While I am very much attracted to you, we are polar opposites with different philosophies on sexual intimacy. Therefore, if you would like to continue a friendship with me, it would have to be one that is purely platonic. I feel I am venturing into something that perhaps I don't have the maturity or experience to deal with.

Respectfully yours,

Kaisa

Damn. I ended the last sentence with a preposition. I'm going to have to work on that. Kaisa put the letter aside, deciding to give herself another 24 hours to think through her situation.

The next evening, Kaisa was working on her economics assignment while Jill was hard at work being an asshole, calling the suite's phone line, and hanging up. She kept calling every five minutes and wouldn't stop. Kaisa initially fell for it, but after a few more times, she figured out who was the crank caller. She picked up the phone, brought it to the toilet, and flushed it in her ear. But it didn't deter Jill. The next time the phone rang, Deborah picked up, saying she too was getting sick of Jill's obnoxious behavior.

"Will you stop!" Deborah yelled. "Oh, sorry, who is this? I can't hear you very well."

Jill came out of Mindy's room. "I think it might be one of your brothers," Deborah said, handing the phone to Jill.

"Kaisa, I don't know who this is. I don't recognize the voice. But he's asking for you."

"Hello?" she said.

"Kaisa?"

The voice sent a shivering wave of adrenaline through her core.

"Yes?"

"Finally, I got you," he said, uttering a sigh of relief.

Deborah and Jill remained close by. "Is it, Christopher?" they mouthed.

Kaisa nodded with a grin.

"Are you wet?" Jill whispered.

Kaisa mouthed back, "Fuck off," and kicked them out of her bedroom.

"What's going on?" Christopher asked, "I kept getting passed around to different people."

"My roommate Jill was messing with all of us. She kept calling and hanging up. We thought it was her calling again."

"You must not be very busy then."

"Jill is about as much into studying as usual, which is not at all, but I'm swamped. I've been trying to study for my test and finish other homework before the dorm council meeting tonight."

"Is that so?" he said. "Well, I'm pretty busy myself, and I'm sure my curriculum is exponentially more difficult than yours."

"Maybe so, but Economics isn't exactly a walk in the park."

"Have you been thinking about me?" he asked.

Of course, she had… at breakfast, at lunch, at dinner, in the shower, in class, at the T-stop, at the library, in bed, any time there was a quiet moment for her mind to wander. But Kaisa couldn't tell him that. "I was wondering the same thing," she said.

"In fact, yes, I have been fantasizing about you. I have a little time for you now if you would like to come over."

"Sorry, as much as I would love to, I'm really busy tonight. I have a meeting in a few minutes. Plus, I have a big Economics test tomorrow."

Christopher didn't seem to care about her commitments. "It has to be tonight. Otherwise, I am going to be busy for at least two weeks because I have a twenty-page paper that is ten days overdue."

"What about this Thursday or over the weekend?" she suggested.

Christopher refused. He said he would be in Cambridge because he had a section meeting for one of his classes. It was now or never. "If you come over soon, I'll walk you home."

"Fine. I'll see if I can get out of the dorm council meeting tonight," she said, opting for now versus never.

"Good. I'll see you in about an hour."

Kaisa went downstairs to tell the resident director she had a bit of an emergency. Fortunately, she was kind enough to let Kaisa out of the meeting, but it still didn't give her much time to shower and change. She hadn't washed her hair in a couple of days, and it would take too long now. A ponytail was an option, but that usually made the oily strands around her ears stand out even more. Kaisa took a quick body shower, shaved her legs, and selected a white turtleneck, Northeastern sweater, Gasoline skinny jeans, and high-top sneakers.

Next, she applied her makeup, carefully covering the pimple rupturing on her chin. She dabbed on some extra foundation and concealer, hoping it would do the trick.

"How do I look?" Kaisa asked Deborah.

"You look fine. Here, put on a spritz of my Lagerfeld perfume," Deborah said, handing the bottle to her.

Kaisa aimed the bottle at her neck and was about to squeeze the atomizer when Deborah jumped in. "No, that's not the right way to put on perfume. Let me have it for a second." Deborah held the perfume bottle up, sprayed the mist into the air, then walked into the scattering droplets. Kaisa followed suit. Given Deborah's success with the opposite sex, she seemed to know what was effective.

The frigid January evening met Kaisa at her front door and accompanied her on her trek to the Symphony Road

T-Stop. It wasn't long before her hands were numb. She shoved them into the thinly lined pockets of her coat to discover the fabric ripped on one side. The bulky headphones from her Walkman made great make-shift earmuffs that blocked the piercing wind. She got off at Copley Place and walked the rest of the way admiring the brownstones and twinkling city lights. When she arrived at 293 Marlborough Street, she rang the bell marked Morton. A few moments passed before Christopher appeared at the front door. He had a short new haircut that made him look exceptionally handsome.

"Nice to see you. Thanks for coming." He held out his hands, and Kaisa grabbed on, "Your hands are freezing!" he said, clasping them between his and rubbing them vigorously. Christopher's hands were soft and supple, not like her dad's, which were rough and calloused from all the manual labor he had done throughout his life.

"I know. It's like fucking ten below out there."

"Such a potty mouth for a pristine girl."

"Yeah, sometimes it just feels right."

"I don't find it appealing when women curse. I wish you wouldn't do it." He wrapped his arm around her shoulder as they walked up the stairs. Kaisa welcomed the body heat. After entering his apartment, Christopher helped Kaisa take off her coat then turned to hang it on the side of his closet door. His shorter hair revealed a large bald spot on the back of his head that she hadn't noticed before. It seemed unfortunate that he was already losing his hair at 26.

"So, what's new in your life?" he asked

"Nothing much, same old grind," she replied, pulling her turtleneck over her nose.

Christopher laughed. "Do I make a pleasant change from your routine?"

"Yes," said Kaisa. *That's an understatement.*

"I like whatever fragrance you are wearing. What's it called?

"KL Karl Lagerfeld," she replied.

"It's really nice."

Good call, Deborah.

He ushered Kaisa toward the window. *This again? Is he trying to make someone across the street, jealous?* He put his arms around her waist and drew her close. Christopher leaned in. His lips met hers, and she kissed him hungrily. For this, she didn't mind being on display. A Northeastern freshman embracing her Harvard man in a quaint Back Bay neighborhood on a moonlit night. Could it be any more romantic?

"You know, you can be a very passionate person," he said, holding her gaze with her face in his hands.

"I'm glad you think so," she said.

He observed her Northeastern sweater. "You had to wear it?"

"Hey, I had like no time to change," she said, knowing she wore it intentionally.

"That's okay, I'm going to remove it from your body

now anyway," he grinned. He turned her around and, with one stroke, pulled off the sweater and threw it aside, then caressed her torso as he knelt before her. His warm lips laid soft kisses on her braless breasts. "Does that feel good?" he asked, as he nipped and fondled each one.

"Mmhmm," Kaisa hummed and nodded at his profoundly dumb question.

A trail of gentle pecks followed the course of her body toward her stomach while he stroked her legs and inner thighs. Strips of crackling Velcro echoed in her ears, signaling her to step out of her sneakers. That meant her jeans were next. But these jeans were like armor. They were tightly cropped at the ankles and were always a challenge to take off. Kaisa wondered if these were a subconscious choice. She laughed to herself as Christopher tried to peel them off her legs. But they didn't hold Christopher up for very long. After a couple of missed attempts, he was able to overcome her denim obstacle.

"Will you let me fuck you in the ass tonight? Please, please, let me fuck you in the ass," he begged.

"No," she exclaimed. "I think I'm done with that."

"Why?"

"You went too fast last time, and it hurt."

"This time, I promise I won't go as fast."

"I thought our friendship was supposed to be about mutual pleasure. It was painful, and I didn't enjoy it," she stated. "That is literally out of my comfort zone."

Christopher was tickled by her choice of words and

chuckled in response. "Alright then, since you won't let me put it in your butt, can I finish in your mouth?"

Kaisa half-heartedly agreed because it was the better option, and it would still make him happy. She recalled a pre-college birds and bees talk with her more experienced cousin Lara and her friend. They both said they swallowed, so maybe it wouldn't be that bad. But Kaisa was not looking forward to her first taste of semen.

"Women I know have found this to be effective," Christopher interjected. "If you roll your tongue in a U shape like this," he said, demonstrating with his tongue, "you can take me deeper, and it makes a clear path for the semen to go down."

Great tip. Better write that one down.

Christopher guided her along, coaching her through the process, while Kaisa responded to his cues. "That's great, sweetheart; you are doing so well," he praised. "Can you go deeper?" His erection stiffened and throbbed as he pumped harder and faster. Kaisa prepared herself for what was about to happen. He moaned and gasped, grabbing the hair on either side of her head just as he ejaculated. With each pulse and wave, the warm, salty secretion flowed into her mouth, over her tongue, and down her throat. As predicted, it was disgusting, and she was not a fan.

Kaisa pulled away and rolled onto her soured face while he hummed and whistled like it was no big deal. She looked up at him with a defeated look to see him smirking in triumph. Kaisa figured since this was over, he would probably usher her out.

"Here, now I just want to stay like this for a while," Christopher said as he laid down beside her. He picked up a pink wool blanket, covered himself, and partially covered Kaisa leaving her naked behind exposed.

After laying there for a few minutes feeling the chill on her butt, Kaisa turned onto her back. She stared up at the cracked ceiling, eyeing a cobweb near a light fixture. *Where is this going? What am I doing? Am I enjoying this? Yes, the physical part where he pleasures me is excellent, but is that enough?* Despite her doubts, Kaisa was relishing this post-coital exchange.

A loud snore interrupted her thoughts. He had drifted off, as most men do after sex, as far as what she had read in Cosmo and heard from her roommates. As he slept, she examined the man she chose to engage with in these extra-curricular activities, his sleek frame, the tiny crow's feet along his eyes, and his otherwise flawless complexion. She snuggled closer and startled him awake.

"Sorry, I dozed off," he said. He gazed at Kaisa and pulled her close in a firm grip. He drew his fingers across her innocent face, and when they reached her lips, she kissed them.

"Now, what can I do for you this evening?" he inquired with a seductive look in his eyes.

"Tell me more about yourself," Kaisa said.

"There's not much to tell. I have a younger brother and an older sister. My parents live in Nashville. Our relationship, at times, has been strained. I don't really like to talk about it. But most kids don't get along with their parents, right?"

"I have a good relationship with mine," Kaisa said proudly.

"Are you sure? Does your mother love you?"

His inquiry threw her for a loop. No one ever asked her that because those who knew her would think the question was ridiculous. "She practically lives for my love," she answered.

"What about your dad?"

"I'm Daddy's little girl."

"How do you know?"

"There's no question about it." There were plenty of things that Kaisa was unsure of, but this was not one of them. "My dad goes out of his way for me all the time. He always has breakfast and dinner for me. When I used to work in the summer and was running late, he would iron my clothes, even though he had his own job to get to."

"So, you are quite spoiled?"

Kaisa didn't think so. She just thought her parents behaved the way they did because they loved her, and that's what parents were supposed to do. Why would she complain about being the center of attention?

"How much does your father make?"

"That's a bit bold of you to ask."

"You don't have to tell me if you don't want to."

"No, I guess it's okay. My mom and dad both work,

and maybe they bring in about $40,000 a year together. I mean, they don't share their tax return with me. It's a lot less than most other parents make in my town, but I never felt deprived or anything," she said. "Why do you ask?"

"Just a question. But then how can they afford to pay for college?"

"I'm pretty much covering it."

"How are you so independently wealthy?"

"I'm not. I've been saving all my life. Whenever I got money as a gift, I asked my mom to put it in the bank. With that and the money I earned from chores, babysitting, and other part-time jobs, I had enough to pay for the first year. I desperately wanted to go away to school like everyone else, so I decided to use it for that."

"Wow, pretty impressive."

"Are you a full-time student?" she asked.

"Yes."

"Then how do you support this apartment?"

"College scholarship."

"No way, you're kidding," she said doubtfully. *This sure as hell isn't campus housing.*

"Do you have a part-time job?" she asked.

"School keeps me busy enough."

It was getting late, and she had more studying to finish if she wanted to do well on tomorrow's exam. "I have to go and study," she said, borrowing a line from Christopher's playbook.

"I'll call you a cab after I watch you get dressed."

"I hope I can find my clothes, now that you threw them everywhere," she stated as she got up from the mattress to retrieve them. He casually reclined on the pillow as Kaisa collected her things and put them on.

"Now, please call me a cab," she requested.

"I'm too lazy," he responded, grinning and not moving from the mattress.

"Does the phone cord stretch to the bed?"

"No, you call," he said indignantly.

She stuck her tongue out at him.

"How juvenile. You ARE a spoiled brat," he said.

Kaisa called several different cab companies but kept getting busy signals and couldn't get through. Was there a strike she didn't know about? Why the shortage? It was after 10 p.m., which meant there was less of a chance of hailing one down in this residential area. After 20 minutes, she was able to reach one dispatcher. Kaisa pulled her coat off the closet door as Christopher got up off the mattress.

"Oh sure, now you get up," she said.

"No need to rush, the cab will probably take at least 15 minutes to get here." He lowered his boxers and guided her hand to his genitals. "Rub it lightly," he whispered.

She wrapped her perfect ectomorphic fingers around his penis and kneaded it gently, looking into his ocean blue eyes before they rolled back into his head. She rested her head on his chest as he lightly pressed it downward.

Knowing what he was after, she reluctantly took him into her mouth. But as his breathing sped up, she removed her lips. "That's enough. I'm not swallowing twice in one night. I do have standards."

A car horn beeped. He met her at the doorway, grabbed her shoulders, and gave her a short, sweet peck goodbye. Kaisa put on her coat, double-checking she had her keys and ID.

"Here," he said, grabbing her waistband and shoving her loose turtleneck into her jeans. "You'll stay much warmer this way." Christopher picked up his pants from the floor, reached into the pocket, and handed Kaisa a few dollars. "I know I promised to walk you home. It's all I have right now. I hope it's enough."

"Thank you," she said. "When will I see you again?"

"Give me a call. I'd like to know you are thinking of me too."

"I better get this cab before it leaves," Kaisa said.

"You sure you have everything?"

"Oh, my Walkman!" Kaisa swiped it from the desk and sprinted downstairs

"Thanks for waiting!" she said to the driver. Kaisa crouched down in the backseat, put on her headphones, and pressed play. She stared out the window into the clear cobalt night as the song played: *'Belief is the way, the way of the innocent, and when I say innocent, I should say naïve.'*

CHAPTER 7
No Place for Beginners or Sensitive Hearts

I sn't it always the way - Feast or Famine? Now that Kaisa wasn't actively looking for love, other men she'd found attractive seemed to be seeking her out.

One such individual was Mac, her cute neighbor from across the hall. She ran into him one night in the laundry room, where he asked if she wouldn't mind helping him with his English paper. She said she would be more than happy to help him write it sometime over the weekend. But he never came over.

Kaisa had a slight crush on Mac. But she wasn't sure if Mac was interested in her beyond helping him with his paper. Heather had a crush on him too. Even though he and Heather were in the same class, he didn't ask her for help. No surprise, as she could barely write her way out of a paper bag. Like Heather, he was in the Alternative Freshman Program, which was like college on training wheels. It was an option for students who barely met the admission requirements. They had little to no homework, and their curriculum consisted of concepts that Kaisa learned in the 10th grade.

On Monday, when Kaisa returned from the study room downstairs, she found Mac at her front door with paper in hand.

"Hey Kaisa, I was just about to see if you were home. Is this a good time for you to help me with my paper?"

"Yeah, sure," she said, inviting him into the suite. On the way to her room, they passed Heather and Jill before shutting the door for a little privacy. No more than two seconds later, Kaisa heard a knock.

"Come in," Kaisa said.

"Sorry to interrupt, but do either of you have any gum?" Heather asked, sticking her head inside.

Really? You have to ask this now?

"Oh, by the way, James called earlier. I just realized I forgot to give you the message," Heather said in a sing-songy voice.

Of course, she had to relay the message at this opportune moment.

"James is my old school friend," Kaisa explained to Mac. "He goes to Boston College. We've known each other since we were five years old when we sang in the children's church choir."

Mac smiled and nodded without any regard.

Out in the common area, the phone sounded its

cricket-like chirp. Kaisa hoped it was for her. She and Christopher had exchanged a couple of calls over the last few days. She called him on Saturday for a study break. He told her he liked that excuse, so he rang her back on Sunday afternoon for the same reason. But it seemed each time he phoned; he came through on call-waiting when Kaisa was on with someone else. She worried this gave him the impression that she was darting for the phone each time it rang because she always answered after the first click.

Even when the girls were right next to the phone, they would follow the suite's answering protocol, casually waiting for at least two rings before picking up.

Jill emerged behind Heather in the common area. "It's for you," she calmly stated, holding the phone out.

Kaisa rose from her chair. "I'll be right back, Mac," she giggled.

"It's Christopher. I guess the man just can't get enough?" Jill said, handing her the phone.

"I told you he's intelligent," Kaisa beamed. It felt great being in demand. James called, she was in the middle of helping Mac, and now Christopher... Trifecta. She leaned her head in the doorway to her bedroom. "Do you mind if we pick this up in a few minutes? I've been waiting for this call."

"Sure, I didn't realize you were so popular," he joked. "Come by across the hall when you're done," he said as he got up to leave.

"Oh, by the way, don't forget when you finish writing

your paper, I can type it for you for a dollar a page if you want." At 70 words per minute, she could rapidly convert a written assignment into a finished product ready for submission, while other students, who didn't have these skills, would hunt and peck for hours.

"That sounds good. I might take you up on it. I failed typing class in high school."

Was she being overly ambitious, offering her services now that she had a new part-time job? That was the other area where the famine had ended. One of Deborah's co-workers got fired and, with Deborah's help, she was able to land a job at Mrs. Fields Cookies. This meant Kaisa could retrace the steps of when and where she met Christopher each time she went to work and, better yet, relieve her mom of the monthly stipend even though Kaisa knew she would continue to send it nonetheless.

"Kaisa," Christopher said, "who are you typing papers for?"

"My neighbor across the hall."

"I didn't know you did that."

"Yes, it's one of my many talents," she quipped.

"I'll have to keep that in mind. I never learned how to type. Sooo, are you in your room alone now?"

"Yes."

"Good, because I don't want anyone listening to our conversations. I hope you aren't telling anyone of our antics."

"Why?"

"I get paranoid when people make judgments about me and try to influence others with their opinions. I'm afraid if you tell them too much, the girls will get jealous and start resenting me because I make you so happy."

"I don't foresee that as being a problem," she said.

"I would appreciate your discretion, nonetheless."

Kaisa agreed, knowing it would be a challenge to keep their further antics to herself, considering what she had already divulged. "So, to what do I owe the pleasure of your call?" she flirted.

"You were distracting me from writing my paper."

"How could I be distracting you? I've been here the whole time."

"I couldn't stop fantasizing about you and wanted to hear your voice."

It was nice to know she was having an effect on him.

"What are you wearing?" he asked.

"A T-shirt and my best sweatpants," she taunted.

"That's not very hot. I like it when women look feminine. Do you have any skirts?"

"Yes, I have skirts."

"How about the kilt kind, like one a Catholic school girl would wear?"

Kaisa replied, "I don't own any of those. They are not my style."

"It would be great if you could get your hands on one. I'd love to see you in a short kilt skirt with knee socks and pigtails," said Christopher, expanding upon his fantasy.

Kaisa didn't get it. She was trying to act closer to his age, and he wanted her to appear even younger. That was a little weird. But at least he wasn't into whips and chains. "I have a sexy black lace bra and panty set I just bought at Filene's Basement. I could wear it next time," she said, suggesting more adult lingerie. But that did not raise his interest. His reaction couldn't have been more apathetic. She might as well have been talking about her Garfield underwear.

"See what you can find. I will call you later in the week. It was nice talking to you. Take care."

Now Kaisa was on a mission. She did live with four other girls that were around the same size. "Hey guys, could you help me out with something? Do any of you have a kilt skirt I could borrow?" she said, thinking Mindy would be her best bet with her preppy style.

"What for?" Jill asked.

"I'm trying to put together an outfit for Christopher."

"I do," Deborah replied, "you can check my closet."

Kaisa rummaged through Deborah's clothes AND Bingo! Behind her new fringed suede jacket was a red, white, and green tartan kilt skirt, complete with a large gold safety pin accessory that fit his description perfectly. "Do you have anything to go with this?" she asked Jill, holding up the skirt on its hanger.

Jill returned with a cropped white cotton sweater.

Kaisa combined the items with her sheer red knee socks and her black loafers. After the outfit was complete, she put it on, and much to her surprise, she didn't think she looked that bad. But pigtails were a bit over the top. She went out into the common area to model it for the girls. "Thanks, guys, this is awesome."

The thought of surprising Christopher was getting Kaisa excited. She wanted to go now to show off her new ensemble, but Jill told her it would make her look too desperate. If not for her accounting exam tomorrow and the fact that she was on the tail end of her period, she might not have had the will to hold her back. Fulfilling his fantasy was going to have to wait.

Anticipating her next visit with Christopher was no small feat. The days she didn't hear from him dragged. He consumed her thoughts and distracted her from her schoolwork, appearing in her mind throughout the day. From the moment she woke up, during her classes, and especially at night when she was alone in her room in bed.

Kaisa laid in her bottom bunk, listening for her roommates, but heard nothing. They all must have gone to bed. Deborah was out with someone and most likely wasn't coming home. Her body ached for Christopher. The thought of him pleasuring her and how amazing that felt was getting her aroused. Maybe it was time to complete Christopher's assignment. He did have a point that she should familiarize herself with what felt good and what drove her over the edge.

Kaisa closed her eyes, envisioning their next encounter and fulfilling his school-girl fantasy. Slipping her hand under her T-shirt, she glided it around her full breasts, caressing her areolas, then slid her other hand underneath to give both a pinch and a slight tug. Her nipples hardened. One hand traveled further down her body, raking her fingers down her chest then to her stomach, pausing at every sensitive pulse point - until she discovered the most delicate area between her thighs.

She moved her fingers in a circular motion, pressing down to increase the friction, visualizing Christopher between her legs, working his magic with his tongue. She thrust her hips back and forth, increasing the sensation. As she neared the peak, she massaged more vigorously, feeling herself approach the climb to euphoria. It was as if her knees represented a mountain she had to get over. Her body rose as this new sense of awareness welled up and intensified. "Oh my God. Oh my God," she panted, then let out a silent satisfied cry as the final contraction sent a tingle down her legs, her heart pounding heavily in her chest. Kaisa let out a long breath. Suddenly, a peaceful calm washed over her as the morphine-like endorphins flooded her system.

I guess this ends tonight's anatomy lesson. Christopher would be proud. Not sure why I waited so long. She slowly extracted her hand, and within a few minutes, she drifted off to sleep.

Kaisa's day kicked off with a 69 on her accounting exam, even though she studied super hard for it. Later that evening, on her way home from work, she bought a pint of Ben & Jerry's Chunky Monkey to drown her sorrows. As she sat back to watch her 10-inch black and white TV, with carton and spoon in hand, she heard the phone chirp once, twice, then a third time.

"Do you want me to get it?" Kaisa yelled.

Jill answered. "Just chill, I got it."

She returned to her TV and ice cream.

"It's for you," Jill said.

She put the phone to her ear.

"Kaisa?" said a breathy hypnotic voice.

"Yes?" she answered, her body tingling.

"It's Chris. What are you doing?"

"Oh nothing, watching television. 'Growing Pains' is coming on."

"Well, if you're so busy, why don't you come over and see me?"

"I'm a little tired. I just got back from work about a half-hour ago." She told him about her new job in Copley Place and asked him to guess what kind of store. Kaisa was flattered that he guessed a bookstore. In her experience, only intelligent people worked in establishments like that. "I wish you would come over here. It's been a long week."

"Kaisa, you know how I feel about the dorm scene. I wouldn't feel comfortable around a bunch of kids. Plus, it wouldn't be very private."

Perhaps she could muster the energy to go over since she had waited so long for his invitation. "I guess I could be there in an hour or so."

"I'll see you then."

"I have a surprise for you," she teased.

Christopher grew quiet, and his tone changed. "I don't like surprises," he said.

"Well, I'm sure you'll like this one," Kaisa responded, trying to lighten his mood. "See you soon."

She jumped into the shower and lathered her hair with Deborah's strawberry-scented shampoo, which she later paired with lemon mousse. Now that she smelled like some sort of tart, she assembled the fantasy outfit to look like one.

Jill's powerful blow dryer was not working fast enough. Too impatient to finish, she put her long damp hair in a single braid, which Heather tied into a bow with a white lace ribbon. Mindy offered her a red purse to complete the ensemble. Even though each roommate contributed to her attire, the girls were not happy about Kaisa venturing out alone after 9 p.m. in their neighborhood, especially in that outfit. But Kaisa couldn't be held back and confidently stated, "I'll be fine."

Westland Avenue was nearly deserted with several flickering streetlights. She sped up her pace on the dark street, keeping her eye on the much busier thoroughfare up ahead. A set of heavy footsteps trudged behind. Kaisa curled her fist as she clutched her keys with the biggest, sharpest one protruding between her fingers. Across the street was an angry homeless man ranting outside of the Stop & Shop. She contemplated turning around and going back more than once, but her desire to see Christopher outweighed any of these variables or her common sense.

She arrived at Christopher's doorstep, unscathed, and pushed the buzzer for his apartment. Kaisa bubbled with anticipation as she listened for the muffled thumps of his feet coming down the stairs. When he opened the door, Kaisa slowly and seductively unbuttoned her coat.

"Nice outfit!" he said, scanning her up and down. "Is this my surprise?"

"Yes."

He put his arm around her and escorted her upstairs. When they entered his cluttered apartment, Christopher sat down on the mattress and invited her to join him. "I was planning on us just watching TV tonight," he said. "I hope you don't mind."

"Sure. That's fine."

They sat with their legs extended, watching TV for about a half-hour with Christopher holding and caressing her hands. She tilted her head and leaned on his shoulder, privileged to be in his company. It was wonderful to just spend time with him, but she couldn't help but feel disappointed that her fantasy outfit wasn't turning him on. "If you just wanted to hang out and watch TV tonight, we could have done that at my place," Kaisa whined.

"You're such a little brat," Christopher teased. "You know, seriously, I was going to be a boring person tonight. But you look so hot in that outfit."

Maybe it wasn't a total bomb.

He got up and stretched out his hand, pulling Kaisa off

the mattress. "Unbutton me, please," he said.

Kaisa innocently reached for the buttons on his shirt, but he redirected her to his pants. He was wearing light blue boxers, which were a lot sexier than the plain white nut huggers Josh wore.

"Pull them down a bit," he said. "Now, touch it lightly."

She massaged his erection while Christopher guided her hand up and down the shaft.

"That's a good girl, now grab firmly and rub it hard. Tell me you love to suck my cock."

Kaisa gazed downward, pretending she didn't hear what he said.

"Say it," he commanded.

"No, I feel stupid. I don't want to."

"Miss Potty Mouth doesn't want to talk dirty? Oh, come on, just do it."

"I love to suck your cock," she mumbled through her teeth.

"Look at me. Say it again. Make me believe it."

"Christopher, I love to suck your cock!" she said, blushing. Kaisa put her mouth on him and began sucking. Although it wasn't her favorite thing, she was impressed by how quickly she was getting the hang of it and how much further she could go without gagging. But this time, it was taking him a lot longer to finish.

"I'll give you a little break," he said.

"Is it my turn now?" she asked, sitting back on the mattress.

"Do you like it when I pleasure you?"

"Without a doubt," she purred. "Hey, remember when you asked me to describe how oral sex from you felt?'"

"Did I?"

Kaisa was beginning to wonder if he listened to a word she ever said. "It bothered me that you chastised my word choice. So, I thought of something better. A tingling yet erotic sensation that sends my senses into ecstasy."

"Did you write that one down, so you could remember it?"

"No," she lied. "What do you think?"

"It's passable," Christopher said, "but I do like the part about sending you into ecstasy." He lightly pushed her onto her back, propping her head up on a pillow by pulling on her braid. Next, he casually slid off her white lace underwear, first complimenting her on how pretty it was.

"Do you want me to take off the rest of my clothes?"

"No, I like what you have on, especially that naughty little skirt."

Kaisa laid back and prepared for her treat.

"I want to see you touch yourself first?" he said.

"What do you mean? Masturbate? No."

"Why not?"

"Because it is more exciting when someone else

stimulates you," she insisted.

"But I want to watch you make yourself come."

Kaisa eventually gave in to Christopher's voyeuristic request. To avoid his gaze, she closed her eyes and pretended she was alone. She placed her fingers on her special spot, reviewing in her head what actions pushed her over the edge the last time. Occasionally, she peeked to see if he was still watching before quickly closing them when his eyes met hers.

"Are you getting close? Do you want me to lick your pussy?" he asked.

Biting her lip, Kaisa nodded in answer to both his questions.

He stroked his palms along the inside of her thighs. "Does that give you a tingling feeling?"

"Yes," she gasped.

"Say, Chris, eat my pussy!"

"Chris, eat my pussy," she enunciated, her eyes still closed. With that, the magic began, no question years of practice. She peered down between her legs to watch him in action noticing the thinning hair on top of his head. He nibbled on her clitoris in a rapid, rhythmic motion alternating his blissful technique with gentle tugs. His fingers penetrated her most sensitive area at unsuspecting intervals giving her unexpected jolts of rapture. Kaisa twisted and turned with every pulse until her breath grew heavy, and she exhaled with an audible sigh.

He presented his manhood to her once again, which she took into her mouth willingly in repayment.

Christopher tutored Kaisa on her technique to maximize his satisfaction. His gratifying moans and groans had to mean she was performing up to his standards. His penis throbbed, and she was relatively certain he was about to release.

A tsunami of salty liquid rolled over Kaisa's taste buds. He let out a hiss and then a sigh of relief as he firmly held the back of Kaisa's head against his groin despite her attempts to release his grip. Then he extracted himself and laid down breathlessly on top of her.

"You're on your way to a first-class blow job!"

Kaisa grimaced. *Sure, just what every girl wants to hear.*

"Come here, sweetheart," he said, gathering her close as he rolled onto his side. "What are you doing here with me? You are such an old-fashioned girl."

Kaisa paused for a moment, trying to craft her response. "I like hanging out with you. You are not like anyone I've ever met. I do wish we could do more things together outside of here. I mean, I come over, we mess around, and I leave."

"Yeah, you're right. I guess we haven't gotten to know each other on another level."

"It would be nice, don't you think?"

"Sure. Give it a chance," he said. "You aren't planning on breaking up with me anytime soon, are you?"

Kaisa smirked and shrugged her shoulders, baffled by his question.

"I like you," he said.

"Yeah? How much do you like me?" Kaisa asked with her hopes propelled into the air.

"I really like you," Christopher responded. "You give such great blow jobs. I'll never break up with you!"

Not exactly what Kaisa wanted to hear, but perhaps she could warm him up to the idea of getting to know her outside of the apartment. "Have you seen 9 ½ Weeks yet?" she asked. "I've heard it's pretty crazy."

"I saw it two weeks ago," he said.

"Why didn't you invite me to go with you? That would have been fun."

"We didn't know each other two weeks ago."

Kaisa raised her voice. "We met on January 9th, about a month and a half ago."

He seemed oblivious. "What a memory you have," he said. "God, doesn't it seem like we only met three days ago?"

Kaisa didn't appreciate his sarcasm. Was he messing with her? "That's ridiculous; we've already seen each other several times over the last few weeks."

She decided to assess his knowledge of their recent history. Sadly, he had no recollection that she went to his apartment on the first day or literally the first hour. He acted as if he was astonished that he would make such a bold invitation only minutes after meeting someone, and more so that Kaisa accepted.

"It had to have been more than 15 or 20 minutes," he said.

"Half an hour at most," she replied.

"Weren't you scared?"

"Yeah, but I decided, I started this adventure, and I'm going to finish it. You also told me you weren't going to molest me, so I took your word for it. I consider myself a decent judge of character."

Kaisa reiterated that he teased her for not exerting her full sense of spontaneity that day. Christopher appeared ashamed that he said that, which surprised Kaisa, even though he did not recall that item either. The details were sharply etched in her brain after replaying them so often in her head and re-reading what she had captured on paper. Sadly, it didn't stand out in his mind at all. "Anyway, who asks for street directions in the middle of a mall?"

"'Do you know how to get to Symphony Road' wasn't a line," he assured her.

That he remembers?

"What did you think of me when you first met me?" he asked.

"I thought you were cute," knowing it was more like love at first sight.

"So, the first impression was superficial," Christopher said.

"Isn't it always?"

"What did you think of me? Did you think I was pretty?" Kaisa asked.

"I couldn't say I thought you were a conventional

beauty, but definitely attractive. I spotted you about two seconds before I approached you. I thought, here's a girl whom I'd love to suck me off," he jested.

"How ROMANTIC," she said, pursing her lips and raising an eyebrow.

Christopher laughed and gave her a peck on the cheek. "Come on, I'll walk you part of the way home. I want to get something to eat. I'm supposed to meet up with my study group near your dorm."

"Can I meet them?" Kaisa asked.

"It's not a good time. We're pulling an all-nighter studying, and I don't want you to break their flow."

Just as they were about to leave, he moved her hand to his crotch and then weighted his hands onto her shoulders.

Kaisa protested. "I don't feel like it."

"Why do you have to be so stubborn?"

Kaisa didn't think she was being stubborn at all. "I did you already tonight!"

"My cock likes you and wants more of you. Here, make it your friend."

Kaisa scowled. "Yeah, I want you to be my friend, not your cock," she argued.

Christopher chuckled, "It's part of me."

"Yeah, but it's not the part I want to get to know better."

"Let's try a 69 then," he suggested, offering to make

their last encounter of the night more mutual.

"What's that?" Kaisa asked.

"I love that you don't know what that is. Come here and I'll show you."

"No, just tell me first."

"In that position, each person simultaneously performs a favor for the other one. So, you straddle my face while satisfying me, and I please you in return."

That sounded weird. She had already received one 69 today and this kind didn't sound much better. Kaisa cringed at the thought of hovering the crack of her ass over someone's nose, and she surely wasn't in the mood for more sucking tonight, even if she was supposed to get something out of it. "Maybe next time. I don't want you to be late for your study group."

"Come on, it won't take too long, just for a few minutes."

"I really don't want to."

"I thought you might be more adventurous," Christopher said pompously as he rummaged through his small closet. He selected a brown cashmere sweater, jeans, and an overcoat from his closet while Kaisa looked around for her underwear.

Out on the street, they walked a completely different route back toward the dorm side by side. When they reached the 'iffier' side of Hemenway Street, Kaisa clutched his arm. Around the corner, they spotted a hooker waiting just outside an alleyway.

"Do you know what that girl is doing?" Christopher asked.

Kaisa knew, but she chose not to answer.

"Do you think if you were desperate enough, you would do that?" he continued.

"No," Kaisa insisted. *Well, don't I already, sort of.* She was feeling a kinship with this girl, particularly tonight. So far, all he did was call her to a private space for some form of sex. And Kaisa wasn't getting paid for it, in any sense of the word. But that was what she had agreed to.

Christopher wrapped his arm around her neck and shook her lightly, "Yes, you're so innocent, such an innocent girl!"

"You want to get a slice of pizza there. I'll go with you," she said, directing him to the pizza joint.

"Oh, that must be new," he said. "Um, not now, I'm already late for the study group."

"But you said you were hungry?"

"Thanks for the tip. We'll order from there later."

She looked up at him, holding on to the lapels of his coat. "Don't I get a kiss goodbye?"

He gave her a light peck and was on his way.

CHAPTER 8
You Lead, I'll Follow

K aisa was avoiding the telephone. She intended to blow Christopher off, but not in that way, and asked her roommates to answer and say she wasn't there if he happened to call. She needed time to process her mixed feelings about their arrangement. There was the concern that he would get bored with her soon and dump her, coupled with how much she wanted to see him again, overlaid with the thought of being coerced into something cock-related.

Fortunately for Christopher, when he called a few days later, he caught her unexpectedly picking up the phone when her roommates were still at dinner.

"Kaisa?"

Her intestines rumbled at the sound of his infectious voice. Perhaps she felt queasy from the questionable canned soup-based chicken casserole from the cafeteria that she had just forced down. Her hands and feet grew cold as an army of nerves marched up her arms and around her shoulders. The sensation was familiar when she was anxious, but this reaction was a potent combination of jitters, adrenaline, and nausea.

"How are you doing?" he asked.

Not so great right now. The tingling in her muscles had escalated to uncontrollable shaking. "Uh, fine."

"I'd love to see you tonight," he said. "Are you busy?"

She didn't have other plans except for the usual looming cloud of homework, but he didn't need to know that. "I have a couple of things I have to get to. I'll see if I have time later on," she said, trying to keep her teeth from chattering.

"Oh, YOU'LL SEE?" he said.

"I have to go now. Bye."

Consumed by an overwhelming sense of anxiousness and emotion, Kaisa wanted to jump out of her skin to escape it. She collapsed on the floor and started thrashing around, pounding her fists on Deborah's "husband" (a moniker Mindy made up for her throw pillow with arms). *What do I do? Jesus Christ!* Her brain and heart were saying: You know you want to see him. But the rest of her body was singing from a different songbook.

Kaisa turned on the TV to try to get her mind off Christopher. Instead, she happened upon a news story about condoms, AIDS, and teenage pregnancies. Even the media was sending her subliminal messages urging her to slow down and take a step back.

Kaisa was still shaking when Jill, Deborah, and Mindy came back from dinner.

"Are you okay?" Jill asked. "What's going on?"

Through a quivering voice, Kaisa explained her predicament.

Deborah left the decision up to Kaisa, saying to do what she thought was best. "Let me know what you decide. I have to get ready for my date."

"She doesn't know what's best. It's obvious." Jill insisted. "Kaisa, you're shaking like a leaf. Something must be telling you this isn't right. Why don't you stay home?"

But as the minutes passed and her symptoms eased, Kaisa began leaning toward visiting him. There were a few things she wanted to address with Christopher anyway. Perhaps she would feel better if she were open about what was bothering her instead of obsessing about it. She swore to Jill it would be strictly platonic, and she would keep her clothes on. Noting that she remained fully dressed last time (well, except for her underwear).

"Suuuuure," Jill said, her voice dripping with skepticism.

"Kaisa, can you come in here, please?" Deborah yelled out from their bedroom.

She sounded mad. Through the doorway, Kaisa could see Deborah holding up the kilt skirt she had borrowed. Kaisa entered the room, with Jill following close behind.

"There appears to be something on my skirt. Do you happen to know where it came from?"

"What do you mean?" Kaisa asked, looking confused. *What is she talking about? I returned it in pristine condition.*

Deborah tilted the skirt toward the fluorescent light revealing a dry, crusty, gelatinous stain.

"Eww, that's jizz on your skirt," Jill cried out, pointing and giggling.

"I, I'm so, so sorry. I didn't notice that when I gave it back. I promise to have it dry cleaned," she stammered.

"I guess I'm wearing something else tonight," Deborah said, throwing it on Kaisa's bed.

Kaisa called Christopher to let him know her plans opened up. She was still feeling a little anxious as she got herself ready. "Don't worry; take it easy. Everything will be all right," she chanted silently. Maybe listening to some music could help distract her. She pressed play on her pink boombox: *'I'm not going down on my knees, begging you to adore me...'* "Maybe not that song," she said, before pressing stop and selecting another cassette.

Deborah and her date, another guy from the crew team, were headed in the same general direction and invited Kaisa to walk with them. After her experience on Westland Avenue last time, she welcomed it. Kaisa made it halfway to Christopher's before Deborah and her date took a different route. It was then she started rehearsing aloud what she would say if the subject of sex came up. She had prepared a few clever comebacks and solid arguments but kept hoping she wouldn't have to use them.

At Christopher's apartment, she rang the buzzer two

times. Kaisa stood there for a couple of minutes until he opened the door, which seemed like hours in the bitterly cold weather.

"Hello," he said.

"It's cold out there," she said, pushing him aside.

"Nice to see you," he said, leaning in to kiss her.

Kaisa turned her cheek. In keeping with her formal theme, she focused straight ahead as they ascended the stairs toward the apartment. Kaisa hung up her coat and sat down at his desk. In the top corner was an opened letter postmarked from Gainesville, Florida, where her high school crush and Gina's current boyfriend was attending school. Along with the letter was an enclosed check, peering out from behind a couple of photos.

"Who's this letter from? I actually know someone in Gainesville."

"That's my sister Selma. She sent me a letter with a picture of herself and her new boyfriend. Look at the couple. Do you see something wrong there?" he asked.

"What's wrong with them?"

"You see nothing strange about that couple?"

"Do you mean their age difference?"

"Yes, how old do you think they are?"

She guessed the woman was in her 30's with a gray-haired man, possibly late 50's, but otherwise, nothing else looked out of place. Her guesstimate was correct. It seemed the Morton's didn't mind substantial age differences between their partners. At least the one between her and Christopher wasn't as substantial.

"So, how is your paper coming along?" she asked.

"Fine," he replied.

"What's it about?"

Christopher engaged her question, describing his paper about some ancient civilization based on the Mississippi River, called Cahokia. They spoke about the primitive Native American tribe that lived there, their ceremonies, and social customs. Thankfully, this paper was far more interesting than the other one he made her listen to on their second "date." Plus, this exchange was keeping her fully dressed.

Kaisa looked at her watch. She was happy to see she had been there nearly 30 minutes without Christopher asking her to take off either of their pants. He seemed to be enjoying her company. Could she get through this visit without having to perform sexual favors?

"Would you like to see some slides I created for the presentation?"

"Sure, that would be great," Kaisa agreed wholeheartedly.

"This will have to be short. I'll show you the slides, then I want to make out with you a little bit, and then I have to get back to studying."

This was her cue to use one of the lines she had rehearsed. "What am I some sort of recreational vehicle – I had this absurd notion that I was a person!"

He responded matter-of-factly. "Yes, you are a

recreational vehicle. Where did you get any other idea?"

Kaisa's jaw dropped, amazed that he would be so blunt.

"It's obvious you don't want me to lay a hand on you tonight?" he said.

"Yes, I would like to keep ALL my clothes on today."

"I'm not sure what you are trying to prove. You realize you are pre-empting any more progress between us, and you can't erase what you've already done."

Well, that is true. Right? Christopher had a knack for twisting her point of view and making her see things from his perspective. She knew it was only a matter of time before he would manipulate her into doing what he wanted. But she would do her best to resist.

"Okay. Take a seat over there. Let's see how self-conscious we can make Kaisa feel," he said, toying with her.

Kaisa sat on a green easy chair facing him while he lounged on the mattress.

"Now take your clothes off."

She shook her head. "I told you I don't want any type of sex tonight!"

"I'm not going to touch you. I just want to look at you."

"No."

"Why do you have to be so stubborn? You know, I don't always want to be the aggressor. I wish you would act more sensually sometimes and voluntarily undress yourself."

"Understood, but how about not tonight, please?" she cooed, hoping to wipe the scowl from his face. Kaisa slowly strolled over and sat next to him. "To your point about progress, I'd like there to be more between us than just these encounters," she said, resting her head on his folded arms.

Christopher nudged her aside and got up to make some herbal tea. "I was so looking forward to seeing you and having fun tonight."

"Do you want me to go home then?"

"No, I don't mind you being here, but I need to work on my assignment a little longer." Christopher looked around to find something else to occupy Kaisa's time. "Here, why don't you read today's newspaper," he said, offering it to her. "Sorry, I already did the crossword."

"No, thanks," she said. "Do you have anything else?"

"You should be more interested in current events," he preached.

"Unless it's major news, I just don't care."

"Well, then what interests you?"

"Music, celebrities, pop culture, whatever's in People Magazine."

"That's so trite. Are you interested at all in art?" he asked.

"Sure, what kind?"

He pulled out a book on Austrian Expressionists. "You could use a little more of this type of culture," he said.

She wasn't aware of any Austrian expressionists, or

interested in them either, but smiled as she took the pretentious book off his hands.

Kaisa sat quietly occupied for a good long while, mostly using the book as a prop while he worked on his paper. Occasionally she would catch his eye when she looked up from the pages. He seemed to be getting more agitated as time passed.

"I'm never going to get any work done with you here," he exclaimed. "All right, you've got to go. I have to study, and I can't wait anymore." He picked up the phone to call her a cab.

"What's this, an ultimatum? I won't play your way, so I have to leave?"

"I don't know why you are acting this way. You knew going in what our friendship was about. I don't want to argue with you."

That was true, but it hadn't stopped her from growing attached to Christopher and wanting more from their relationship.

"No one is forcing you to be here. If our arrangement isn't for you, then why do you continue seeing me?"

"I just don't understand why we always have to play by your rules?" she whined, dodging the question.

"Because you're in my apartment." He calmly rose from his chair and approached her in slow motion, like in a movie. He took the book out of her hands and let it fall to the floor. Kaisa could not help getting aroused as he gently pushed her back into the chair, kneeled before her, and pulled off her pants. Then he placed his hands on her inner thighs and parted her legs. Kaisa went through the motions, letting him pleasure her orally. She then reciprocated when it was his turn, as he always seemed happier after it was over. She didn't want him to be angry with her, and besides, it wasn't like she wasn't getting something out of it too.

His eyes softened. "Don't mess up what we have going here," he whispered in her ear. "I'm not saying there couldn't be more between us down the road, but I'm not there yet. I have been thinking about fucking you for real. I know you want to fuck me, but we have to get you laid first."

"What do you mean?"

"Oh, I don't want to be your first."

"What about when you had anal or oral sex with me? That was the first time I did those things."

"That didn't count," he said.

Kaisa averted her eyes and parted her lips, letting out a sigh of disbelief. "That doesn't make any sense!" she argued.

"There are so many more emotional implications with traditional vaginal sex?" Christopher explained. "Think about it, when a woman refers to her first time, that's usually the orifice she means."

In her case, that orifice was still intact, so maybe he was right?

Out of nowhere, an urgent rumble surfaced in her stomach. It was those crazy nerves kicking in again. Was it that lousy dinner acting up, the situation, or both?

Regardless, she wasn't feeling well. She excused herself and quickly ran to the bathroom.

It took some time for Kaisa to pull herself together. She sat analyzing his nonchalant suggestion of getting her laid first. Did he not care if she was faithful to him? Was their special friendship exclusive? Or was she one of many? As she got up from the toilet to wash her hands, Kaisa spotted a girl's red hairband on the edge of the sink. She grabbed it in her fist and stomped into the living room, glaring at Christopher.

"Is something wrong, he asked?"

"No," she said, seething under her breath.

"You sure?"

"I found this hairband in your bathroom. It doesn't seem to fit your style."

"There's no need for your sarcasm," he calmly responded, "there is a reasonable explanation. My neighbor across the hall lost her keys at the office the other night and asked if she could stay here for several hours until someone could come and let her into her apartment." Christopher smiled. "You girls are all alike, so suspicious."

"Well, sometimes those suspicions are right," Kaisa answered in defense, not buying his story. "How do I know how many girls you bring back from Copley?"

He laughed and hugged her hard. "Come here, you crazy girl, we'll cuddle for a bit. Would you like that?"

She laid down next to him. Christopher eased her mind by diverting her attention to more neutral subjects.

The next time she checked her watch, it was after 11 p.m., about four hours since she had arrived. Kaisa hadn't expected to stay that long or that late and wasn't sure what she was supposed to do. She had barely enough money for a cab, especially with the evening surcharge, and she sure as hell wasn't going to take the T now.

Kaisa truly didn't want to leave. She was thoroughly enjoying these precious moments of intimacy, warm and cozy, wedged into the grooves of his body, like a perfectly matched puzzle piece. But it was unlikely Christopher would ask or want her to stay over, especially since he already got what he wanted.

Without a word, he got up and turned off the light. He kissed her on the cheek, threw a well-worn wool blanket over them, and then fell asleep almost immediately. Both stunned and surprised by his gesture, Kaisa took this as a sign that she was staying over, like a real girlfriend. It was also comforting that he wasn't expecting the owner of the hairband to come home that night.

Sleep didn't come that easy. The Prudential Building's bright glow seeped through the three-windowed bay, barely veiled by Christopher's sheer drapes. Kaisa honed into the hissing white noise from the radiator that dripped and clanked at random intervals. She eventually dozed off but kept waking up every hour on the hour strangled by her turtleneck. It was the only thing keeping her warm besides Christopher's residual body heat a few inches away. Kaisa could have done with a few more layers to mask the draft circulating around his shallow mattress from beneath his doorway. She didn't know where or if he had anything she could borrow and didn't want to wake him by rummaging through his things.

The sound of a garbage truck startled Kaisa awake. With the faint morning light building over the horizon, and Christopher still asleep, she collected her things in preparation for her walk of shame. Kaisa checked his wallet. It appeared he was in a similar financial state with only a one and a five-dollar bill. She took the dollar, figuring that, coupled with the $4.35 she had, would be enough to get her home. Kaisa called a cab and waited by the window watching the early morning sunrise. A car horn sounded, but it wasn't the cab.

"You're leaving, sweetheart?" he asked sleepily.

"Yes, I was just going to slip out," she said.

"Wait, I'll walk you downstairs." He threw on his jeans and followed her down. "I'm glad you stayed with me last night," he said, putting his hand on her thigh. He leaned in to kiss her, which she abruptly returned with a little peck before running out.

So, our visit wasn't completely platonic, but at least he had to work for it a little more this time. Kaisa got into the cab. She slumped down on the padded red leather seat and closed her tired eyes. The driver's radio was playing softly: '*Should I let go now, would I even know how to anyway.*' Kaisa sang along with the lyrics in her head, amazed by her telepathic connection with the dee-jay. She got home with his dollar to spare, and this time she gave it to the cab driver.

Kaisa unlocked the heavy suite door and opened it slowly so as not to wake anyone.

"Where the fuck have you been?" Jill snapped, standing in the doorway of her room.

Kaisa jumped, completely caught off guard. "I was at Christopher's."

"You don't do that!"

"Do what? Can't I stay over a guy's place?" she remarked. What the hell? Jill wasn't her mother, and she didn't owe her an explanation. Besides, Christopher said she should run her own life and shouldn't have to answer to anyone while she's at school - not even her roommates.

"No, dumbass," growled Jill. "We all live together and are friends. We care about you and were worried something bad happened. I mean, you just met this dude, face it, like a month and a half ago, you've only seen him a few times; then you disappear one night. We don't know him, and quite frankly, we don't trust him. Next time you call and tell us where you are!"

Kaisa did appreciate the concern, no matter how harshly it was delivered. "Well, I'm sorry. I didn't think I needed to check in," she said, trying not to internalize Jill's tirade. *No one checks in with me when they stay out all night,* she wanted to say. But she was too tired to deal with this right now. Deborah was awake and waiting with a similar speech when Kaisa entered their bedroom. *Lucky for me,* she grumbled in her head.

Later that morning, Mindy was equally irate with Kaisa. She was the R.A., and how would it look if something terrible happened to one of her suitemates? Heather had come home late from a party, too drunk even to realize Kaisa was missing. At least she didn't have to worry about hearing it from her as well.

CHAPTER 9
Wrapped Around Your Finger

I t had been a long chaotic day at Mrs. Fields cookies. Deborah and Kaisa had only one 15-minute break each during their whole eight-hour shift. It didn't help that Deborah was in a nasty mood. She kept freaking out over the most trivial things. "The brownies are not proportionately sliced. There is a major inequity in the sizes!" Deborah huffed.

Kaisa offered to help her eat those that bothered her the most, hoping the chocolate might make her feel better. They ate quite a few, but, unfortunately, that didn't help Deborah's mood. Every time Kaisa asked her what was wrong, she said she didn't want to talk about it.

While on her break, Kaisa spotted Christopher circling the area where they first met. "Hey there," she called out.

"Oh, hi, Kaisa. What brings you here today?" he said as if he wasn't expecting to see her.

"You know I work right over there? I thought maybe you were coming over to visit ME, for a change," she joked.

Christopher didn't confirm or deny her statement. "That's right. How much longer before your shift is over?" he asked.

"Not for a few hours. I get off at five."

"Yeah, I've been procrastinating. I really should go home and get back to studying. It was great to see you. I'll call you around six. Maybe we can get together later," he said before giving her a brief hug and meandering away.

When Deborah and Kaisa returned to the dorm that evening, Deborah had a burning urge to rearrange their room. She had a knack for decorating and design, so Kaisa wasn't opposed to the idea but wasn't sure where her energy was coming from or why she had to take action now.

"Maybe we should clean up first before moving the furniture - like pick up the stuff on the floor," Kaisa suggested.

"Fine," Deborah said reluctantly.

While Kaisa wasn't a neat freak, Deborah was a whirling dervish of slobbery. Keeping up with her mess, much less tolerating it, was a challenge in itself. Sometimes Kaisa would get fed up and spend a solid hour cleaning and straightening up their room, so she didn't have to study among the chaos. Deborah continued not to study, so whether the room was neat or messy didn't seem to matter or bother her.

After pushing the last piece of furniture into its new spot, Kaisa took a step back. She was pleased with Deborah's reimagined space and thanked her for agreeing to keep Kaisa's desk by the window.

"Hey, I almost forgot." Deborah said, admiring her new layout, "A guy from my class is having a party tonight at his apartment on Gainsborough Street."

Kaisa wasn't sure if she wanted to go. Her stomach felt a little uneasy, and she wasn't hungry for dinner at all. "That sounds cool, but I'm not feeling that great right now. I think I'll hang back." She peeled off her cookie-flavored uniform and undergarments and threw them in her overflowing laundry basket. Kaisa put on her robe, some soft music, and laid down on her bed, eagerly awaiting Christopher's call.

A couple of hours later, she was feeling slightly better, at least physically. Going to a party was sounding more and more enticing. It was only around the corner, and she was feeling well enough to check it out. *Why should I miss out on the fun waiting by the phone?* Kaisa didn't put too much effort into getting ready. She picked out a pink sweater and jeans from a pile on top of her dresser that were cute and clean enough, kind of like Deborah's boyfriends, and took a French bath by spraying on perfume.

The party was standard college fare: loud music, kegs,

underage drinking, smoking, and snorting of various substances; a recycled version of the last one she went to, including most of the same people. Kaisa had passed on the cafeteria that night and was happy she was getting her appetite back. There wasn't much to eat except pretzels and chips until someone brought in a bunch of cheesesteaks. She grabbed half of one for herself. Along with the sandwich, throughout the night, Kaisa had two and a half Solo cups of beer, a few hits off a joint, and a can of Diet Coke.

Around one in the morning, the remaining girls of 401 returned from their respective social outings and gathered in the common area. Kaisa was still a little buzzed and woozy, feeling like she had a little too much of everything at the party when the phone chirped.

"Yello?" Kaisa said in her heightened drunken enthusiasm.

"Kaisa? It's Chris. I'm sorry I didn't call you earlier, but I came back here, then I realized I was missing something and had to go back to school to get it."

"Suuuuuuure, you went all the way back to school. Did you think I would wait around all night by the phone?" she slurred, making the most of her liquid courage. "I went to a keg party instead and just got back!"

"Is that why you sound so silly?"

"I thought we were going to meet up tonight?"

"I said maybe, but I did say I was going to call."

"Technically, you said you'd call me yesterday. Now it's too late," she insisted. "Are you going to be busy this weekend?" she asked, swaying back and forth.

"Most likely," he said.

"It figures. When I call, you always use the same lame excuses: 'I have to study, I have a paper, I have a section meeting,' whatever that is. But when you call and want me to visit you, I'm supposed to drop everything."

"I wouldn't have it any other way," he snickered.

"Ha, ha, you're funny."

"If you want to see me, why don't you come over now?" he said.

A feeling of oncoming digestive rebellion immediately followed his impromptu invitation. She didn't know if his suggestion threw her off, or it was what she ate, drank, or smoked, but suddenly, she was not feeling her best, by a longshot.

"It's after 1 a.m.! I don't think so."

"Oh, that's a shame. I was hoping you would want to come over," he carped. "I wish you were more spontaneous from time to time."

This wasn't the first instance that he mentioned her lack of spontaneity like it was a character flaw. "You're so annoying. First, you say you don't like surprises, but you're encouraging me to be spontaneous."

"No, I don't like it when people show up without warning. I just asked you to come over, and I'm hoping you'll be free-spirited enough to accept my spur of the moment suggestion."

She found herself wrestling with what she initially felt

was a stupid idea that had now manifested into a challenge. If she went over, she could prove that she was just as much of a free spirit as he was. "I may come, and I may not. You'll have to wait and see," she said before hanging up.

"You're not going to go see the Marlborough Man now, are you?" Mindy asked.

"Yes, I'm going to Christopher's." *At the very least, he won't be able to question my devotion or my ability to follow through.*

"You just said you were feeling sick like five minutes ago," Jill chimed in. "Stay home."

"Yeah, but I'm sure it will pass. It did earlier tonight. Maybe I need some air to divert my attention away from my sickness."

Jill said Kaisa was nuts for A) going out this late, B) going when she said she felt sick, and C) going to his apartment in the first place. Kaisa ignored her lecture because she had enough on her mind, and ultimately, it was her decision.

"Good night, we're all going to bed. Have fun. At least we know where you'll be this time," Jill said, slamming her door.

Kaisa called a cab to take her to Christopher's, but about five minutes later, she was feeling sick again. She tried to call the cab company to cancel it, but no one was picking up the phone. She dialed Christopher, but his line was busy. *At 1:20 a.m.?* Kaisa hung up and hit redial until she got through. "Could I put my spontaneity on hold?" she asked.

"Why?"

"Because I'm really not feeling well."

"Alright, if you don't feel well, fine," he said, sounding more disappointed than sympathetic.

"But I really want to come," she replied desperately.

He chuckled.

"Okay, I might come." With that, she put on her coat and went outside to wait for the cab.

The fresh chilly air provided some minor relief. Up ahead was a somewhat intoxicated but cute guy.

"Hey there. What's your name?"

"Kaisa."

"Hey Kaisa, you want to go to a party?" he asked

"Yeah, thanks. I think I was already there. I'm waiting on a cab to go visit a friend."

"Male or female friend?" he inquired.

Like it was any of his business, but she was not in a state to care. "I'm not sure I even know yet."

"You're not sure if your friend is a male or female or if they are your friend?"

"What?" His question was far too complicated for her current state of mind. Fortunately, a yellow car with numbers on it was approaching the curb so she could politely end the conversation. "I think that's my cab, have a good night."

"It was nice meeting you. Can I have a kiss goodbye?" he asked.

What did he say? Too drunk and not in the mood to protest this handsome stranger's bold request, Kaisa played along by kissing him on the cheek.

"Oh, not on the lips?" he said like he was crushed.

That was pushing it. But she gave him a light peck instead. *What a night this is turning out to be. Who am I?*

The cab ride was as fast as one would expect for 1:45 a.m., but she had a little trouble pointing out the brownstone because most of the porch lights were out. As the cab crawled down the street and the meter continued to spin, she worried she wouldn't have enough money to turn around and go back home if Christopher had decided to go to bed or did not answer the door.

When she finally arrived, Kaisa realized she probably should have stayed home. Her queasiness was getting worse.

"How are you doing?" he asked.

"I could use a hug," she pouted. Kaisa leaned her head on his chest, hoping he would cradle her in his arms, but he only lightly tapped her on the shoulder.

"How was your party? Did you get picked up?"

Still feeling slightly buzzed, she rehashed her night in full detail, including the part about the guy she kissed on the street. As she was telling the story, it felt like she was talking about somebody else. "This is not me," she wailed. "I don't do things like this. It's like I've been possessed by some demon who is controlling my actions."

"See, I knew there was a wild side to you. There's a great force that's trying to break out from inside that innocent little girl. Let's keep exploring this wild side."

He reached for her pants, boldly unzipped them, and shoved his fingers underneath. His digits twirled and twisted as he attempted to get her or something going. Kaisa was not in the mindset to give in, but he didn't seem to care. At this point, what else did she expect? "Christopher, seriously, I'm feeling nauseous tonight. I'm not up for any shenanigans right now."

"Fine then, I'm craving a late-night snack." He strolled over to his tiny kitchen area and came back with an open can of tuna fish and a fork. As he began eating it right in front of her face, it was clear that he was taunting her on purpose. She tried desperately to divert her attention away from its odor, which was only making her delicate digestive situation worse, but the smell was overwhelming. That demon that had taken over was about to make its exit.

"I have to use your bathroom!" she called out before making a run for it.

What happened next wasn't pretty. Kaisa made every effort to muffle the horrible noises. It was not a version of herself she wanted to share, especially with Christopher. What made the humiliation ten times worse was she was sure he could hear everything through the thin wall. She just wished he would move to the opposite end of the studio apartment, which wasn't that large, to begin with, turn on the TV or some music or leave altogether. About 15 minutes later, there was a knock on the door.

"Are you okay in there?"

"Yeah. I hope to be out soon," she whimpered, feeling slightly less miserable but eternally embarrassed. Kaisa slowly rose off the cold linoleum floor. She cracked open the medicine cabinet, hoping to find something to ease her upset stomach. Under the dim fluorescent light, she rifled through, shoving aside aspirin, cold medicine, and razor blades, until one item made her pause. *What's this doing here?* Kaisa opened the bathroom door.

"Are you feeling any better?" he asked.

"In some sense, yes, in another sense, no," she said, reeling from her latest discovery.

"What do you mean?"

"Do these belong to you?" she yelled, waving a half-used box of tampons in his face.

"Those have been in my medicine cabinet since I moved in."

"I don't see the need for you to hold on to them. It's not like you use them unless they have some sentimental value."

He rolled his eyes. "Why were you looking in there?"

"I was looking for Pepto-Bismol or something. I think I will go home now," Kaisa said, her nausea now fully suppressed by her anger.

"Maybe you should," he said.

Kaisa spent the cab ride home thinking about her impulsive actions but mostly regretting them. Could she have made any more mistakes that night? One thing was clear. The next time she felt sick, she vowed she would never leave the creature comfort of her dorm.

Kaisa slept in late the next morning, almost missing breakfast hours. She threw on a sweatshirt and jeans and raced to the dining hall before it closed to get some toast and tea.

"So, what happened last night?" called Jill from a nearby table.

Kaisa pulled up a seat. "I don't think you want to hear about it over breakfast."

"You got sick?"

Kaisa grimaced and nodded. "I'm so embarrassed. God knows what he thinks of me now. I don't think he'll ever call me again."

Jill took a breath. "You know, I'm worried about you. That was a little crazy going to his apartment at 2 a.m. last night, especially when you said you weren't feeling well."

Well, technically, it was 1:30. "I know, I feel like such an idiot. It didn't paint an attractive picture of me. More like a drunk college party girl, and that's not who I am, at least not regularly. I just couldn't turn him down. I'm so afraid of losing him."

"What exactly would you be losing?"

Kaisa paused, slightly thrown by her question. "I could never land someone like that again."

"Is he all that great? Yeah, maybe he's hot and goes to Harvard. But I'm sure you could find someone else who would treat you better and take you out occasionally."

Jill did have a point. Although Christopher had qualities that Kaisa loved: attractive, intelligent, well-educated, exciting, and sexually stimulating, his not so flattering characteristics outnumbered the positive ones. He only seemed to care about himself. He could be condescending and forget about generosity on any level.

"Why not take a break from him and figure this thing out?" she added. "Let him miss you for a while. If he likes you, I'm sure he will call again."

Kaisa was doubtful. She had yet to find that mutual connection with someone, and the likelihood of that happening in the near future was non-existent. But it was sound advice and a logical plan of action. "Okay. I'll try," she responded, not sure if she could follow through. "By the way, I found out what the deal with that girl was."

"Oh yeah. Why has she been so friendly with my boyfriend lately?"

"I talked to her. I don't think there's anything to worry about. She's going with one of the other crew guys and just knows your man from the parties, and they have a class together. She's cool," Kaisa said.

"That makes me feel better. Thanks for getting me the low down. You're a good private investigator."

"No problem. You're not the first person who's told me that. Hey, do you know why Deborah was in a foul mood yesterday?"

"If I tell you, you have to promise not to mention it again or tell anyone I told you."

"I promise," Kaisa said.

"Deborah's new guy broke it off with her."

"Oh, really, why?"

"Remember when she got the little VW Beetle car and the plush Boston crab at Christmas?"

"Yeah?"

"They were STD references."

"What? No way. I get the reference to crabs, but VW?"

"Venereal warts," Jill said. "That guy Ian gave her crabs, and Benjamin gave her genital warts. Ian apologized to her, but when she confronted Benjamin and told him that she got it from him, he refused to believe he gave it to her. I can't say I was surprised. I've heard Benjamin is known for sleeping around and isn't very selective with his sexual partners. I told Deborah a while back, but she didn't seem to care. My boyfriend told me that everyone on the crew team heard about it. We think maybe Dave spread it. Deborah's new boyfriend asked her if it was true, and when she admitted it, he just broke it off."

Kaisa felt lucky that she hadn't been unfortunate in that area with Christopher. "I'm glad I didn't know. I wouldn't have been happy about sleeping on my bottom bunk. I would have been paranoid that her pubic lice would rain down on my bed when Deborah changed her sheets or crawl into my hair during the night."

Jill laughed. "You're dumb," she said, pushing her over.

"I'm not that dumb. My grades this quarter have been the best in my whole school career." It was true. She was on her way to getting straight A's.

"Well, you deserve it. You sure as hell study enough."

Ironically, it was Christopher who inspired her to push herself academically. Her grades just provided further validation that perhaps she was intellectually on par and worthy of a Harvard man.

CHAPTER 10
Can't Fight This Feeling

K aisa was laying low since the previous incident with Christopher. It was becoming painstakingly clear that the possibility of him developing or expressing any feelings toward her was slim to none. She was beginning to accept that she was more or less a plaything, mostly more. Maybe that last encounter was meant to be a metaphorical exorcism from his grip, complete with projectile vomiting.

As Jill suspected, Christopher started calling again, but now Kaisa put him off, saying SHE had to study.

"Why don't you come by and see me. It's been a while," he said, attempting to lure Kaisa to his den of iniquity or, more like, inequity.

She fired back. "Look, you promised to take me out sometime, but you never did. All you want is for me to suck your cock and satisfy you whenever the urge strikes. I'm tired of this shit."

"Nice language. You know I hate it when you swear."

"I don't give a flying fuck. How about that? You know, I think we should stop seeing each other for a bit."

"Is that your decision or what your friends told you to do?" he implored.

Kaisa hung up without answering his question, knowing it was a combination of both. Her feelings were torn. The romantic side didn't want to give up yet and worried this break might forever sever the possibility of anything between them. The rational side of her screamed, 'Good for you!'

It was hard having no prospect of hearing from Christopher. As much as she tried to put him out of her mind, she continued to see daily signs and reminders. At Store 24, the guy in front of her was buying Marlboro cigarettes. The next day someone was wearing a Harvard sweatshirt. And, of course, she was reminded of him when she picked up Deborah's kilt skirt from the dry cleaner. Then there was work around the corner from where they had met, so how could she not think of him.

This was one of those weird days, maybe because it was Saturday, the 14th. Her mother phoned at 9 a.m. and woke her for the first time that morning, which wouldn't have been so bad if she had fallen asleep before 3 a.m. Deborah had rebounded with Joseph, another one of her on-again-off-again beaus. Kaisa had to listen to them in the upper bunk for about two hours before she fell asleep. When Kaisa awoke again, it was nearly lunchtime. At least she didn't have work until early afternoon.

"Are you coming with us?" Deborah asked.

"Go along without me. I'm not ready and don't want to hold you up." But the truth was she didn't want to spend any more time with Joseph.

Later, at the dining hall, she selected a table in the far corner to people watch. Mac casually waved hello and, much to her surprise and pleasure, came over to her table. He told her he blew off his rugby game that morning because he got so drunk and was hungover. (Not her favorite conversational subject matter, but she smiled and nodded because he was adorable). As he was about to sit down, his roommate called him to another table. *What a puppy dog. I wish he were more of an individual than a follower.*

When she finished, she put her tray on the belt. On her way out, another cute but hungover guy grabbed her attention. Even though they didn't know each other, somehow, he felt compelled to tell her a story about how drunk HE got last night. Kaisa recycled the same smile and nodded accordingly. *Hoooo-ray more drunk stories.* "Sounds like a blast. As long you had a good time," she said. *If the Christopher thing is indeed over, is this my alternative?*

Kaisa had work in about an hour, and it was payday, so there was something to look forward to. She put on her standard uniform: a white shirt and black pants and threw on her light denim jacket. It was chilly outside, but not cold enough for something heavier. She was only scheduled for a short two-hour shift. According to her manager, they were expecting Mrs. Fields herself to make a surprise appearance sometime that week. But Kaisa had heard that before, and she had never shown up. She believed the store manager just told the employees that to make sure they didn't goof off.

Mrs. Fields was uneventful that afternoon, except for one of her co-workers burning a whole sheet tray of cookies. Another employee had called in sick, so the store manager asked Kaisa to stay an extra hour and a half. She craved a snack during work, but her relationship with Mrs. Fields' brownies was also on hold. They no longer were appealing and would be off her menu for some time.

By the time her shift was over, it was getting dark. As she stepped outside, she immediately regretted her jacket selection. The temperature had plummeted at least 20 degrees since earlier that afternoon. That, plus the cold March wind penetrated through her skin.

In miserable weather, Kaisa had become accustomed to navigating through as many covered passageways as possible to minimize her exposure to the raw conditions. She usually took a short-cut around the buildings just outside Copley Place's plexiglass exit. But today, the space between the buildings was a nasty wind tunnel. The harsh gusts tossed her around before enveloping her in the vortex. There had to be an alternative route. Just a few steps back was Saks Fifth Avenue. If she cut through there, it would provide a place to warm up before she set forth on the next stretch of her walk home. Going through

Saks was not her usual route. Entering Saks Fifth Avenue was like crashing an elite event. She didn't fit in with the affluent shoppers nor felt welcome by the snooty salespeople. But today's bone-chilling cold was a lot more potent than her insecurity.

As she entered the ornate revolving door, a warm burst of air welcomed her inside. The store's fragrance tickled her nose with a bevy of floral and musky notes emanating from the perfume counter – like bits of Obsession flirting with Eternity. Kaisa set her tired eyes on the exit straight ahead when out of nowhere, someone grabbed her by the shoulders and began playfully shaking her.

"You little squirt, who do you think you are, calling me names on the phone? You little squirt!"

Kaisa froze. She knew those hands, that voice. He obviously hadn't taken to heart what she said on their last call, considering the fact that she meant it.

There was Christopher, smiling. He was dressed in torn jeans and a flannel-padded denim jacket, carrying his familiar backpack over his shoulder. She didn't want to admit to herself that she liked how he looked in his outfit with his Converse high tops, but she took comfort that he looked more out of place than she did.

Kaisa figured her best move was to be Joe Cool, or more like Joe Cold. "This is the last place I would expect you to be," she snapped, still processing the situation.

"Yes, it is quite fragrant in here but a lot warmer than

outside. What have you been up to? I've missed you," he said.

"Mostly school stuff, I got straight A's last trimester," Kaisa said, omitting it was the first time ever.

"See, I told you, you were intelligent and don't belong at Northeastern. The curriculum must not be challenging enough for you."

"It's right for MY LEVEL," she emphasized. "Do you think the only reason I got straight A's was because the material was easy?"

"That's not what I meant. I was paying you a compliment."

"Okay."

"You look a little tired," he said.

"Gee, thanks for noticing," she huffed, responding on autopilot. "I'm beat, and I'm not working on all cylinders today."

"Do you want to sit down for a minute?"

He led her to a couple of chairs by two mannequins. She was positive these seats were part of the décor and not intended for people like Christopher or herself to use as furniture.

"Were you just coming from work?" he asked.

"Yes."

"So, are you free now?"

Kaisa avoided the question, shifting their conversation to other things, like interviewing for her first six-month co-op assignment. She shared her aspirations of working for an advertising agency in New York. It dawned on Kaisa that he never mentioned having a job during any of their talks, except for working in a clothing store a long time ago. Assuming he had nothing to contribute to the conversation, he redirected his focus onto the two mannequins.

"She's pretty," he said.

"Yeah, you could drill a few holes in her, and you'd be all set."

"I don't think she's my type," he joked.

"Why not? She is perfect for you. You could stick her in your closet like you want. Take her out when you feel like it. She won't give you any trouble. And you don't have to take her anywhere because she doesn't eat."

"But you do need a response," he countered.

"Right, and with that comes consideration for the other person."

They continued with their verbal ping pong. Despite working on major sleep debt, Kaisa was on her game, which was rare. Instead of stumbling over her words, she had a witty or cutting remark for every one of his innuendos. She touched on everything that bothered her about their "relationship," all the while showing little emotion. "I don't understand why we couldn't have gone out one time, like for a burger or something, nothing elaborate," she stated.

"Because I have a lot of work to do."

She shook her head. *Really, is this the best he could come up with*? "Right, you have work to do, so shouldn't you be home now working on your papers? You seem to have time for procrastination, but not the time to sit down and get your shit done."

"You know I don't like that language."

Kaisa didn't care. "I've known you for like three months. I'm sure somewhere along the way, you could have worked it into your schedule and set aside two hours for me outside of your apartment."

"You're right. I should have taken you out somewhere. I do miss you and can't stop thinking about you," he said, placing his hand on her thigh.

Kaisa was enjoying this heavy-duty well-earned guilt trip. But amid her strength, she revealed a crack in her armor. "To be completely honest, I've missed you too."

Christopher slowly leaned in and rested his forehead on hers. "What are you doing now?" he said, as his hypnotic whisper chipped away at her bitterness.

"I'm going home. That's where I was heading before you intercepted me. Why? Do you want me to visit you?" she said, anticipating his invitation,

He moved his head away and sat back in his chair. "No, forget it," he said. "So, I guess if I ever want to run into you, I'll just have to go to a retail store," Christopher said.

"Maybe?" Kaisa stated, lingering.

He asked once more, "Do YOU want to come back?"

This was unfamiliar territory. He was empowering her

to make the decision. Or was he? Was she now in control? 'No thanks, I gotta go. It was nice seeing you.' That's what she felt she was supposed to say. Instead, Kaisa found herself willingly following him back to 293 Marlborough Street with the wind slapping her in the face. Despite their past, her craving for Christopher consumed her. Truth be told, she still felt deeply for him and could not abandon what little they had. There must have been a reason fate brought them together again, and she knew better than to mess with that.

When they arrived, he held the door open like a proper southern gentleman. "Why does this scene look familiar?" she said as they walked up the stairs, probably because it was. There were a couple of parallels between today and the day they first met. For instance, they met up in the late afternoon and in the same vicinity. But this time, there was a history between them, and his behavior was different. His disposition was warmer, considerate, and he seemed less selfish.

His apartment had changed personalities too. The old familiar smell was present, but there were different pieces of furniture, including a new couch and artwork. He had adorned his walls with a couple of Christopher Morton originals. One sketch was of a girl on her back who looked like she had just been "done" by Christopher. He assured Kaisa that she was a model for the class. The other portrait struck her fancy. It was a self-portrait of him holding a cat, standing in a cathedral with the light breaking through the stained glass. The more she looked at the painting, it indeed resembled him, and she was impressed by the talent she didn't know he had.

"Why are you sitting so far away from me," he asked.

"I'm keeping a safe distance."

"Don't worry. I am not going to pressure you anymore into anything you don't want to do. If you just want to hang out, that is fine too. I'm just happy that you're here with me."

"I know. You never forced me into anything, but you can be very persuasive," she admitted.

Slowly he melted Kaisa's limited willpower with his sweet demeanor and coaxed her over to the mattress. She relished being near him again, cradled in his arms. Christopher remained a perfect gentleman, not making any moves beyond kissing the top of her head. It seemed if anything was going to happen, it was going to be up to her. She laid there quietly, contemplating.

"You smell like a cookie," he said.

Kaisa lifted her sleeve to her nose and inhaled her Eau de Margarine. Indeed, in those short hours, her clothes had absorbed the sweet buttery scent of the store.

"Wouldn't you like a bite?" she teased.

"You know I would," he said as he gently cupped her face in his hand.

"I can't believe I'm saying this, but I want to fool around," she stated.

"Are you sure? I mean, nothing would make me happier, but it's totally up to you."

Kaisa nodded as she bit her bottom lip then confirmed

her desire with a long, hard, passionate kiss. It was fine because this time, it was on her terms, and she was in control. She surrendered any thoughts of guilt or questions about her decision and resigned herself to just savor the moment. "I want you to lick my pussy," she ordered. "But I'd like to use your bathroom first."

While Kaisa was in the bathroom preparing, she discovered another parallel: She was wearing the same Garfield underwear as their first meeting. This encounter was meant to be.

Christopher's eyes widened when she returned, wearing only her lacy sugar-scented bra. She laid back on the mattress and shut her eyes to revel in his oral gratification. "Lower," she ordered, guiding his performance. "Yes, that's the spot, now suck me hard," she demanded, as she flung her legs over his shoulders. His lips clamped on hers. With each sweep of his tongue, the tender spot between her thighs grew more sensitive to the touch setting the stage for a powerful finish.

He gently eased his fingers inside. With each thrust, Kaisa edged closer and closer to climax, twitching and turning, until the final pulses of his flickering fleshy organ launched her into her sexual zenith. Her bottom lip quivered as intensely pleasurable contractions echoed throughout her bloodstream.

Figuring 'why prolong this,' she went directly for his pants.

He put his hand on hers and looked into her eyes. "You don't have to," he said.

That was a first, and it blew her away. Was he using reverse psychology?

"It's okay, you did something to please me, so I want to do something for you in return."

"Are you still a virgin?" he asked.

"Yes," Kaisa answered. "I want my first time to be with you."

"You know how I feel about that, but maybe we could one day soon. But for now, if you are willing to do me another favor, that's perfectly fine with me."

Before she could answer, either way, the phone rang. Once he knew who it was, he moved his conversation into the bathroom.

"Who was that?" Kaisa asked.

"That was one of my classmates. I'm so sorry. I forgot I had a section meeting with my group, and I need to go now."

Once they both got dressed, he offered to walk her part of the way to Commonwealth Avenue. "It was so nice running into you," he said.

"Yeah, I thought so, as well."

He kissed her goodbye and gave her a wave.

Their encounter swirled around Kaisa's head the rest of the way home. Perhaps there was hope that Christopher's feelings might catch up to hers, or at least they were heading in that direction. Fate had intervened and brought them together again, for what reason she wasn't sure. But she was happy she hadn't entirely written him off, even though everyone, including herself, thought at times he was an asshole. This was a chance to start over. Their friendship wouldn't be the same old bump and grind. Well, maybe it would be, but only in the literal sense.

CHAPTER 11
Oh, Mickey, You're So Fine

A fter a long, grueling week of classes and tests, Friday finally arrived. Jill and Deborah were planning to go to a movie after dinner and invited Kaisa along. Neither of the girls had seen "9½ Weeks," and it was still playing at Copley Place Theatre. Deborah stood in line for the popcorn and candy while Jill and Kaisa scoped out three seats together.

"I heard this is good," Jill whispered to Kaisa.

"Yes, Mickey Rourke is in it, and he's really hot. It's funny. I've been seeing Christopher for about that long now."

"Is that right?" Jill said, facing forward, looking at the blank screen. She was not thrilled that Christopher had somehow weaseled his way back into Kaisa's life and had no issue expressing how she felt about it.

Deborah shuffled into her reserved seat with snacks in hand, just as the lights started to dim.

As the film progressed, Kaisa felt more connected to the main character, who meets a charming, attractive man in New York City. At first, the woman was intrigued by his sexual games and erotic situations that pushed her to and past her boundaries. But each encounter led to more peculiar behavior and events that not only tore at her emotionally but began affecting her outward appearance and her daily life.

When the movie ended, Kaisa remained seated, thinking for a moment while the rest of the audience got up to leave. This film was new in the theatres, yet aspects of it seemed so familiar. As a hopeless romantic, Kaisa was sad to see this intense and exciting "love story" end badly. *Is my friendship with Christopher headed in this direction? I mean, my grades have started to take a nosedive since last semester. No, the leading man was way more demented than Christopher. Mickey's character went to sex clubs and hired hookers, so how could it not drive her away?*

"Come on," Jill barked, "we're not staying for the credits."

Kaisa got up from her seat and grabbed her purse.

"What did you think of the movie? Did it remind you of anyone?" Jill asked.

"It wasn't what I expected, but I kinda felt bad for the guy afterward," Kaisa said.

"Why?"

"He realized that he went too far with his behavior at

the end and lost a great thing. Maybe she shouldn't have given up on him so easily if she cared for him."

"Only you would have sympathy for that guy," Jill said as they walked out of the theater.

It was only 10, still early by college student standards. The girls did not want to go home yet, but they were too young to go bar hopping, at least legally. Besides, they couldn't all share Mindy's old fake ID. Now that she was 21, she had given it to Jill to use because the photo was taken when she was still a brunette. It was her indirect way of buying alcohol for her suitemates and promoting the true freshman experience.

"Hey," Jill said, "doesn't your friend Christopher live near here?"

"Yeah, so?" Kaisa replied, wondering where Jill was going with her question.

"I think it's about time we meet him. Why don't we go over and visit? You always go to his place. It would be nice since you guys are seeing each other again."

"Yes, that sounds like a great idea," Deborah concurred.

Kaisa kept silent, hoping they would immediately forget what they had just suggested. Was their desire to see him fueled by curiosity or concern? Possibly both. Either way, it did not feel like a bright idea. The last time she invited him to come over for their 'first date,' he was not happy about it. "Let me call him first to make sure he's home and cool with it," she said. "Christopher would not like to be surprised, much less ambushed." Kaisa slowly approached the payphone near the theatre exit. She fumbled through her purse and fished out some change, placed a quarter into the slot, and dialed. Kaisa anticipated this phone call would not be fun, and she was not in the mood for one of his lectures. The phone rang, once, twice, three times while Jill and Deborah hovered nearby. "I don't think he's there," she said. *Thank God.*

"Hello?"

"Oh, hi Chris, it's Kaisa."

"Hi," he said in a sweet whisper, "What are you up to?"

"Not much. You busy now?"

"Just studying. Why don't you come over," he sighed.

She sensed his smile over the phone. "Well, that is kind of what I had in mind. I'm nearby at Copley Place."

"I was wondering from where you were calling. I can barely hear you over the background noise."

"I'm with my roommates. We just got out of a movie and were wondering if we all could visit."

"How many roommates?" he probed.

"Two: Jill and Deborah."

The line went silent. *Here we go.* Kaisa waited, anticipating a response like: 'I don't enjoy being on display.'

"Wow, you're bringing over two girls for us. I've never had a foursome."

"Ha-ha," she said, not entirely sure if he was joking.

"Don't get any ideas."

"I'd like to meet them. Bring them over."

Kaisa's jaw popped open. Did he just agree to her proposal? "See you soon," she said, giving Deborah and Jill a thumbs up. She put the phone back into its cradle and gave a bewildered shrug. "He never ceases to amaze me."

The girls walked the few blocks to his apartment under an unseasonably warm and overcast sky. When they came upon the brownstone, Kaisa rang the buzzer.

Christopher's shadow soon appeared behind the sheer draperies in the foyer's window. He opened the door and greeted the girls dressed in a Vanderbilt sweatshirt and jeans. "I was surprised when Kaisa said all of you were coming," he said, "but how could I refuse a visit from three beautiful women?"

Kaisa proceeded with the introductions. "This is Jill."

Christopher shook her hand and gave her a cordial, "Hi."

Jill smiled politely in return.

"And this is Deborah." She noticed Christopher immediately perk up as he scanned her up and down, blatantly taking note of her more than ample breasts. Kaisa squirmed. It was not the first time she introduced a curvy friend to someone she liked, which ultimately contributed to the demise of any possible relationship with that guy.

How could she forget about what happened with Gina? More than once. It was bad enough she currently dating someone Kaisa loved and pined for after she made the mistake of telling him Gina liked him too.

Her old classmate, who had transferred to a local prep school, had set her up with one of his new friends for the Homecoming Dance. Everything seemed to be going fine with her date until Kaisa made the mistake of suggesting Gina show off her robot dance. As she showed off her mechanical stop-motion moves to a synthesized, digitally enhanced beat, Kaisa's date kept encouraging her to keep going. From then on, Kaisa's date seemed distracted.

Two days later. She and Gina were talking on the phone after school when Gina's doorbell rang.

"Wait a second, someone's at the door," Gina said. "You won't believe this."

"What?"

"I just got flowers from YOUR date."

Wow. MY date sent the robot dancing queen flowers.

Upstairs, Christoper had arranged some chairs in a semi-circle. Kaisa chose the seat closest to him.

"I'm sorry I don't have anything to offer you, ladies."

Kaisa wasn't surprised, as he never offered her much more than his penis.

Jill responded on the girls' behalf. "It's fine. This visit

was a spur of the moment thing, and we're still full from the movie snacks."

Kaisa sat back and watched as her roommates, but especially Jill, grilled Christopher with questions like: 'Where are you from?' 'How long have you lived in Boston?' 'What are you studying?'

He answered without hesitation in rapid succession, managing their inquisition without missing a beat, providing Kaisa with some sense of comfort that none of the "facts" waivered from what he had said in the past. Kaisa glanced back and forth at her friends, looking for some sign of approval, hoping neither would bring up the recent skirt incident, even as a joke. She hadn't told Christopher, and it would be humiliating for both.

As she feared, Christopher directed most of his questions at Deborah. Maybe agreeing to invite and introduce her was not the best idea. But her doubt alternated with feelings of pride. He was his ever-engaging self, and he was her man. She got him on her own. This attractive, intelligent specimen clearly measured up to — No, exceeded Deborah's boyfriend, Benjamin. He also beat the pants off any guys she met at Northeastern or those her roommates brought back to the dorm.

"Wow, it's getting late, so I guess we're going to go now," Deborah said. "It was nice to meet you."

"Yes, the pleasure was mine," he agreed. "I'm glad I had a chance to meet you both finally. I'm sorry for not being very social when I visited your dorm; I was feeling out of sorts that day."

Kaisa got up with the other girls and grabbed her coat off the back of a chair. As she started to make her way to the door, she felt a slight tug. Christopher whispered a barely audible invitation into her ear: "I was hoping YOU could stay a little longer."

It was late, and she was more interested in hearing what the girls thought of him versus what more than likely lay ahead. Nor did she want any part of satisfying Christopher while he imagined Deborah. "I can't," she politely declined. "I will see you, maybe tomorrow?"

"Fine then," he said, in a tone that communicated otherwise. She could see the disappointment in his face, like the scorn a parent shows when their child disobeys them. But she wasn't going to be shaken this time.

"Can I use your phone to call a cab?" Deborah interjected.

"Of course," he said with a flirtatious smile.

"Deborah, we'll meet you outside," Jill jumped in, ushering Kaisa toward the door. "Nice meeting you, Christopher."

But Kaisa stood firm as if her boots were nailed to the floor. No way was she leaving Deborah alone with him. "You can wait outside if you want," she said.

"It's coming in a few minutes," said Deborah. Let's go."

Out on the street, Kaisa was dying to hear their evaluations. "So, what did you think?"

"I think he's full of it," Jill said. Not exactly what Kaisa wanted to hear. "He's no different from the guy we just saw in the movie. I would even say he looks about the same age."

"That guy was in his 30's at least. Christopher told me he was 26 when we met, so he's 27 now," Kaisa insisted.

"Are you sure?" Jill said.

"Yes, why would he lie about that?"

"Because he's not. Would you have continued seeing him if he told you he was like 36?" Jill remarked snidely.

"I don't know, maybe?" Kaisa replied.

"He's definitely an interesting one," Deborah said. "Does he have a brother?"

Well, yes, he does. But doesn't Deborah already have her hands full?

As soon as Kaisa returned to the dorm, she wanted to call Christopher. She didn't like how he looked at Deborah, and she needed to make sure he wasn't mad at her for not staying behind. But Kaisa didn't want Jill or Deborah to hear her conversation. Jill would say calling him so quickly would reek of desperation since she was just there. Deborah would probably not have as strong of an opinion but would definitely snitch on her to Jill.

Kaisa, however, needed to resolve a few things and was too riled up to sleep anyway. She picked up the phone from the common area and stretched the long cord into the hallway.

"Hello," he answered.

"Hi."

"Who's this?"

"It's me, Kaisa."

"Weren't you just here?"

"Yes, I'm lying in my bed naked, thinking of you," she flirted.

"Is that right?" he said, sounding disinterested. "Well, the mood has passed."

"Don't worry, the next time I see you, I will make it up to you."

"You're damn right, you will," he said, his voice deepening.

"So, what did you think of my friends?" Kaisa asked.

"I haven't stopped picturing you with them since you left."

"You're sick," she responded.

"Have you ever done anything sexually with your roommates?"

"No." *Where did that come from?*

"I would especially love to see you with the blonde one; she is gorgeous. You should bring her over next time."

"I've never been good at sharing, and I am not about to start with you."

"That's a shame; I'll try anything once."

Kaisa countered. "I've always wondered what it would be like to jump off a bridge, but I'm not dumb enough to try it. It's one of those things you don't do. And if you do try something sexual with her, see if I come back."

He laughed.

Kaisa's hunch was right. He was attracted to Deborah. She had to think fast. She wasn't about to give up her sovereignty over Christopher to another successor. "I don't think she's the kind of girl you would be into."

"Why not?" he inquired.

Kaisa lowered her voice. "Well, she's already had crabs and genital warts this year. Unless that doesn't bother you?"

"Are you kidding?" he said. But when Kaisa assured him she wasn't, he seemed immediately turned off. "Yeah, I think I'll pass."

"I'll see you soon," she said.

Kaisa laughed to herself, satisfied that she had put him off Deborah. If only her friend Gina had contracted any kind of venereal disease, her life in high school might have turned out so much better.

Kaisa went back into her room, put on her nightshirt, and got into bed. She lay there, reflecting on the evening's events. Agreeing to meet her friends was a good sign that their friendship was progressing. Maybe he finally wanted to get to know her more as a whole person, beyond her private parts. But she was getting antsy. Spring Break was approaching, the year was almost over, and she still held the sole title of The Virgin of 401. While she wanted to hold on to her philosophy that her first time would be with someone she loved and someone who loved her back, Kaisa was in love with Christopher, and he said he "really liked" her. That was going to have to be enough.

Kaisa made good on her promise and visited Christopher the next day. He was kind enough to carve out some time for her.

"Can you give some thought to us, taking this friendship to the next level?" Kaisa asked during their pillow talk.

"I would love nothing more than to have intercourse with you, but you know how I feel about not being your first... in that sense," Christopher said.

"Why not?" she whined.

"I'm afraid you'll get too emotional. It would mean more to you than it's supposed to."

She was concerned he was right. But she had made up her mind, and he was going to be the one. "At this point, I'm looking for the experience. I want to know what it is all about," she assured him. "Didn't you say our friendship is about making each other feel good?"

"Yes, but you won't see it as just sex. I don't want to give you the wrong idea."

"I'm not as naïve as you think I am anymore, thanks to you. I know the deal," she said. "Don't worry. You don't have to answer now. I'm going on Spring Break starting Friday."

"Oh, for how long?"

"I'll be gone until March 24th. I wanted to let you know in case you called looking for me."

"Are you going anywhere fun?" he asked.

"No, just home. I have some stuff to take care of and need some quiet time."

"I'm going to miss you. I do love the time we spend together. Maybe it's good that we get a little vacation from each other. I'm becoming a little too attached to you," he said as he rolled on top of her.

His words warmed her heart. "Can you think about us while I'm gone?" she said, looking into his eyes. "You know what I mean. Promise me you will at least consider it?"

Christopher agreed to think about it while she was away. She could only hope her absence would make his heart grow fonder.

CHAPTER 12
You Better Love Somebody

A s a former girl scout, Kaisa understood the merits of being prepared. She was hopeful Christopher would want to make love with her when she returned from Spring Break. Given his sexual prowess and expertise in other related activities, she was confident the experience would be nothing less than memorable.

She knew he was not a condom kind of guy and that it would be her responsibility to take the initiative and provide her own protection. Before she left for home, she made an appointment with her OB/GYN. Being 18, she didn't need her mother's permission to get a prescription for birth control pills but chose a female doctor because she wanted to discuss this decision with a more experienced woman.

"So, you found a man that you want to sleep with?" the doctor asked.

"Yes!" Kaisa said emphatically.

"Is he another student?"

Kaisa nodded. *Technically yes, he is a student. A much older one at that, but the doctor doesn't need to know the details.*

The doctor explained how the circle of pills worked. She stressed that Kaisa needed to make sure she took one every day, then noted the possible side effects. Bloating and spot bleeding seemed to be a small price to pay for what Kaisa thought would be the experience of a lifetime. "One more thing. If you smoke, I suggest you stop as it poses risks," the doctor advised.

The next day Kaisa threw out her three-month-old pack of cigarettes and started her first cycle of pills.

During the break, she thought of Christopher at almost every moment, picturing them together in the ultimate human connection. While their encounters were still rooted in sexual activity, the intimacy between them had been growing, and the ratio of sex to pillow talk had flipped. Basically, there was a lot more banter between blow jobs. Since their run-in at Saks, he was more affectionate and called her often just to chat, and he did agree to meet her friends. His feelings for her had to be getting stronger.

The second Kaisa returned to school, she called Christopher. "Oh, please be home, please be home," she chanted, getting more anxious with each ring.

"Hi Christopher, it's Kaisa."

"Hi. How are you? Where are you calling from?" he asked, sounding distracted.

"I'm back in Boston."

"I thought you weren't coming back until next week?" he said.

"I told you, March 24th. You forgot or did not pay attention. Can I come over?"

"I'm sorry, I have a major paper that's overdue. I can't spare any time today."

Kaisa sighed, her body aching to feel his touch. "I've heard this before. You've been telling me the same thing since January. Are you sure you can't find a little time today?"

"I'm swamped. I'll call you tomorrow, sweetheart," he promised.

The next day dragged. Kaisa jumped each time the phone rang and slid back into a depressed state when it wasn't Christopher. Every spare moment, when her mind wasn't occupied on something else, she held the phone to her heart, rationalizing why she could call him again.

"Put the phone down," Jill said, passing by. "Stop acting so desperate. You called him yesterday, and he blew you off."

Kaisa couldn't help herself. It was probably the tenth time that day she almost dialed his number.

"I'll bet you a book of stamps that you can't call him before he calls you."

This bet would be tough, but Kaisa accepted the challenge, hoping it might deter her from calling him. But the very next day, she got the urge again. While Jill was lying in her bunk, Kaisa picked up the phone as quietly and as slowly as possible, hoping Jill wouldn't hear its soft click.

"You lose!" she yelled from her room.

"I technically didn't call him."

"Doesn't matter. You were going to if I didn't catch you."

Three days and a book of stamps later, Kaisa finally heard from Christopher.

"Kaisa?"

"Yes?"

"Did you want to see me?"

Duh? "What do you think?" she said. "I just stepped out of the shower. I'll be there as soon as I can."

She pulled out a frilly, light blue frock with a flowing skirt which she bought over break with her hard-earned Mrs. Fields money. At least if he made a mess on it, she would not have to answer to Deborah.

Kaisa added a mist of Deborah's fragrance that Chris favored and quickly ventured out, looking like a sexy southern belle. The anticipation of being in his presence again fizzed inside her like carbonated bubbles. Her body and her senses were on overdrive. As she neared his apartment, she tried to slow her breathing, flicking her wrists in an attempt to shake out the excess stress.

Upon reaching the frosted glass door, she announced her arrival and eagerly listened for those muffled thumps on the staircase. After a few moments that seemed like forever, he met her at the door wearing a lavender polo shirt and khaki pants and was as attractive as she remembered. It had been too long since he was close enough to touch. Kaisa could not wait to melt in his arms. He smiled, leaned over, gave her a hug and a quick peck on the cheek, which was hardly satisfying.

"I guess your roommate wasn't able to catch you in time?" he said.

"What do you mean?"

"I am so sorry, but I forgot I had to be somewhere in an hour. I called back, but you had already left."

Kaisa deflated. She had waited so long and now could only enjoy him for an abbreviated time. "Well, can I stay while you get ready?"

"Of course. You know I was thinking, I really did miss you." Christopher said as they ascended the stairs.

It was exactly what she wanted to hear. She kept her trench coat buttoned so that he couldn't see the dress except for a hint of lace trim peeking out from beneath the hem.

His apartment was a giant mess. Papers cluttered his desk, and dirty plates surrounding an empty pizza box lined his floor. Evidently, he hadn't made any effort to clean before her arrival or possibly since she left for Spring Break. "Sorry, I had a section meeting here yesterday and haven't had time to straighten up."

"Never mind. What do you think?" Kaisa asked, revealing her new dress as she twirled around with her skirt flaring in the air.

Christopher smiled, "You have an incomparable ability to make me so hard," he said, proudly displaying the bulge in his pants. He put his hands on her shoulders and pushed down. "Get on your knees and undo me."

"Already?" she moaned. "But I wanted to talk to you."

He nodded. "We don't have much time."

"You haven't even kissed me yet," she said.

"I did before."

"That didn't count."

"Please, Kaisa, I've missed you so much. We'll talk after this, okay," he begged.

She traced her fingers along his belt buckle and effortlessly unfastened it, then lowered his boxers, and knelt before him. Kaisa obliged his request but wasn't focused or engaged in what she was doing. Her mind was occupied, mentally strategizing the best way to get him to agree to take that next step. She bobbed on his shaft, moving her tongue on the underside, happy she didn't gag as much as she used to.

"Oh, that feels so good. Take me deeper. You are amazing," he praised in the background.

Before she knew it, she had completed her task. Apparently, mastering the mechanics of satisfying him enough that he came with no problem and didn't seem to notice that she was on autopilot.

"Wow, you've become an expert really quick."

She withdrew his penis from her mouth. "I guess practice makes perfect. So, I think we need to address the elephant in the room," she said.

"You don't look like you've gained weight since I last saw you?" he joked.

Kaisa's face soured. The birth control pills were making her bloated. "I think you should know that I got a prescription for the pill, and I've been taking it."

"Why?" he asked.

"Why do you think? So, I'm prepared when one of our escapades eventually leads to that."

"Leads to what?"

"What we discussed before I left?"

"What did we discuss?" he inquired.

Kaisa had a sneaking suspicion that he was well aware of what she was referring to, but he was going to make her say it. "Intercourse," she muttered, gritting her teeth.

"It hasn't before. Why should it now?"

"Because I want to make love with you," Kaisa said. As the words left her mouth, she wished she could have grabbed them out of the air.

"I don't 'make love, I fuck." His crude description didn't make her want him any less. "I already told you. I'm concerned you won't be able to separate the two – love and sex."

"You don't know that for sure."

Christopher gave her a knowing smile and a look of doubt. "You are still a virgin, right?"

"Yes, in the vaginal sense, you took it in other ways, so what's the big deal?"

"That was early on, and it was wrong of me. Traditional intercourse holds more meaning and risk than other types of sex. Look, when we mess around, I've never been turned on by anyone more than you. You are the best partner. I've never had such a satisfying sex life without intercourse. I fantasize about you constantly!"

"You must say that to all the girls," she teased, hoping she wasn't right.

"Actually, I don't. You should know that. As much as I would love to be with you in that way, I've thought about it, and I don't think your first time should be with me."

"Wow, I never thought getting you to have sex with me would be this difficult." Kaisa threw up her hands, then fired back. "Are you afraid of disappointing me?"

"No. I'm pretty sure I'd rock your world."

"Would you feel differently if I wasn't a virgin?" she asked.

"Sure, I probably would have been fucking you silly," he said with a chortle.

"Are you serious? Is that all that is standing in the way?"

"Let's talk about it another time. I have to get ready now."

While Kaisa pouted over her shattered expectations, Christopher arose from the mattress and went to his small closet. He put on a blue and white striped shirt, khakis, a red silk tie and completed his ensemble with a tweed jacket and leather loafers. "Where are you going so dressed up?"

"I have a meeting with my professors about some overdue papers. I can't believe it slipped my mind today. Come on. I'll walk with you part of the way."

"Can I kiss you when you look that good?" she asked swooning over his Harvard preppy outfit.

"Of course," he said.

Christopher placed his hands on either side of her cheeks and cradled her face. She examined his expression, attempting to decode the thoughts behind his eyes. He guided her face toward his and pressed his lips tightly against her mouth. "I must go now," he said.

Outside his apartment, on this beautiful spring day, Kaisa strutted proudly linked arm in arm with Christopher looking like a couple dressed up for their date.

"Have you ever been there?" Christopher asked, pointing to a restaurant and bar called Daisy Buchanan's.

"No."

"Do you know where that name comes from?"

"Isn't it a character from the Great Gatsby?" Kaisa

stated, thankful it was required reading for a high school English class.

"You're right. You're more well-read than I thought."

"Maybe we should go there sometime and discuss F. Scott Fitzgerald," she suggested.

"You're always hinting, aren't you? You know we're not boyfriend, girlfriend."

"I know," she said, trying to hide her disappointment, "but you can't blame me for trying. When I set my mind to something, I don't give up easily, that's for sure."

That weekend, Jill and Deborah were planning a big night out dancing at a local nightclub and invited Kaisa to come along. Technically, they were going to two clubs that were adjacent to each other. Celebrations was a club for 18 and up. Narcissus was for 21 and over, or as it was more commonly known – Narsyphillis.

The last time Kaisa went out clubbing, she had a wonderful time. She danced for hours with a bunch of guys and never paid for her drinks. Jill's friend, Aaron, had a new job at Narcissus as a bouncer. He told the girls all they had to do was pretend they were of age, show him their drivers' licenses, and he would give them the over 21 wristbands. Before they left the dorm, they each took a power nap and primed themselves with a couple of shots of tequila.

As planned, Aaron was carding at the door. Jill brought Mindy's fake ID just in case. After he let the girls in, Kaisa broke away from Jill and Deborah to scan the perimeter of the human meat market. The club was hot, dark, and smoky, which made it even harder to see. The music was deafening with a bass that reverberated through her body while seizure-inducing strobe lights flashed in sync with the beat. A couple of acne-ridden, greasy-haired guys approached her and offered to buy her a drink. But she graciously passed as they weren't what she had in mind.

Then someone at the bar caught her eye. She smiled back, and he waved her over. He was wearing a short-sleeve plaid shirt and maybe navy or black pants, looking like he came straight from work. Kaisa seductively strolled toward him through the faint fog of cigarettes, balancing on her three-inch heels.

He offered to buy her a drink, but Kaisa said she only wanted water. They began yelling at each other in the nicest way possible because how else do you talk with someone at a loud dance club? After a few minutes, he motioned to follow him to the opposite side of the bar, which was the furthest point away from the dance floor.

"What did ya say ya name *wass*?" he asked.

"I'm Kaisa."

"That's a different name. I've *nevah* heard that *bee-fah*. I'm Mike."

"Are you here alone?" she asked.

"I came with a couple of my friends, but I haven't seen them in an *ow-ah*. At least I drove."

"Oh, what do you drive?"

"A *Sab*." Kaisa knew he meant, 'Saab,' but that's how it came out in his heavy Boston accent.

"How about you? Are ya *he-yah* by yourself?"

"My friends are around here somewhere."

"Would ya like a drink?" he asked.

Kaisa wasn't in the mood for beer or another shot and didn't know many drink names. Last time she was at this club, she tried a few drinks but could not remember what they were called, except one. "Um, I think I'd like a 'slow, comfortable screw against the wall,'" she said.

Mike's eyes popped out of his head, "I wasn't expecting that, but I'm *shoo-ah* that could be arranged," he joked.

Kaisa felt the blood rush to her face. "It was either that or 'Sex on the Beach.' Those are the only drinks I know and like."

"*Ei-thah* one sounds good. I'm happy to buy it for ya if ya wouldn't mind *awdering* it. I'd feel a little *awd* asking the *bahtender* for that."

Kaisa screamed out her request to the bartender while a couple of other guys sitting nearby turned their heads. Mike reached into his wallet, paid for the drink, and left the bartender a generous tip. *Wow, someone willing to shell out a little cash for my company.* It was a welcome change from Christopher.

They found a less noisy place with tables to sit and talk while she sipped her dirty drink. Each swig of the hard liquor sent a rush into her brain, begging her to slow down. Despite being further away from the blaring speakers, it was still a challenge to hear Mike. Based on every other word, Kaisa was able to make out he was 22, lived in Natick, and worked at TJ Maxx's corporate office. She told him she was a Northeastern student, almost 19, and only got into the club because her friend's friend is a bouncer.

"Do ya wanna dance?" he asked.

"Yeah, that would be awesome."

Unlike other guys she had danced with in the past, Mike had rhythm. They grooved to a string of popular hits and leftover 70's disco seamlessly mixed together by the deejay. With each aerobic track, Kaisa and Mike bounced and gyrated closer to each other as the sweat seeped through their clothes. Kaisa kept praying for a power ballad, so she could lean on him and catch her breath. But no such luck.

"Why don't we go outside to get some *ay-ah*? It's really noisy and hot in *he-yah*."

Kaisa nodded her pounding head. He took her hand and led her outside into the balmy night or more like early morning by then. The cooler air was refreshing, and just what she needed.

"I would like to see ya again. Can I have *yaw numbah*?" he asked.

Mike wasn't precisely what Kaisa liked, but he seemed sweet and cute enough to see again. Besides, how could she turn down a man with an actual job willing to take her out and spend money on her? What a concept. "Sure, I had fun." Kaisa pulled out a piece of scrap paper from her purse and a stick of black eyeliner. "That's all I have to write with," she snorted. "Hope it doesn't smudge." She scribbled her phone number and gave it to Mike.

As they hugged goodbye, he gave her a small peck on the cheek. "I'll call ya," he said.

Kaisa checked her watch. It was nearly 1:30 a.m. She was done for the night and wanted to go home. The club would be announcing last call soon, and she had no idea if Jill or Deborah were still there or had left without her.

"Have you seen Jill?" she asked Aaron, who was still on duty working the door.

"Not in a while."

She held out her wristband (the one he gave her) and waved it at him with a wide grin. "Look, I'm 21 today," she teased.

Surrounded by the other bouncers, Aaron said reassuringly, "Yes, Kaisa, I know you are 21. Happy Birthday. Why don't you go back inside and look around?"

The lights were turned on. Only a few less attractive female stragglers were left who had not been paired up for the night. Were these the 'beer goggle girls,' the crew guys talked about - the ones who become progressively more attractive the more you drink. Kaisa felt bad for them, knowing what it was like to feel virtually invisible back home. Tonight, she was a solid 11:00 p.m. girl,

thinking in her drunken logic. "There you guys are," Kaisa said.

"Hey," Deborah and Jill replied in unison.

"Where did you go?" Jill asked. "We couldn't find you."

"I met someone. He was pretty nice and cute. He asked to see me again."

"You don't pick up guys in bars," Jill said. "You are only supposed to dance with them and have them buy you drinks."

"Well, all people that come here can't be scumbags. I mean, we're nice people, and we came here," Kaisa said.

"We're the exception," Deborah insisted.

Kaisa hoped Mike would call. It had been a while since she had been on a traditional date or part of a normal couple. Plus, Mike had a car so she could explore new places in and around Boston. Christopher didn't need to know and probably wouldn't care because even he said they weren't boyfriend/girlfriend.

So, what if I met him in a bar. Mike might be exactly what I need right now.

CHAPTER 13
How Can I Convince You?

As much as Kaisa wanted love, sex, or whatever else, she had to focus on securing a co-op job between June and December once her freshman year was over. That was the biggest priority, and time was ticking away. Knowing that, she made an urgent appointment with her advisor.

"It's May, and I still don't have anything," she wailed. "Many of my classmates have already received offers. All the positions I interviewed for that were near my hometown turned me down."

There were more opportunities to choose from in the Boston area, but any money she would make would have to go to rent versus tuition. So that would completely defeat the purpose. Truthfully, none of the positions interested her, but she needed something for her resume and to fulfill her school requirement. It was still frustrating. After school and during the summer, her previous work experience included jobs as a part-time office assistant for an executive search firm and an investment banking company. It was supposed to give her a leg up when competing for work with other students who just waited tables or scooped ice cream. But so far, it wasn't making a difference.

"I do have a job that just came up: A Northeastern alum is looking for a Budget Coordinator at his advertising agency," her advisor said.

"That sounds great! Where?"

"It's at OMNI in New York. You had said you were interested in working in advertising."

Kaisa's eyes grew large. "Are you kidding? There is an opening at a major global advertising agency in New York City, no less?" She had been turned down for roles that she didn't want, and now there was a last-minute opening for her co-op dream job. Maybe it was meant to be. If she were ever lucky enough to get that position, she could take the train to the city, which was only a five-minute walk from her house.

"It's not a done deal. You still need to interview for it."

"When?"

"By the end of this week."

Kaisa only had one class on Friday, and for this opportunity, she had no doubt she would skip it.

He gave her the information, wished her luck, and left her with one last piece of advice: "Remember, there is no shame in flat-out asking for the job! It shows you genuinely want it."

Flat out asking for things doesn't always work. But who knows, it's worth a try.

That Thursday night, Kaisa rode the Amtrak train home to Connecticut. She relished the extra time to decompress, sleep in her bed, and prepare for the next day. The following morning, dressed in her new black interview suit and armed with copies of her resume in an imitation leather folder, she walked to the train station for the hour ride to New York City.

The advertising industry, otherwise known as Madison Avenue, got its name because most of the big firms had their offices there at one time or another. OMNI was there, and only a few short blocks from Grand Central Station. The agency was in an old, gray stone building, as dingy on the inside as it was on the outside, but Kaisa didn't care. They did work for Pepsi with all those major celebrities. Even though she was interviewing for a less glamorous client that made synthetic fibers, it could be her foot in the door.

Kaisa first met with Lupe, who would be her Supervisor if she got the job. Lupe was an intimidating heavy-set, middle-aged Hispanic woman. She greeted Kaisa as if she didn't want to be there or already had someone else in mind. If her demeanor wasn't enough of a challenge, Lupe had a strong accent that was difficult to understand.

During the interview, she launched direct and sometimes harsh questions like: 'Why do you want to work here?' and 'Why should I hire you instead of someone else?" Despite being nervous, Kaisa did her best to maintain eye contact, be polite, and not be distracted by the giant mole above her lip with two long gray hairs growing out of it.

However, Lupe did seem to perk up and smile when Kaisa spoke about her experience and her strong work ethic. Even though she was from the same affluent town as Lupe's boss, Kaisa took the bus to various jobs in a neighboring city. She didn't mention it to Lupe, but on her way home, she was always the last person on that crowded bus by the time it crossed over the border into Westport.

"Do you have any questions for me?" Lupe asked.

"No, I think you explained everything thoroughly. But I'm curious, why are there boxes everywhere?"

"Most of the agency is moving to a new office on 6th Avenue and 51st street in a couple of weeks, except for Accounting. So, if you got the job, you would work in the new location."

Kaisa knew where that was – across the street from Radio City Music Hall. It would add an extra 10 minutes to her commute, but it was still within walking distance. She thanked Lupe for the interview with a firm grip and a smile and moved on to the next one, not knowing what kind of impression she had left.

The interview with Lupe's boss was also challenging but in a different way. Mr. Brenahan was a pleasant balding older man in a brown Mr. Rogers cardigan. He was dressed more casually than the other executives and seemed out of place at the dynamic agency. Living in the same town helped establish some connection and made her reference points easier for him to understand. Kaisa's biggest task was keeping him awake as he kept dozing off in between her answers.

Finally, she met Mr. Crawley. He ran the account as the Management Supervisor and was the reason the position was open. He was an energetic older man with gray hair and warm blue eyes.

"What brings you to OMNI?" he asked.

Kaisa paused for a moment, hoping she wouldn't stumble over her words. "When I first met my co-op advisor, he asked me what would be my dream job? I said: 'to work in advertising in New York City.' So, the fact that this opportunity opened up, and I could possibly work on your team seems like fate to me."

In keeping with Professor Ablom's advice, she expressed her enthusiasm and passion for the position at the end of the interview. "I would work harder than any other candidate and guarantee you no one wants this position more than I do."

While on the train home, she wrote her thank you notes and mailed them the next morning, praying they would hire her.

After a couple of weeks, Kaisa hadn't heard anything from the agency, but Mike from Narcissus called to ask her out. Christopher had been preoccupied and agitated as of late and set little time aside for Kaisa. He blamed it on all the assignments he had to finish for school, but then again, that was always his excuse.

His decision, about not being her first, could not be swayed. He had no interest in breaking through her virgin roadblock. Kaisa hated taking these stupid birth control pills for nothing. Most of the time, she experienced spot bleeding, which prevented her from engaging in what she enjoyed, or at least what she got in return when she and Christopher were together. Kaisa had considered lying to Christopher and telling him that she had sex with someone to alleviate the pressure of being her first time, but she feared he would probably see through her lie. It appeared the only way to get him to toss around the idea of having traditional sex with her was to lose her virgin status, recalling he did say he might feel differently if she wasn't a virgin.

For their first date, Mike suggested they go to Faneuil Hall before going dancing. He opened the car door for Kaisa as she gracefully stepped into his fancy vehicle.

"Oh, this is a stick shift," she said.

"Have ya *evah* driven one," he asked.

"No, I've never ridden, I mean driven a stick shift before," Kaisa turned her head toward the window to hide her embarrassment, hoping Mike didn't see through her Freudian slip.

Driving around Boston was umpteen times better than riding the T. She could take in all the sights in sequence versus being buried underground for most of the trip.

They stopped near the Marriott Long Wharf at a romantic spot along Boston's beautiful "Hahbah" backdrop. She leaned against the railing taking in the crashing waves, stars, and a bright full moon. Kaisa had been there before with Josh. While the conditions were the same, the ambiance did not coincide with her feelings. It was different with Mike. First, she didn't tower over him in heels. It also didn't hurt that he was better looking, which made him an ideal candidate on which to practice her new French kissing technique. Mike also appeared to be an expert.

At Narcissus, Aaron was working the door and hooked Kaisa up with another Over 21 wristband. Mike was full of energy and had his groove on. They danced through another long stretch of songs and had a couple of drinks each. Mike paid for everything. Kaisa had to admit it was a lot better than being summoned to a room each time.

"Tonight's been fun!" Kaisa said. "I don't want it to end just yet. Do you want to come over?"

"*Shoo-ah*, that would be great," Mike replied.

Back at the suite, she was happy to see that she had the place all to herself. She led Mike to her room, in case someone came back unexpectedly, but forgot how bad the room looked. Its pigsty status was at an all-time high. Her desk was overflowing with books, papers, and snack wrappers. Deborah's shoes were everywhere except for her closet. There were piles of clean and dirty laundry on several flat surfaces, including the floor, and damp towels were hanging on the metal rails of the unmade bunk beds.

Kaisa held a hand to her heart, "I apologize for this mess."

"It's no problem," he answered.

She was reasonably sure Mike couldn't have cared less if it had been hit by a grenade, even though it looked damn close to that.

Kaisa straightened out the sheets on her unmade bottom bunk and invited Mike to sit. She leaned her head on his shoulder, and he followed suit by placing his arm around her and gently laying her down on the bed. Now that she was level with the playing field, they began working their way around the bases. His body bumped and grinded against hers as their make-out session grew in intensity. Kaisa was quite aware of which was which thanks to Christopher's lessons. She got so caught up in Mike's passionate kisses that before she knew it, her skirt was up around her hips.

"Kaisa," he whispered.

"What?"

"Do ya mind if I put it in and pull out?"

Her first instinct was NO. "Mike, that's too far for me for a first date," Kaisa said, thinking they wouldn't make it all the way around the bases tonight. "I think we'd better stop now."

He agreed, sitting back up with a huge bulge in his pants. "I don't usually do this, *ei-thah*. I guess we just got caught up in the moment."

The suite door opened, then shut with its heavy thud.

Kaisa got up and opened the door to make it look like they were doing nothing but talking.

"Maybe I should go," he said.

"Okay, if you want to."

They walked toward the dorm steps in awkward silence. He reached for her hand halfway down the stairs and gave Kaisa an assuring grin. She followed him outside to say goodbye at his car, which of all places was parked on Symphony Road.

"I had a good time tonight. You're a *lotta* of fun, and *soopah* hot," Mike said.

Kaisa blushed and looked down from his fixed gaze. He leaned in slowly, lifted her chin with his finger, and gave her a soft kiss goodbye. "I'll see ya soon."

The following Thursday, Mike called for another date. He wasn't going anywhere for Memorial Day weekend, and neither was she. As a bonus, everyone else in Suite 401 was leaving, so the place would be all hers, and she could get ahead of the mess.

Mike and Kaisa planned to grab an informal dinner on Saturday, then leave the rest of the night open to whatever they felt like doing next.

An hour before he was supposed to pick her up, he called. "I'm *sawry*. I can't make *ahr* dinner date. I'm going to be *he-yah* a little while *longah*. I hope ya don't mind."

Kaisa could barely hear him over the rooting and

roaring in the background. "Oh?" she said.

"My baseball game went *intah ova*-time. Then we all decided to celebrate *ahr* win at the *bah*. The guys *awdered* a *buncha bee-yas* and some *appetizahs*. I would like to see *ya laytah* if that's alright with *ya*? But I *haftah* to go home, take a *show-wah*, and change. I hope ya don't mind if we stay in tonight. I'm *kinda* beat. I can be *ovah* about 9:30."

Kaisa congratulated Mike on his win and said that was fine. "Take your time, everyone else went away for the weekend, so at least we'll have the place to ourselves."

When the downstairs buzzer went off, she popped in her Peter Gabriel/Genesis combo tape to set the mood and then went down to get him. He was wearing a cream-colored cable knit sweater, faded acid-washed jeans, and sneakers and was holding a movie, coffee, and soda. Kaisa hugged him and inhaled his just-showered scent.

"The coffee is for me," he said. "I'm tired, but I wanted to see ya. I'm *sawry* again for not taking *ya* out. I got Top Gun at the video store. I hope *ya* haven't seen it. There's nothin' left by Saturday night."

"No, I never saw it. I'll pop this into the VCR." Ironically, she had already seen it on the one mercy date she had with Gina's boyfriend before he became Gina's boyfriend.

The movie served more as background noise, as neither of them was paying attention. In between their chatter, Mike began working his way around the bases again, concentrating on her top half. But when he reached for her belt, Kaisa instinctively pushed his hand away as if by some involuntary reflex.

If ever there was a time and place to lose her virginity, this was it. So, what was holding her back? She was comfortable with making out. Hell, that was fun. She barely knew Mike, but at least they had already seen each other three times, so it wouldn't be as shameful as a one-night stand.

"Do you want to watch Saturday Night Live?" she asked.

"Wow, it's that late already. I have *anothah* game *tomarrow* morning. I should be going."

"If you are too tired, you could stay here tonight if you want," Kaisa suggested. "Most of the dorm is deserted, and it's eerily quiet. I wouldn't mind the company."

"Thanks. That sounds good," he said, planting one of his gentle kisses on her mouth.

"I think I'll get changed for bed," Kaisa said, getting up from the foldout chair in the common area. She chose a T-shirt and a pair of easy-access hospital pants with a ribbon tie in the front and changed in the bathroom.

Mike was in the lower bunk when she returned wearing his tighty-whiteys. Not exactly Kaisa's favorite, but not a deal-breaker. She set her annoying alarm for 6:00 a.m., as he requested, and turned off the light.

The less than twin size irregular bunk was not designed to sleep two, probably on purpose. Kaisa turned on her side with her back facing Mike to maximize the space, wedging herself into the concavity of his spoon.

He pressed his chest against her back and kissed his

way up the nape of her neck. She felt his erection stiffen as it rested in the crevice of her buttocks. The coffee must have taken effect because sleep appeared to be the last thing on his mind. Kaisa turned her head and locked her lips with his. As her t-shirt climbed upward in his fist, she willingly raised her arms, signaling permission to slide it over her head. Mike caressed and squeezed her breasts until her nipples hardened and stood at attention. She could see only a silhouette looming over her in the darkness. A stiff, throbbing penis pulsated against her pubic bone, at least bigger than what she was used to. She gripped his full erection in her hand to assess its size. Kaisa tensed up when she realized how big he was, not so much in length but in girth. Not the below-average starter penis that she would have preferred or something comparable to Christopher's.

He loosened the tie and slowly slipped off her pants. Then with his knee, he parted her legs. He was going for the gusto - HER gusto. She knew "it" was inevitable if she didn't stop him. She should have asked him to put on a condom but just let it go, hoping he wouldn't leave the kind of mark as Benjamin or Ian left on Deborah.

Then he entered her. It took some coaxing and additional maneuvering to absorb his manhood. The euphoric jolt she had anticipated felt more like someone shoving a plug into a dead socket. *That's it? No electrical current? No wave of pleasure?* Fortunately, it didn't hurt as much as she had expected. But his thrusts grew harder and faster, and the friction was starting to burn. "Mike, can we stop, please."

Mike graciously stopped without protest.

"I'll be right back," she said.

Kaisa picked up the phone from the common area, went into the bathroom, and shut the door. It was 1:30 a.m., according to her watch on the sink. Her mind was twisting with an onslaught of emotions that she couldn't process alone. She needed to talk to someone to sort them out. With the girls gone, she dialed her friend Gina at her parent's house, against her better judgment, which seemed to be a theme that night. Gina's boyfriend Fitz was notorious for that. If she were lucky, maybe Gina would answer.

"Oh, hi, Mr. Catrone. I'm so sorry to call this late and wake you. I have to talk to Gina," she whispered.

Kaisa spent a lot of time at Gina's home and was close to her parents, even calling them Mom and Dad at times. Hopefully, they would understand and forgive her for the late call. Within a minute, Gina picked up the other line.

"Guess what I just did?" Kaisa announced, sitting on the edge of the cold bathtub.

"How was it?"

"Not as bad as I thought, but I didn't do it with Christopher."

"Really?" Gina said, sounding surprised.

"I did it with that guy Mike I met at the dance club," Kaisa said, realizing she wasn't sure of his last name.

"Oh well, you should be careful," she warned.

"Too late now."

"Hold on a sec."

Kaisa could hear Gina whispering to Fitz, which just added salt to the wound. Gina had recently lost her virginity to him as well. Her first time had been with someone she loved who, ironically, Kaisa loved first. But sadly, he didn't feel the same way.

"It's so late," Gina finally said. "Fitz was just about to go home, and I'm beat. You can call me tomorrow if you want to talk more about it."

"Yeah, okay, um, have a good night." *Well, that didn't help.* She wasn't surprised that talking to Gina was a bust. It wasn't the first time she had let her down. But with Jill gone for the weekend, Gina was all she had.

Kaisa was not ready to go back to her room. Her brain and her body were still a mess. She couldn't believe she went through with it. This love-starved girl was no longer officially a virgin, even though it didn't work out the way she had always imagined.

Her high school psychology teacher had said that a significant loss brings on the seven stages of grief. There had to be a parallel regarding losing one's virginity. However, it felt like she was experiencing these stages all at once and somewhat out of order. Denial morphed into shock then twisted into uncontrollable giggling. She tried to process her emotions for a couple more minutes, unsuccessfully, then realized she had been in the bathroom for quite a while.

Kaisa flushed the toilet, turned on the water, and washed her hands, to appear that she used it as more than a phone booth. She slipped quietly into bed, then burst into a ferocious giggle once again.

"What's so funny?" Mike asked.

"Nothing," she said. "Um, what day is today?"

"The 24th, why is it a special occasion?" he asked.

"You could say that," she said.

He didn't press for any more information before falling asleep. Kaisa was too wired. She drifted in and out of sleep crowded by Mike and his loud snoring until exhaustion won out.

"What time is it?" Mike asked.

"Kaisa lazily cocked her head to make out the blurry digital figures. "5:30," she mumbled.

Mike rustled around for a few minutes as Kaisa dozed. Within a few moments, Mike's kisses rose from her shoulders to her neck and up to her face. He pulled Kaisa onto her back, then placed his knee between her tightly locked legs. Even though she wasn't interested, she played along. This time it was easier. He complemented each hard thrust with tender kisses as his breath grew heavy. "Oh, you feel so good," he moaned, just as he pulled out and released on her thigh.

There she was with a pool of ejaculate on her body, AGAIN. But now, it didn't seem to faze her.

"Do you have a towel or something?" he asked.

"You can use the one on the closet door."

He got up out of bed and threw the towel to her and went into the bathroom.

Kaisa turned onto her stomach to watch the daylight rising through the window. With her back to the door and in a semi-trance, she was startled by Mike's hand on her bare shoulder. He slowly caressed her back, gliding his fingers up and down her spine for a couple of minutes while she stayed silent, holding her gaze outside the window, having entered the freaked-out stage of post-virginal grief.

The alarm screeched, cueing Mike to get up and get dressed. Shortly after, Kaisa arose, picked up her nightclothes off the floor, and put them back on to see him out. The last thing he said was what she assumed to be the obligatory departure line in these awkward situations: 'I'll call you.'

Kaisa went back to bed but lay there staring at the metal coils of Deborah's top bunk, marveling at the irony that just a day before, she was talking to Mindy about not leaving her freshman year a virgin. Doing "it," as a whole, was weird. Now she had to deal with the aftermath.

She pulled out her cassette collection and selected a few songs she felt were appropriate for the situation and her frame of mind; "Somebody" by Depeche Mode, followed by "Big Mistake" and "Daddy's Girl" by Peter Cetera. As she listened to her personal serenade, she rounded the corner into the grief stage of grief and cried. She turned the mattress over to pretend it never happened, even though she knew the truth. That mattress would be a constant reminder until the end of school, which was fortunately only a few weeks away.

She threw her desk chair onto its side. *What a waste! All this time, I held on to my precious virginity, reserving it for someone special, and the person who helped me cross that milestone didn't even know.*

But maybe the ends could justify the means. It was likely Christopher would be willing to sleep with her now. In fact, she might even be a better lay, with some experience under her belt, or more like below her belt.

MARLBOROUGH MAN

CHAPTER 14
Start Spreading the News

With her cherry popped and the non-virgin box checked, Kaisa desperately wanted to see Christopher. The pressure of being her first was now a non-issue. This new badge of honor meant she had earned the right to approach him for the experience she ultimately wanted.

She tried reaching him for most of the morning, but all she got was a busy signal as if he disconnected his phone. Later, no one was picking up. Kaisa couldn't hold on to her new truth any longer; it had to come out. With what energy she had left from that horrible night of sleep, she set out to find him to share her sexual status.

Kaisa began her search at Copley Place, as both times she had run into Christopher, it was in that general vicinity. She circled the mall's interior a few times, keeping an eye out, hoping he would materialize, but didn't have any luck. Hopefully, he hadn't gone away for Memorial Day Weekend, not that she had any idea whom he would visit.

Around lunchtime, she took a break at Au Bon Pain. It would add at least one positive to her day if she could not track him down. Kaisa chose a single table by the floor to ceiling windows. As she enjoyed her favorite chicken tarragon sandwich, she closely watched the flurry of foot traffic on the other side. But Christopher was nowhere in sight.

With the Sunday afternoon weather working in her and everyone else's favor, she extended her mission to the mall's outer perimeter. While strolling by a bar/restaurant called the Sports Saloon, she spotted Christopher sitting inside watching baseball among a bunch of men. Kaisa waved through the window, trying to get his attention, but either he didn't see her or was avoiding her intentionally. No matter what, Kaisa wasn't going to let the chance of technically being out with Christopher pass her by.

Upon entering the bar, she found an empty chair and dragged it next to him, smiling and mouthing a hello. She reached for his hand, but he yanked it away as if she was a stranger, then adjusted his chair in the opposite direction.

Kaisa heeded his signals and sat silently by his side through two innings of the game as he fidgeted and treated her company as if it was an invasion. The awkward display seemed to catch the attention of the other men. She could see them casually pointing and winking out of the corner of her eye.

"Well, I've seen enough," he said to guys around him, as he got up from his chair, abandoning Kaisa and a partially finished beer he more than likely hadn't paid for.

She followed him outside. "Why were you so cold to me in there?" she asked as the door closed behind them.

"I'm not a big believer in public displays of affection, and I just wanted to watch the game in peace."

"I'm sorry if I made you feel uncomfortable."

"That's fine. You just caught me by surprise. You know how I feel about that."

Maybe this wasn't the best time to inform him of last night's events. "Can I talk to you," she asked, going against her gut.

"Sure, I'm hungry. I was going to get something to eat. This place is expensive."

They ended up at Burger King. It wasn't much, but it was the first time they went to a public eatery besides that first "date" at the cafe.

"Can I get you anything?" he asked.

It would have been perfect if she were hungry or thirsty because an offer like this was rare. "No, thanks. I just had lunch, but I may nibble on your fries."

"Why don't you go get us a table, and I'll be right there," he said.

Kaisa found a booth at the end of the restaurant as far

away from other customers as possible to avoid an audience.

Christopher joined her a few moments later. "What have you been up to?" he asked, taking a bite of his Whopper.

"I had an interview at an advertising agency in New York City."

"How did that go?"

"I'm not sure. Finding a co-op job has been hard. It seems everyone has secured one but me. This one at the agency is the only hope I have left, and ironically, it's my dream job. Either way, I'll be leaving for home in a couple of weeks and won't be back at school for six months."

"Would it be a paid internship?"

How nice he cares more about if I'm getting paid, than I won't be local for half a year. "I'm not sure of the salary exactly, but if I get it, I will have to pay for the commute to New York. Whatever is left will go to tuition."

"At least one of us will have a job. Maybe you could send me a stipend," he suggested.

"You could always get a job."

"I'm planning on visiting family in Nashville after the semester is over, so I won't be around."

"Is that right? I'm going to be busy myself with finals coming up," she added.

It was evident that their relationship was winding down, or at minimum, going on a long hiatus. If she wanted to be with him before her sendoff, this would have to be the time.

"Can we go back to your place?" she asked.

"Wow, now who's being the aggressor?" he said, grinning.

"It looks like we won't be seeing each other for a while. I want to be with you... in that way before I go."

"Kaisa, we've discussed this. It would be too emotional for you."

"You mean it wouldn't mean anything to you!" she snapped.

"We're both going our separate ways soon. I don't see the point in either of us becoming more emotionally involved or attached."

"Who is going to become more emotionally involved or attached?" she prodded.

Christopher took a large final bite of his burger.

"If you're still worried about being my first, you don't have to anymore."

He tilted his head and gave her a sideways glance. "What do you mean?" he chewed.

"Well, I've been seeing this other guy, and -- we had sex. He didn't know he was my first."

"I beg your pardon. When did this happen?" he quietly clamored his face beet red.

It was not the reaction she was expecting, which was

relief followed by lust. "Last night... and... early this morning... twice."

"Last night? I don't believe this!" he hissed, keeping his voice low.

"I did it for you. I mean for us."

"You did it for me?" he growled.

"You didn't want the pressure of being my first, so now you're not. YOU were the one who said that we needed to get me laid," she remarked, looking around to see if anyone was listening to their whispering fight.

"I did not!"

"Yes, you did. I don't understand why you are so mad. We aren't exclusive. You made sure to inform me of that more than once. I thought you saw our relationship slash friendship slash whatever as casual?"

Christopher crumpled up his hamburger wrapper and threw it on the tray. "Yeah, but you don't tell someone you are sexually involved with that you fucked another man," he grumbled, getting up from the booth. "I think I've heard about enough. I'm going home now."

"Will I hear from you?" Kaisa asked.

"Probably not anytime soon. If you get lonely, call the other guy," he said as he stormed out.

Kaisa remained in her seat, partially stunned. *If we were in a normal relationship, of course, I would have been faithful. But this is anything but a normal relationship, so why does he care so much that I slept with someone else?*

A few days later, Christopher called. Their conversation started with safe, non-controversial topics, like the weather and sports, until it segued into a more interesting subject. "I've had some time to process what happened the other day at Burger King. Our friendship was never supposed to be more than an exchange of physical pleasure. But over time, I've become fond of you, and the thought of you giving yourself sexually to someone else was hard for me to visualize, much less accept."

Maybe her escapade had sparked some underlying feelings, which he never openly admitted before. "Would you mind if I came to see you?" she asked.

"Sure. Come by in an hour."

Knowing this could be the last time she would see him for months, she pulled out a small Instamatic camera from her drawer and shoved it in her bag.

When she arrived, his apartment was torn apart. The décor was stripped to a fraction of its original minimalist state. Most of the books on the shelves were gone, in addition to his new couch.

"Are you moving out?" she asked. "Half your stuff is missing."

"I may be subletting my place, so I put some items in storage and have been cleaning out the rest."

Sticking out of an open drawer were two black and white photos that looked like professional modeling shots of a stunning blonde woman. "Who is that?" she inquired.

"She and I used to date a little before I met you. We

went together for about a year or so. I was trying to get over her during the time we started seeing each other. The first time we broke up, she took it really hard and wrote this twisted love letter. It was literally twisted because she wrote it backwards. I had to hold it up to a mirror to read it."

"What do you mean the first time you broke up?" Kaisa probed.

"We saw each other on and off in the past. Something about her kept drawing me back. She is hard to forget," he said, picking up the photos in his hand.

Kaisa knew that feeling all too well. "Is she still around?"

"I spot her from time to time walking around Boston when she's not working. It's awkward. She models, so she travels a lot. Last I heard, she was moving to Europe."

"Why do you still keep her picture?"

"Don't you save things?"

"You never struck me as someone who believed in sentimental value," she said, thinking there might be a heart in there after all. Maybe she was at the other end of those mystery phone calls. And maybe that explained the paranoia he sometimes has. Could that be why he never wanted to go out in public? "Why did you guys break up?"

"For one, she got pregnant. We agreed an abortion was the best thing to do given our situations. But I'm not sure if that's what she wanted. After that, things weren't the same between us." He paused and looked down at the pictures.

"Is that why you refuse to have intercourse with me?" "I mean, I really like you, but intercourse has always made things a lot messier. I haven't had the best luck with relationships, so I prefer to keep my distance."

Christopher pivoted to another subject. "It's a nice day out. Why don't we take a walk together since we might not see each other for a while?"

Kaisa smiled. She liked that he saw her in his "future," however long that would be. He was keeping a door open; it wasn't goodbye. Before they left, he pulled five books off the shelf - beautiful, classic, hardcover art books that could create an enviable display on any coffee table.

Just as they were about to walk out the door, the phone rang. "Do you want me to get it?" she offered, seeing that his hands were full.

"I got it," he said, lunging for the phone. "It's my brother. I have to take this."

Kaisa yelled out, "Hi!"

Christopher turned around with a scowl and waved his hand. He dragged the phone into the bathroom, saying something that sounded like, 'Oh, that's nobody.' But maybe she heard him wrong.

They left the apartment and headed toward Newbury Street. As they passed the alphabetical cross streets, she could see the Booksellers Café come into view. Christopher turned and entered a used bookstore a few doors down on the opposite side of the street. He handed the art books to the man behind the cash register. "How much can I get for these?"

The man seemed to recognize Christopher, greeting him with an acknowledging smirk. He looked through the books, examined their condition, and offered him $25.

"Really?" he said. "That's it? Just one of these cost me 50 bucks!"

The book purveyor wouldn't budge.

"Thanks," he said rudely, leaving the books and grabbing the cash.

"Can we go to the Booksellers Café for coffee?" Kaisa asked.

"No, sweetheart, we can't. This is supposed to last me for the next three days."

As they walked toward Massachusetts Avenue, she lagged slightly behind. This was her opportunity to snap a picture for her own sentimental value and take a small piece of him home. Kaisa readied the camera for a candid shot. "Say cheese," she said, aiming it at his gorgeous face. He spun around, but his expression darkened. The palm of his hand grew larger as it lunged toward the lens.

"Give me that," he ordered like she was committing some heinous violation of privacy.

"Why? I just want to take a picture of you so I could look at it when I'm at home."

He clenched his jaw, demanding she hand over the camera. "I don't like being in photos."

"How come?"

"I'm a very private person, you know. I had a bad experience, and it makes me uncomfortable. You don't want me to feel any worse, do you?"

"What happened?"

"I don't want to get into it, but it had to do with a court case I was involved in years ago."

"What was that about?" she asked.

"Just give me the damn camera," he ordered before grabbing onto it.

"No, I don't trust you not to break it," she said, holding it in a firm grip.

"Then, pull out the film and give it to me!"

"Really?" Kaisa said. Had this been the end of the roll, she would have probably put up a bigger fight. She opened the back of the camera and held it as he yanked the film out to the end, exposing it to bright sunlight, then threw it into a nearby garbage can. Kaisa shook her head in disbelief. *What's up with that?* She continued walking alongside Christopher in silence.

"I'm sorry," he said, "I'm sensitive to having my picture taken."

"Obviously!" she grumbled.

"Do you want me to walk you back to your dorm?"

"No, thanks, I'm going to stop into Tower Records first. I'll take it from here."

"Okay, call me before you leave," he said before wandering off in the opposite direction.

She watched his body shrink as he strolled further and further away, left only with a picture of him in her head.

During the last two weeks of school, she had other priorities to worry about. There were finals for one, and her desperate search to land some kind of work before the trimester ended. She was in a panic. There were only three days left until she had to declare a co-op job. The whole reason she went to Northeastern was so she could graduate with two years of work experience that would look impressive on her resume. But none of the jobs from the Northeastern Co-op Office had panned out. It was in her hands now.

With finals starting later the following week, she took a quick trip home. She ran around like a maniac, calling on temp agency after temp agency, trying to find something for six months.

Kaisa was lounging in front of the TV after one of those long days.

"Did you find a job?" her grandmother asked.

"Yeah, but not the one I really wanted. I got offered one today as a receptionist at a company nearby. I just called them back to accept."

"Hold on a second. The phone is ringing," her grandmother said, picking it up in the kitchen. "Someone from Northeastern is calling for you."

Kaisa slowly rose from the couch.

"It's Professor Ablom, from the Northeastern Co-op Office."

"Oh, hi Professor, I've been running around all day meeting with employment agencies."

"I'm glad I caught you then. Your roommate said you were home. I have good news for you."

"Oh?" she replied.

"You got the job at OMNI if you want it."

If I want it, could that be any more absurd? Kaisa mouthed 'YES' and waved her fist in the air. "Are you serious?" she said calmly, trying to contain her excitement. "But I just accepted a position no less than an hour ago. I thought by now that the agency went with someone else."

"Well, Kaisa, which one do you want more?"

Like this was even a question. "Please let the agency know I accept." She didn't care about the details, the train fare to New York, or even how much it paid. She wanted this so bad; she would figure it out and make it work.

"I will. Come by my office when you get back, and we'll work out the details."

"Thanks, Professor. You really made my day."

She calmly put the phone on the receiver, then shrieked for joy as she jumped up and down. Unbelievable. She got her "dream job" - a Budget Coordinator in Account Services. Well, maybe more like her dream opportunity, a chance to work in advertising at a top five global agency in Manhattan.

Upon finishing her last final, Kaisa returned to her barren dorm room to pack her remaining things and wrap up loose ends. Her parents drove her back the previous weekend and picked up most of her stuff, leaving her with only a few essentials for the remaining days. In her notebook was a letter she had written one late night while studying for her exams.

Dear Christopher –

I'm thinking about you again. It seems I do that more than is healthy for me. It's another midnight shift with the books, but I can't study. If you only knew how many "letters I've written never meaning to send" telling you how I feel. But I just couldn't for fear of scaring you off or losing you altogether. The year will soon be over, and we'll go our separate ways. I do want to keep in contact with you. Unfortunately, physically, that will not be possible. Life sucks sometimes, doesn't it? (Oh, I didn't mean that, literally). I hope you will want to write or, better yet, call me occasionally until we can see each other again. Overall, I've enjoyed our time together and hope you have too.

Kaisa

With no one around, she folded up the letter and opted for a phone call, which was less threatening. She shared the happy news about the job. He congratulated her and wished her luck.

"Well, I guess this is it for now. I wanted to give you my home address and phone number. I hope to hear from you sometime." "Thanks, sweetheart," he said. "Be careful of the men in New York. You don't want to get mixed up with a really strange guy."

Kaisa giggled under her breath at the irony of his words. "That wouldn't bother you?"

"You are free to see other people. I just don't want to know about it."

Kaisa assumed that it meant the same for him. Although his statement made her sad, maybe now wasn't their time. Fate had brought them together more than once. If it were meant to be, it would happen down the road. The question was, did she have the patience to wait until then. "I do hope to see you sometime soon," she said. "I'll miss you."

"Take care. Bye"

I love you. Kaisa hung up the phone and pulled the cord out of the jack.

She popped in a newly created mixtape to listen to while she finished packing. With every last item stowed away in her suitcase, Kaisa took a last long look at the suite lined with her roommates' boxes as she stood in the bedroom that was empty once again. Her eyes flooded with tears as Simon and Garfunkel harmonized through the somber but poignant lyrics of "The Boxer." She had learned so much - from living with new people, developing new friendships, to discovering her sexuality through this strange erotic pilgrimage. It seemed like a whole other lifetime packed into nine short months.

One thing was for certain. She was not the same innocent, morally bound girl who pulled up in the Chevy

Nova not that long ago. In fact, she was even more unsure of who she was now or how to handle her newfound knowledge and experience.

Kaisa locked the door and dropped off her key downstairs at the entrance. While sitting on the T with her last suitcase, headed for the train station, she pressed play on her Walkman then fast-forwarded to "Homeward Bound."

CHAPTER 15
You Give Yourself Away

T he last week in June, Kaisa began her aspiring career in advertising in a stylish, newly designed space on 6th Avenue in Manhattan. Not only was she working for a global agency, but she had an office that she shared with Lupe, her new supervisor. The opportunity she dreamed about was delivering in every respect. Even though she was only an intern, she was certain this was the first step on her way to making it "Big Time." With a New York Times in hand, she waited for the train among the other successful executives, every weekday morning, aiming for the door to stop where she was standing to improve her chances of finding a seat.

The weekends, however, didn't offer much

excitement. Kaisa's mother, who was always on the lookout for love for her only daughter, wouldn't stop singing the praises of their new next-door neighbor, Spencer, and had already given her the lowdown. He was attractive and close in age, having recently graduated from college. Even Kaisa's grandmother, who was still visiting from California, voiced her approval. Spencer had moved in three months earlier and was living next door while transforming their previous neighbor's home from the hole it was to something more inhabitable.

The Hadfields were the previous owners of that hovel and had been Kaisa's neighbors for as long as she could remember. They had a postage stamp-sized corner lot with a two-story white colonial and a one-car garage. Both filled with junk. She couldn't remember it ever looking nice. The house had chipped paint all over, and the siding was dripping with rust-colored stains. Their yard was essentially dirt with a few stubborn patches of grass that refused to die. Behind their garage was an empty, neglected above ground swimming pool that had since become a breeding ground for mosquitoes. About a year before they left, the Hadfield's bought a motor home and parked it in what Kaisa called their side yard and spent most of their time living in it instead of their house.

Kaisa and their son Billy knew each other before kindergarten. He was her first friend. They rode bikes and played on the street with the other kids until they became too old for that. Billy had a learning disability. After the second grade, he joined the other kids of varying special needs and was eventually warehoused with them for the rest of his school years. His mother was not all there. She would stare out the window until someone caught her eye, then she would duck behind a curtain. Billy's mother forbade him to invite anyone to their house. The only occasion when Kaisa was able to get inside was when his parents weren't home. The last time was just before they packed up their motor home and moved to Florida. It was dark, dank, with cracks in the walls, and filled with too much furniture and items they should have thrown away decades ago. The house sat empty for a long time until Spencer finally bought it.

While Kaisa was weeding in the garden one Saturday morning, she noticed Spencer mowing his lawn (or what little grass had grown back). Kaisa gave a slight wave to signal a hello, but he didn't return her greeting.

She attempted to get his attention a couple more times, but every time he would turn slightly in her direction, it was as if she were invisible. *Is he consciously avoiding me?* Finally, the noise of the mower ceased. It was time to make a move. "Hey there!" she called.

Spencer smiled and walked over to greet her. He was wearing a tattered lime green collared shirt with an authentic polo player on his chest. "Hi, "I'm Spencer."

"I'm Kaisa," she said, reaching out her hand.

"It's nice to meet you. Are you Mrs. B's daughter?"

Kaisa felt the blood rush to her face. Mother LOVED to talk and had a knack for oversharing. Knowing her, she probably tried to grease the skids. How much information had she already relayed? "When did you move in?" she asked, even though she already knew.

"I moved in May after my business partner, and I closed on the house."

"Business partner?" she prompted.

"Yes, my buddy Brent and I recently started a real estate investment business. This house is one of the three we are currently renovating. The other ones weren't remotely livable, and this one is close to home."

"Where is home?" Kaisa asked.

"Delafield Island."

Wow. One of the most exclusive and affluent areas of town. Why is he slumming it here? Seeing how the other 99.5% lives? "Must be a few steps down for you living here?" she joked.

"It's quite a change. My friends think it is hilarious. They also rag on me that I'm driving a pick-up truck."

"I grew up here," Kaisa said.

"Yeah, your mom told me you guys have been here for a long time. Are you back from school for the summer?" he asked.

"Yes and no. I'm here for six months. I go to Northeastern and am working in New York City. I don't go back until January."

That seemed to be the end of the conversation. Kaisa tried to come up with the next question to fill the awkward silence, but 'what are you up to?' didn't seem appropriate because that was painfully obvious. "So, I'll let you get back to what you were doing. It was nice meeting you," she said as she started to walk away.

What was her mother thinking? She wasn't of Spencer's ilk? She didn't have a prayer with someone like him. But then again, she didn't think Christopher would be interested in her either, and he most definitely had been. She just had to try a little harder. Kaisa spun around one last time. "Hey, Spencer, if you don't mind, I'd love to see how your renovations are going. The last time I was inside, it was pretty scary."

"I'd show you around, but I'm supposed to meet my parents at The Club now. But feel free to stop by any time."

Kaisa smiled and nodded. She appreciated the invitation but wasn't sure if he meant it since she kind of invited herself.

Kaisa stopped by one hot summer day wearing a thin, clingy tank top with no bra that clearly displayed the change in temperature when she entered his pleasantly chilled house.

"That's some, um, pretty bad sunburn?" he said, shifting his glance to her shoulders.

"Yeah, right? I should know better with my pale skin tone than to lay out in the sun during midday. I usually only go to the beach at night. Do you or your friends ever go there?"

"Yeah - but mainly to get our drugs."

"Hmm," Kaisa said, with a smirk, unimpressed by his response.

"I get burned too, working outside on these flips. My mom gave me some good stuff for that. I'll be right back." Spencer returned with an expensive-looking glass-etched jar of aloe vera cream. "This stuff feels great. Turn around, I'll put it on you." He lifted her hair and moved it to the side, while Kaisa held on to it at the base of her neck. Her red glowing skin welcomed the soothing chill of the cream as he gently massaged it into her shoulders. "Wow, the sunburn is all the way down your back," he said, lifting her shirt and spreading the cream with his fingers.

"That feels so good," she sighed, her senses tingling as he slid his fingers down her spine, veering off into areas that didn't have any sunburn.

"Yeah, that was fun. We should do this again, even when your sunburn gets better," Spencer suggested.

That led to further invitations of Spencer's own accord, but rarely when anyone else was around. Kaisa loved visiting Spencer. Mainly for his attention, but mostly for the air conditioning. That was one of the best upgrades to the Hadfield's house. Her one-floor 756 square foot home had none. It was built on a slab, so escaping to a cooler basement wasn't even an option.

They had nothing in common, except they were both in complicated, long-distance relationships. He had an on-again-off-again girlfriend, Regan, who was spending her summer in Italy. Spencer Vanderbrook was from old money. The price he paid for the house wasn't a real stretch for him or rather his family. This guy was bred from people with a long history of frequenting society pages - a blueblood through and through. When he wasn't around, he was spending weekends on Martha's Vineyard, attending a charity golf or polo tournament, or just hanging at his parent's country club. Whenever Kaisa mentioned she would be interested in attending one of these events, he would say there wasn't an extra ticket, or it was strictly for members only.

Kaisa felt his desire building, but Spencer said he didn't want to abandon his current relationship. He suggested they engage in a new ritual during her visits. While he referred to them as "sexual backrubs," these sensual massages were not limited to the back. It meant they massaged each other within an inch of each other's privates while partially clothed. Spencer said it was a way of engaging in something remotely sexual while remaining semi-faithful.

The intimate exchanges fueled her feelings for him, and she hoped that she could influence Spencer to move on from Regan. The fact that he was from a wealthy family and had a house with air-conditioning didn't hurt.

Another Saturday morning, Kaisa spotted Spencer in his yard. "My friend Gina is working tonight at Baskin-Robbins in New Canaan. Would you be able to take me there? My parents are out of town, so I don't have a car. There's ice cream in it for you."

"Sure. No problem. I'll come by and pick you up

around 7:30. I may be meeting some friends there tonight anyway," he said.

That evening after dinner, she changed her clothes, refreshed her makeup, and got ready to leave. By now, Spencer's dirt driveway and most of St. Charles Street was lined with a slew of BMW's, Mercedes, and an Audi or two. It looked like he was having another one of his exclusive parties with the trust fund babies from metaphorically and geographically the other side of the tracks.

Around eight, she got up the nerve to go to his house and gently remind him of his promise. A slightly inebriated, attractive, and tall man with dirty blonde wispy hair that was beginning to show its fate of male pattern baldness greeted Kaisa at the door. He had on plaid shorts and a light blue oxford shirt with another one of those embroidered designer horses. His shirt had one too many buttons undone, revealing the long hair on his chest, and he reeked of a strong musky fragrance. Kaisa was fairly sure it was privilege.

"Hi, is Spencer here?" Kaisa asked.

"Whom shall I say is calling?" he said in an overly exaggerated English accent while clenching his jaw.

"I'm Kaisa from next door."

"Hey there. I'm Brent," he said, coming out of his impression. "I didn't know Spencer had such a hot neighbor."

"Oh, thank you," she said, blushing. "You're his business partner, right?"

"That is true. How did you know that?"

"Spencer and I hang out from time to time."

"I'm sorry to say that he's never mentioned you."

Kaisa's smile deflated.

"But I'm sure it's because he just wants to keep you all to himself," he said as if he was trying to extract a foot from his mouth. "Hold on a sec. I'll get him."

After a couple of minutes, Spencer emerged through his latest flock of guests. "Hey, Kaisa, what's up?"

"Remember you said that you would give me a ride to New Canaan tonight."

"I'm sorry, I totally forgot. I'm not in the best state to drive right now, I'm afraid."

"Are any of your friends planning on going there? Maybe I could get a ride with one of them?"

"We were planning to hit some bars later, but I think the plan changed to Rowayton."

"Oh. Well then, can I come in and hang out with you and your friends for a bit?" she asked.

"I'm not sure how comfortable you would be around them," he said, gripping the door handle. "I'll talk to you tomorrow."

Sighing, she returned to her stifling hot house to call Gina and let her know she wouldn't be able to make it. Outside the picture window, the sky was a kaleidoscope of hazy fading pastels. Kaisa couldn't let this night entirely go to waste. She would go to her beach. That's where she went when she needed solace or to find some inner peace - and in summer, to get a break from the heat. She cleared the pellets of perspiration from her forehead, went out the back door to her father's toolshed, and pulled out her old 10-speed bike. Despite the weather, she knew she could make the two-mile trip. It was nearly all downhill — at least one way.

Kaisa climbed on her bike and headed toward the main road. A refreshing summer breeze wrapped around her body as she weaved through the side streets to avoid heavy traffic. She pushed hard on the pedals pressing out her frustration as she raced feverishly to get there.

Finally, she reached the last leg of her journey with the long stretch of trees that hung over the road like a canopy. On either side were grand mansions set far back from the road, some with spectacular water views. Kaisa coasted along until she arrived at the gated entrance at the far end.

"Where's your beach sticker?" the guard joked.

"It's in Atlantic City with my mom, dad, and grandmother. That's why I only have these wheels."

He smiled and let her through.

There were two distinct sides to the beach, separated by a formation of gray rocks. The right side had a small strip of beach plus paddle courts, picnic tables, and a smaller parking lot where troublemakers gathered in the evening. That's where people like Spencer scored their pot, cocaine, or other controlled substance. Kaisa avoided that area and the people that hung out there.

The left side was where families gathered during the day, laying out their towels, blankets, and umbrellas on a wider expanse of rocky New England sand. The daring swimmers braved the chilly water, the occasional jellyfish, and the sharp rocks that felt like shards of glass if you waded without caution. When the sun set and most of the beachgoers emptied out, the left side became deserted, and the action shifted to the other side. On occasion, Kaisa could time her arrival so that the left side was exclusively hers. Tonight, was one of those nights.

Kaisa parked her bike next to a birch tree, kicked off her sneakers, and dug her feet into the coarse warm sand. As she struggled to catch her breath, Kaisa looked out into the bay overlooking Long Island Sound that offered her answers many times before. She panned over to the berth where she and her dad fished, barely visible now because of high tide.

Taking a seat on the sand, she watched the sun melt into the horizon. Her mind wandered as she imagined romantic moments and scenarios that seemed unlikely to ever come to fruition. She opened a new pack of cigarettes from her small purse and lit one. She took a drag, blowing smoke into the cool ocean breeze at her back as the evening grew dim and nightfall blanketed the sky.

"Hey, what are you doing there by yourself?" someone yelled.

She turned to see three preppy guys in a BMW convertible parked on her side of the beach. "Just enjoying the evening," she said casually.

"We've got something better if you want to smoke?" one said, as he discreetly waved a small bag of whatever he must have just purchased from the other side. He got out of the car and walked toward her, leaving the door open.

Kaisa scanned the parking lot looking for her dad's car until it dawned on her that's not how she got there tonight. In her haste, she hadn't thought the round trip through. "No thanks, I'll take my own transportation," she said with authority, puffing herself up like prey when confronting a predator.

She threw her second cigarette in the sand, got on her bike, and rode past the gate into the pitch black, cavernous road. The car's engine roared as it edged closer to her back wheel. "We'll throw that bike in the back and give you a ride."

Realizing that continuing her journey into the black abyss of Edgewater Lane would be stupid, she turned her bike around and pedaled toward the security booth, then parked it next to the payphone. First, she tried Gina, but nobody was home. Maybe Spencer could help. He owed her a ride somewhere tonight. Hopefully, he could take his pick-up truck and drive her and her bike home if he and his friends hadn't left.

"Hello, Vanderbrook residence," some girl answered, followed by a drunken snort of laughter.

"Hi, is Spencer there?"

"Who's calling?" the girl asked.

"It's Kaisa."

"Who?" she asked quizzically. "Spencer, some girl is on the phone for you. I should tell Regan about this!"

When Spencer came to the phone, Kaisa explained the

odd situation. "I'm here at Longshore Beach. I took my bike, and I stayed here too long. Now it's dark, and I'm freaking out about riding home."

"It can't be that bad. I mean it is Westport."

"Well, for one, these three dudes keep following me with their car."

"Ask them for a ride," he mocked.

Kaisa placed her hand over her face in dismay. "Could you please come and pick me up. It should only take a few minutes. I'll be waiting at the front entrance. But please come soon because the beach closes at 10."

He half-heartedly agreed but said he would come.

Kaisa stood under the glow of the streetlight near the security booth, waiting.

"Who are you waiting for? We told you we'd give you a ride," the guy in the driver's seat yelled out.

Kaisa continued to ignore them.

"Come on, guys, leave her alone. Get out of here," said the security guard.

"Shut up, rent-a-cop. I'm sorry for interrupting your TV show and your $5.00 an hour job?"

"Fuck off, scumbag," he said. "Go bother someone at whatever goddamn country club your daddy belongs to."

The obnoxious bastards finally drove away, but it was nearing 10 o'clock. It had been 20 minutes since she had called, yet there was no sign of Spencer. At that moment, she recognized his pick-up truck.

"Hey, Kaisa? Spencer said you needed a ride."

Brent put the truck into park and let Kaisa into the passenger door.

"Where is Spencer?" she asked.

"He said he felt too hammered to drive." Not that Brent looked like he was in much better shape. "I needed to make a beer run and such."

"I'm glad you're here," she said.

"I just need to make another pick up before we go." Brent loaded the bike into the back and drove to the other side of the beach. "I'll be right back," he said.

Kaisa waited for Brent to return taking in the light of a full moon, dancing on the rippling waves. A small crisp stamped envelope on the dashboard caught her attention. She picked it up and held it under the glow of the streetlight. It looked like a reply to an invitation addressed to someone, *Rockefeller? Wow!*

"All set, let's go," Brent said as he jumped into the truck.

In a panic, she threw the invitation on the floor.

"What made you ride your bike to the beach so late?" Brent asked as they passed the half-closed gate.

"Well, it wasn't dark when I left. I come here all the time, but my parents weren't home tonight, so I didn't have my dad's car."

"Your parents aren't home tonight?" he inquired.

"No," she said, strictly relaying information.

They rounded the corner onto St. Charles Street past Spencer's house. Kaisa could hear the music and people through the closed windows as Brent parked the truck in her driveway.

"I'll get your bike out of the back," he said, stepping out of the truck.

Once she was alone, Kaisa reached for the envelope and shoved it in her purse. Before exiting the passenger side, she left the window open a crack to slip the card back in after she read it. Kaisa thanked Brent and sprinted into her house, throwing the bike in her backyard. She was overheated, and sadly, her cooling-challenged home wasn't offering any respite from the mugginess. Even opening the windows around the house didn't yield any movement of air, only the residual noise from Spencer's party.

She pulled the envelope from her purse. It WAS an RSVP, but it was only partially sealed. Perhaps the humidity had pried it open. It was going to be easier than she thought to access. Before she could open it, there was a knock at the door. "Hello?" she called.

"Hey, can I come in?" Brent asked.

"I was just about to get in the shower and go to bed. It's been a long week," she said.

"I won't keep you long, I promise?"

She shoved the invitation into the cushion of her dad's well-worn brown vinyl recliner with tears in the armrests. Kaisa already had enough this evening, but she didn't want to be rude since he was kind enough to pick her up.

Despite feeling embarrassed by it, she invited him into the small, brown-paneled living room.

"God, it's hot in here," he commented.

"Yeah, don't remind me." Kaisa sighed.

Brent wobbled to the old tweed couch with threading in varying shades of mustard, brown, and green, centered on the arc of matted down carpet created by back-and-forth foot traffic from either side of the small house. "Why don't you come sit here and join me," he said, holding out his hand.

Kaisa chose her dad's recliner with the tears in the armrest.

"So, Spencer tells me, you are good at giving backrubs."

"Yeah, that's between Spencer and me," she said, locking her jaw to keep it from dropping.

"You know he has a girlfriend. He's just killing time until she gets back. Listen, I think you are way cute. I recently broke it off with someone and am looking for something casual. Spencer thought you might be interested."

Kaisa's face flushed from the simmering blood in her veins. *What am I some sexual hand-me-down?*

"Come on, why don't you see if you like me. Which way is your bedroom? My guess is that way?" he said, pointing to the tight hallway. "This house is so small it can't be too hard to find." Brent rose from the couch and lunged at Kaisa, grabbing either side of her arms. He yanked her toward him and pressed his lips firmly against hers as Kaisa tried to squirm away.

Kaisa took her knee and jammed it swiftly into Brent's genitals, releasing his grip.

"Hey Kaisa. Is Brent there?" As much as she was annoyed with Spencer right now, she was happy to hear his knock. "I just wanted to make sure you guys got home safely," Spencer said on the other side of the door.

"Thanks for checking in on me. Brent was just leaving," Kaisa said, giving Brent a piercing look.

"Yes, she did. We were getting to know each other a little." Brent squeaked, regaining his stance.

"I need to talk to Kaisa for a second," Spencer said. "I'll catch up with you back at the house."

Kaisa joined Spencer on the front step as Brent made his exit.

"First, I'm sorry I couldn't drive you earlier. I've been thinking, Regan is coming back soon, and that means we need to stop what's going on between us. I don't want to ruin it with her. Our parents are also good friends, and it could get awkward."

"Really? So now that anything we had is over, you think it's acceptable to pawn me off to Brent?"

"Brent told me he liked you. Just to be clear, we didn't have anything. We were just enjoying each other's company."

Where had she heard that before?

Spencer gave her a quick hug while Kaisa stood like a soldier with her arms at her sides. "See you around," he said as he walked away.

"Uh-huh," she uttered, assuming more than likely it was sign-off like Mike's 'I'll call you,' which he never did.

Kaisa returned to the recliner, dug her hand in between the cushions, and pulled out the RSVP. At this point, she was fairly sure what was on the inside:

Spencer Vanderbrook – Accepts, September the 26th

Guest's name: Regan Wilson

Entrée Choice: Chicken

You got that right. Wouldn't it be fun to cross out her name and put hers instead? That could cause quite a stir. But what would be the point? She tore the RSVP into pieces, throwing it and the idea in the trash.

Kaisa jumped into a tepid shower to cool down from the heat of the night and her emotions. Draped in a light cotton nightdress and her underwear, she positioned her small fan toward her face and climbed into bed just as the pungent smell of skunk bloomed through her open window. "Motherfucker," she groaned.

She darted to each room, pushing down on the open panes, but failed to stop the odor from permeating inside. The mushroom cloud of sharp, nose-hair curling stench consumed her tiny, sweltering home and clung to the heavy, humid air. As Kaisa flung herself back into bed, she couldn't help but think, w*hat a perfect ending and metaphor for tonight.*

CHAPTER 16
Because the Night

N ow that Spencer was out of the picture, Kaisa couldn't help but wonder how Christopher was doing and if he was still in Boston. Craving a little fun and adventure, she arranged a weekend trip. Luckily, Mindy was taking a summer class and offered Kaisa a place to stay.

After an abbreviated summer Friday at work, she took the Amtrak train from New York's Penn Station. Mindy had forewarned her that Boston was a different city in the summer. Different, in a not-so-nice way, and advised her to stay alert.

When Kaisa arrived at the T-stop closest to Mindy's campus apartment, she realized she wasn't kidding. It was not the same booming college town overrun with emerging adults. Another population had emerged, or one that wasn't as visible during the school year. Now, streetwise locals outnumbered impressionable students, and the fact that Northeastern bordered a rough area of town became more apparent.

As she walked down Huntington Avenue, she caught sight of a gang of loud, streetwise Hispanic girls approaching ahead. Even with a little daylight left, she felt uneasy. Kaisa casually looked around for an escape route, holding her head up high. Sadly, there was no way to cross over to the other side with the subway's underground tunnel entrance bisecting the street at that particular spot. The girls eyed her as they got closer, alternating their conversation between English and Spanish. Kaisa walked up the steps of the YMCA to get out of their path. Suddenly, one girl ran up and grabbed onto Kaisa's purse while the other girls surrounded her. They teased and bounced her around from one girl to another as she stood helpless, unsure of what to do next.

"Hey, leave her alone," yelled a police officer storming out of the YMCA building. The girls backed off immediately as if nothing happened but continued to mock Kaisa as they scurried away. Kaisa blew out a sigh of relief and thanked the cop. *That was close.*

Kaisa ran the rest of the way to Mindy's apartment and hugged her at the door. "You weren't kidding about how Boston is not the same as during the school year."

"Why do you say that?" she asked.

"I almost got mugged by a gang of girls. I was really scared there for a minute."

"Oh my God, are you okay?"

"Yes, luckily a cop came out of nowhere. When they saw him, they bolted."

"Does this mean you just want to stay in tonight?" Mindy asked.

"That depends. I have to make two calls first."

"Without missing a beat, Mindy said, "Let me guess: your mom and Christopher?"

Kaisa called her mom first to assure her that she arrived safely. She omitted what happened, knowing it would have worried her mother even more. Once she hung up, she proceeded to call Christopher, hoping to reach him. As far as this visit was concerned, he had no idea she was coming to town. She had a sinking feeling that if she told him ahead of time, he would make up an excuse or say he was busy.

"Hello?" he answered.

Yay, he's home! "Hey, it's Kaisa. I haven't heard from you in a while, so I thought I would call to say hi."

"You sound close," he probed.

Was he excited or anxious? She wasn't sure. "No, it must be a great connection," Kaisa said, keeping her cover.

"What's new with you?" he asked.

"Not much, just working a lot. I got a second job on the weekends at The Limited. I start next week. What are you doing now?"

"Reading the newspaper. Have you been keeping up with the Iran Contra crisis?"

Like I care. "As you know, I'm not into politics. It's a dry subject," she said, listening for the sound of Christopher rolling his eyes.

"Oh really, what's wet then?" he asked.

"Besides you," they said in unison.

They bantered some more about her job and his excuses for a lack of one. Their verbal sparring picked up where it left off. His tone wasn't what she expected for someone who hadn't seen or heard from a close friend in some time. She wasn't sure if his acerbic banter was annoying her or getting her sexually riled up, probably both.

"What are you doing tonight?" she asked.

"Nothing much, just staying home and writing. I'm supposed to go to the beach tomorrow with some friends."

"Me too, just writing, but in my journal."

"You keep a journal?"

"I've kept one since we met. The entries have been pretty boring lately."

"I'm sorry to hear that. It was nice talking to you. I should be getting back to my assignment. Take care," he said before hanging up.

"Does he know you are here? It didn't sound that way." Mindy asked.

"I don't know, maybe."

"Why didn't you say you were in town?"

"If I told him in advance that I was coming, I would get my hopes up, and then he would probably cancel on me last minute. I didn't want to jinx it. I know he doesn't like surprises, but this way, if I show up unannounced, he has to deal with me. At the very least, I get to see him in the flesh. Plus, I can get a better take on what he's really doing. But he was such a dick on the phone, I want to go over and punch him in the face."

"You should have done that a long time ago. Sit down for a few minutes, calm down, and try not to act so immature."

But Kaisa knew she had to get over there before Christopher ditched his place, perhaps suspecting she was in town. She went outside to hail a cab. No more walking alone tonight.

During her ride to Christopher's apartment, she questioned whether surprising him was smart but figured it was about time she caught him off guard. She couldn't let the opportunity of being back in the same city pass her by.

Outside his building, she scanned the notification system for apartment #5. There were new tenant names that she hadn't seen before. In fact, the whole paging system looked new. For a moment, she got a little scared that she wouldn't find "Morton." Maybe he had moved and took his phone number with him. After frantically skimming the list again, she happened upon his name and pressed the button long and hard.

"Who is it?" asked a vaguely familiar voice over crinkling static.

"Come down and see," she replied.

Kaisa stepped aside to let a man go by on his way out. He smiled and held the door open for her. She thanked him and quickly sprung inside. Checking herself in the hall mirror, she tried patting down the straw-like frizzy strands of her hair amplified by the steamy summer weather. As much as she wanted to go straight upstairs, she decided not to invade his privacy altogether and wait until he appeared. God knows who else she might meet.

Within a minute, there he was, slightly tanned and strikingly handsome in a torn pinkish plaid shirt and khaki shorts. "I thought you sounded like you were nearby," he said with an unwelcoming smirk.

"I know you don't like surprises, but I thought you wouldn't mind a pleasant one."

"Why didn't you tell me you were coming to town?" he said as if she did something wrong.

Kaisa pouted. He had not seen or talked to her in over two months, and he looked annoyed at best. "So, are you going to invite me up?"

"I can't," he said.

"I won't stay long if you're busy," she said, as she pushed him aside, attempting to shoot upstairs.

Christopher bared his teeth and grabbed her arm as she cleared the first step. "Where are you going?"

"I just want to see your apartment."

"Don't be a brat. I can't invite you up now. I have a friend coming over in 15 minutes."

Kaisa wasn't buying his excuse. Either he already had a friend there, or there was something else to hide. She neglected to remind him that he told her no more than a half an hour ago that he was staying in to write tonight. Of course, that was when he thought she might be in Connecticut. "Fine. I'll stay until your friend arrives, and then I'll leave."

"That might be a bit awkward."

There was little doubt in her mind that another woman was coming to visit. "Well, you told me that you were staying in and studying tonight, but apparently not." Figuring any chance of a rendezvous was over, she turned around to leave. As she yanked the front door open, his disposition seemed to change.

"I wish you would have told me you were coming to Boston. I haven't seen you in a long time, and I would have made plans with you. How long are you staying?"

"Only 'til Sunday morning," she said.

"That's it? All right then, why don't I go put my shoes on."

And tell my friend I'll be right back, she surmised.

"...and I'll walk around town with you a little while. You wait here."

If she was going to spend any time with him, she had no choice but to take his offer. At least she was lucky enough to find him home, thinking the last time they saw each other, he said he would be moving back to Nashville.

In a few moments, he came back downstairs. He was hers for now.

As they headed down Marlborough Street, Christopher started lecturing Kaisa again. "You know, I had other plans tonight. I hope you appreciate that I altered them for you."

"That's not what you said on the phone. But I'm honored," she sneered. "I had this crazy idea that you might want to see me since I'm not as readily available now."

"You can't expect people to drop everything and go along with whatever you want when you want it," he argued.

Hah! Seriously? "Why? You do. You do what you want because it pleases you. Sure, I go after what I want, but that doesn't necessarily mean I always get it."

"YOU DON'T?" he mocked.

Seeing Christopher again was supposed to be fun, but two blocks later, he was still lecturing on proper social etiquette. Kaisa stewed in silence, ignoring his rant and focusing on the street noise. "So, work is going fine," she burst out, trying to change the subject.

"What are you doing now, answering questions that weren't asked of you?" he said in a condescending tone. Kaisa's stew increased to a rapid boil. He seemed to be enjoying riling her up. If that was his objective, he was nailing it.

At Boylston Street, near the Boston Public Library, a short, fat, punk girl around her age with a platinum blonde mohawk headed in their direction. As they walked past the girl, Christopher tapped her on the shoulder, pivoted around, and waved hello. She turned her head and acknowledged him with a surprised grin.

"Who is she?" Kaisa asked, unable to quell her jealousy.

"She's a little squirt, who hangs out in squirt corner," he said, showing her the protruding stone around the library's perimeter. "Don't worry about her. I'm spending quality time with you," Christopher interjected.

"Yes, I know. I'm having a blast," she snarled, exasperated by his behavior.

"So, how is your job?" he asked.

"Oh, am I allowed to answer now?" She took a breath and switched to a more pleasant tone. "It's great. I love working in the city. You should visit me sometime in New York."

"Yeah, maybe," he said, giving a non-committal shrug.

They had been walking for quite some time, a half a mile or more. The August air was hot and heavy, and after her long train trip and the incident with the scary gang of girls, Kaisa wanted to sit next to or, better yet, dive into the refilled reflecting pool in the middle of the Christian Science Center. "Where are we going? I'm tired. Can I take a break for a minute?"

"I like this; we're going for a nice stroll. You'll be fine. It's not much further," he said, refusing to stop. Christopher would not divulge their final destination. It seemed he had a surprise of his own in mind. They passed the Sheraton Hotel and turned onto Westland Avenue, heading in the direction of where she was staying. At minimum, it would be a short trek back to Mindy's. "I like this street. It reminds me of New York," he said before taking her hand. From there, not much more was said.

He led her into the nearby pharmacy attached to the Hotel Hemenway, less than a block from her old dorm. "There is a way to get into the hotel from the pharmacy," he said, "I used to live here."

Kaisa followed close behind. The door was locked, but their timing was perfect as an artsy looking girl, with spiky hair and an attitude to match, pushed her way out of this secret passageway. Christopher held the open door for Kaisa, then headed towards an elevator in the dark hallway. The elevator took ages to come. Thinking it might be broken, Kaisa asked another tenant who passed by if it was in working order. He assured her it was working; it was just slow.

"You know, one time I went to a party here and got lost in the basement," Kaisa said.

Christopher did not respond. He was somewhere else. When the elevator door finally opened, the same girl who let them in returned with her items. She pressed 5, and Christopher pushed 8 – top floor.

"Are you visiting someone?" the girl asked.

"Yes," Christopher lied.

"Well, then I probably shouldn't have let you in. It's against policy to let in other people's guests."

As she stepped off the elevator, Christopher made a

face and gave her the finger behind her back. "I hate uptight bitches like that," he said after the doors closed.

Kaisa was taken aback by his lack of maturity, mainly because he was always calling her on it. The elevator rumbled and creaked as it continued its slow ascent to the eighth floor.

"By the way, how long did you live here?" she asked, desperate for any new piece of personal information.

"Four years ago, for about two years."

"Too bad you don't live here now. It would have been a lot more convenient."

They got off the elevator onto another dingy and dimly lit hall. The overhead lights were in bad shape. Burned out blackness consumed most of the once fluorescent white rod. He pointed to his old place then continued down the hall toward a decrepit flight of metal stairs. "I want to see something," Christopher said. He climbed the short flight, cracked opened a heavy metal door, and motioned to Kaisa.

"Where are we going?" she panted, suffocating from the heat in the musty hall.

"You'll see," he grinned. "I'll give you something for that journal."

As they exited, a refreshing summer breeze welcomed Kaisa to a deserted rooftop nine stories up. The sky was ablaze with orange and magenta shades igniting the

Boston skyline, creating pink marshmallow clouds from its fiery reflection.

She smiled for the first time that evening as she took in the spectacular sunset with Christopher. "Are we going to get in trouble being up here," she asked.

"You worry too much. Isn't this great? When I lived here, a couple of friends and I used to come up to the roof all the time. It was an awesome place to catch some rays and entertain guests."

"I'm sure you were an avid participant in that," she said.

Christopher gave her a sly grin. "And there's your beloved university," he taunted, outstretching his arm in the direction of Northeastern.

"Oh, shut up. Will you leave my university alone!"

She remained close to his side as he silently visited each edge of the roof, taking in the different views of the city as the gravel crunched beneath their feet. Each time he stopped, Kaisa anxiously waited for him to scoop her up in his arms and take advantage of the romantic vista, but he did no such thing. *Does he want me to beg? Why did he take me up here if he keeps ignoring me - just to see the view?* Sure, it was breathtaking, but it seemed like a big waste to be on this roof so close to heaven on a sultry summer night with the most incredible man doing nothing.

The red and orange glare was fading into dusk as the windows of the surrounding buildings gradually filled with artificial light.

He pressed his back on a chimney in the middle of the roof, then grabbed her hand and yanked her forward until she collided with his chest. "You didn't think I would let you get away this easy, sweetheart," he whispered, giving her a seductive glance.

Calling her sweetheart was music to her ears. Kaisa smiled in sweet surprise as a hot trail blazed under her skin. Maybe he was waiting for this moment when their actions would be better cloaked by the coming night. He nibbled hungrily at her neck with little Dracula bites while one hand disappeared beneath her flimsy summer dress. Two fingers plunged inside. She could feel them circling vigorously and aggressively between her legs as Christopher thrust them at unsuspecting intervals. Kaisa closed her eyes and let out a satisfied gasp at every erotic jolt teetering between pleasure and pain.

"Oh, sweetheart, I love playing with your pussy."

"And I love when you play with it," she exclaimed as he cracked up in amusement.

"Am I hurting you?" he asked.

"A little," she whimpered, writhing and panting on her tiptoes.

"I like to hurt you a little. It hurts, but it feels really good, right?"

"Yes," she moaned and nodded her head.

"Does this make you weak in the knees?"

"Everything you do makes me feel that way," she uttered, revealing more than she wanted, but it was not like that was something he didn't already know.

The Hotel Hemenway was by no means a skyscraper with the world below. Here she was, back on display.

Kaisa could see more windows in the surrounding buildings and high rises lighting up, along with the people inside. Standing with her back against his chest, akin to the cover of a romance novel, she closed her eyes to shut out her potential audience and turned her face to meet his. His lips touched hers. She kissed him with an open mouth just as he had taught her.

"I want you to suck my cock," he whispered.

Kaisa obliged, kneeling on the large, sharp, and dirty pieces of gravel that scraped at her knees. Changing her position to a squat, she clutched it with one hand and massaged his jewels with the other. She placed his penis in her mouth and savored it as she glided her lips up and down, persisting until he appeared to be in a frenzy.

The growing shallow light made her feel a little less self-conscious as Christopher coached her along. "Yes, deep throat, you are the greatest cocksucker that ever lived," he praised, grabbing the hair on either side of her head, and pulling her face closer to his pelvis.

Kaisa gagged and pushed him away. "I can't anymore. I feel like I'm going to throw up. I'm out of practice."

"Well, you can throw up over the side of the roof; I need you to finish."

"I think you've had enough for now," she said as she rose to a standing position.

"Is that so? You're such a tease."

"I believe it's my turn," she commanded.

"How is that going to work up here?" he asked.

"You go to Harvard. I'm sure you can figure it out."

He looked around, then pointed to two metal bars. "Here," he said, "put your leg up there." He lifted her short summer dress, then knelt, and put his head between her thighs. He pulled her panties to the side and began pleasuring her with his tongue.

Kaisa relished the sensation in the cooling night air as he tickled the exact spot that always sent her into overdrive. She stroked his thinning baby fine hair in gratitude while she wriggled in delight. Christopher pleasuring her atop a building in her favorite place in the world against a fading sunset backdrop was heavenly on so many levels. And not even close to what she could have ever imagined.

Christopher stood up and escorted her to one side of the roof. He held her at the waist and leaned her over the side of the building. Already close to the metaphorical edge of orgasm thanks to his talents, now all she could see was a dark alley nine stories down.

"What are you doing?" Kaisa asked, holding on for dear life.

"You didn't let me finish before, and you asked for this." Christopher laid his chest on her back and whispered in her ear. "This will give you something to think about when I'm not around." He pulled down her panties and entered her, traditionally.

Kaisa let out an audible sigh as she took in his manhood. It wasn't exactly how or even where she imagined intercourse with him might be, but it was finally happening.

"Oh sweetheart," he moaned, "you are so tight and feel so good. If I knew you would feel like this, I wouldn't have waited so long," he panted.

She gripped the rough stone, feeling an odd combination of passion and fear as he thrust his hips back and forth, hammering her backside. Then he quickly pulled out, sucked in his breath, and finished with his signature hiss. "I think we better be going now," he said. "You've probably had enough of me tonight?"

"I should say so," Kaisa answered, overloaded with emotion, still processing this celestial experience.

Kaisa held on to her daze as they left the roof for the elevator. Under the light, she noticed both their hair was a mess. She took a small brush out of her purse then reached over to fix his.

"Stop, that hurts," he griped, lightly slapping her hand. "Besides, your hair is thick," he said, grabbing a fistful at the back of her head, "and mine's falling."

Back at the pharmacy, Christopher slowly perused the merchandise while observing the skeletal staff. He eased toward the refrigerated section in the back of the store. "Do you want an ice cream sandwich?" he quietly mumbled.

She did, but not in this way, after sensing he was not planning to pay for it. "I'll have a bite of yours."

Nearby, a stock boy was shelving inventory. Kaisa calmly let Christopher know that he looked like he was watching him. But that didn't deter him at all.

"Come on, let's go," he said, taking her hand and rushing out the door in the direction of her old dorm.

Now it was her turn to lecture. "That wasn't smart," she said. "I stole a couple of things from stores during high school, but I don't steal now because I'm not a minor. Having a record could mess up your chances of getting a job. It doesn't make sense to ruin a fantastic opportunity over a Good Humor bar. You know what it says on all job applications, right?"

"Yes, have you ever been convicted of a crime?" he said in a snarky nasal voice.

Did I touch a nerve? "Yes," she replied, "and I can still check no."

By this time, Christopher had unwrapped the evidence and was eating it. "You sure you don't want a bite?" He held it to her mouth as she took a small sexy nibble. "Now you're an accessory to the crime," he joked. "I better let you go now. Do not broadcast what just happened, okay? I know how you like to kiss and tell. And next time you plan to come up, please tell me ahead of time."

How would next time ever top this? "I'd love it if you would come to New York to see me."

Christopher paused for a moment. "I do have a couple of friends who might let me stay with them. We'd have a much easier time finding a tall building," he flirted.

"That would be great." She pulled out a business card from her wallet with her number and extension scribbled on the back." Here is my contact info at work if you ever want to meet up or surprise me. I don't mind surprises, as long as they are good ones."

"Isn't this your old dorm?" he asked, pointing to the building in front of them.

Kaisa shook her head, disappointed that they were still several doors away. Not only had he been there before, but he requested the address numerous times when he called for cabs. He gave her one last kiss as they parted.

Back under his spell, she watched him walk away, already thinking about their next encounter.

"How did it go?" Mindy asked when Kaisa returned.

Kaisa could hardly hold in her giddiness. "Oh fine," she replied, trying to avoid going into detail.

"Why are your knees all dirty?"

Kaisa looked down at her black soot-covered kneecaps. "I was, um, ah -- praying," It was the best and lamest excuse she could think of at that moment.

"I'll bet," she said. "Did you want some ice cream?"

"No, thanks."

She had already had her fill.

A couple of weeks later, Kaisa could not get Christopher out of her mind. Still riding high from their encounter, she wanted to talk to him but worried she might look too desperate if she called. Christopher was right. She could not turn off her emotions when it came to sex. She kept replaying their rooftop escapade over and over in her head, feeling a fiery tingle through her body each time.

She just wanted to hear his voice. But long-distance phone calls cost a lot of money. Her mother waited for the rates to go down every Saturday night so she could call her mother in California. It was weekday peak time now.

However, the advertising agency was enormous. They probably wouldn't notice. Her extension wasn't an option, as it was only set up for local calls or at least no further than northern New Jersey. Kaisa got up and wandered the floor until she found an empty office. She dialed his number by heart.

"The number you have reached has been temporarily disconnected," said a recording, finally picking up the line.

I must have dialed it wrong. She slowly pressed the numbers once again but got the same annoying recording. *What happened? Where did he go?* Kaisa felt helpless. It wasn't like she could run to his apartment to find out if he was there anymore. She was 200 miles away. The recording did say "temporarily," so maybe it was out of service for some reason. But there was no forwarding number, and she didn't know how else to reach him.

Any future meetings were now in his control. The only way she could talk to him was if he decided to reach out to her. *Will I ever hear from him again?* She could only wait and see.

CHAPTER 17
I Wonder if You Think About Me

S itting amidst a large stack of invoices on her desk, Kaisa wanted to crawl underneath. It had been a bad week. She had a big fight with her mother, her boss Lupe said she lacked confidence in her approach with the Account Executives. And last night, the automated recording she got each time she dialed Christopher's phone number changed from temporarily to permanently disconnected with no further information. *Why didn't they just say that from the beginning instead of torturing me for a month?*

Despite that, she needed to focus on getting those invoices processed, but her phone would not stop ringing. Most of the calls were from the Account Executives regarding the status of their budgets or requests for last-minute accruals. OMNI's phone system had two distinct ringtones. Calls within the building were identified by one long ring after another, while external calls had two short rings before they repeated. Ever since his phone was disconnected, every time Kaisa got an external ringtone, she wished it would be Christopher. Of course, it never was. She had little doubt he had misplaced or even threw away the card she gave him with her work number by now.

RING, RING—RING, RING. "Kaisa speaking." Click. *Wrong number, no doubt.*

She went back to updating her budget report when another outside call came through.

"Kaisa speaking. Oh, hey Bob, what's going on?" It was only Bob from Accounting calling from the old office building. "I'll process those invoices ASAP and send them over via Interoffice Mail," she assured him. "I know you need them for month close."

No more than two seconds after hanging up, the phone rang again — two short consecutive rings.

"Bob?"

"Kaisa?" said a breathy soft-spoken voice.

"Yeah?" she replied in anticipation as that quivering nervous energy reemerged in her gut.

"I apologize for calling you at work. I lost the note that had your home phone."

Kaisa couldn't have been more thankful that she gave him her work number, just in case. "Oh my God, how have you been?" she asked.

"Things are not so great. I'm no longer at 293 Marlborough Street."

She didn't want to admit she figured as much since his phone was disconnected. "So, where are you living now?"

"In a monastery."

"Really? Where? Why?"

"Yes; In Cambridge; Because it's free," he replied, claiming it was part of a Harvard Divinity School requirement and that he was also staying true to a life of solitude and chastity.

"You? I don't buy it."

"Believe it. It's making me horny as hell for you."

"I thought you were done with school and were going to take some time off?"

"I'm still working on some incompletes."

"Do you work on your assignments in between prayer?" she gibed.

"You're a riot," Christopher said.

"You could say I'm mon-hysterical. Anyway, I'm so happy you called. I am planning a trip to Boston at the end of October for the Head of the Charles."

"Can you come up any sooner?" he asked, sounding anxious.

"I can't. I don't have any time off with my weekend job at the mall, nor do I have any extra money saved up," she groaned.

"Well, you have more than me. I'm calling you from a

payphone. I want you to know that I'm spending my last three dollars on you, so I hope you appreciate it."

Just as he finished his statement, a recorded operator's voice interrupted their call. "Please insert 50 cents for the next five minutes," she ordered.

"Can you ring me back?" he asked.

"Sure. Give me the number. Uh-huh. Okay. Got it."

"Hurry, because it looks like some people are waiting to use the phone."

Kaisa promptly hung up, picked up her extension, and began dialing. In her excitement, she forgot her phone was not enabled for long-distance.

"Who was that?" Lupe asked. "Your boyfriend from Boston?"

Kaisa and Lupe had become fast friends sharing the same office. While she had her rough edges, Kaisa liked her very much. It wasn't the only time a person she wasn't keen on at first ended up as a great ally. Ironically, most people she liked right off the bat didn't have the same outcome.

"Yeah, I haven't heard from him in months. He was calling me from a payphone and asked that I call him back, but I can't from my line."

"Here, you can use my phone. I was going to go down and have a cigarette anyway."

"Thanks Lupe, I really appreciate it."

Kaisa waited for Lupe to collect her purse then shut their office door.

"So, what's new?" he asked after they reconnected.

"Nothing," she replied.

"You haven't met anybody?"

"Nope, no one worth mentioning."

"I might be passing through New York City soon. What is the train fare from Boston?"

Her stop was the prior one in Connecticut, about an hour earlier. "I think 25 dollars," she said, padding her estimate, "but I'm not positive about that. Are you going to stop by and see me? There are many skyscrapers, really high ones, with roof decks to choose from," she said, twirling her hair.

"Yes, that sounds like fun," he said. "I have to go now; you're making me hot."

"Remember me in your prayers," she joked.

"Don't worry. You're on my mind. I'll call you soon."

"Okay, bye. -- Is there a way I can get in touch with you?" she quickly added but not fast enough before he hung up. Once again, her connection to Christopher was lost.

Christopher's call was exactly the pick-me-up Kaisa needed. She kept repeating their exchange in her mind as she floated down 6th Avenue toward Grand Central for the train bound for home. Could he be falling in love with me and not know it? Why else would he have called?

The train station was uncomfortably and unusually crowded. That never meant good news. The giant rotating schedule board was full of delays and cancellations, with a massive swarm of angry people below.

"Excuse me, what's going on," she asked a passerby.

"I heard a fire broke out in the Grand Central tunnel. There's been no service for hours."

An announcement sounded over the intercom. "We apologize for the inconvenience, we are resuming service, but trains are limited." It was fitting, given the week's chain of events, except for today's uplifting phone call.

Kaisa maneuvered through the chaotic crowd, wielding her oversized bag like a weapon, searching for a coveted spot on one of the few available trains. The temperature on the underground platform was nothing short of a sauna. The heavy air magnified the acrid bouquet of smells, fuel, exhaust, bodies long overdue for a shower, a freshly opened bag of Fritos, and the fragrant stench of marijuana.

She managed to squeeze into one train bound for a couple of stops past hers. She could always call her dad for a ride home. Kaisa leaned on the metal railing, just inside the doors, surrounded shoulder to shoulder by other sweaty commuters. Thankfully, it was an express, so she would only have to stand for about an hour. On any other day, she would have been steaming like the other passengers. But today, she was the only person on the train with a smile.

In October, Kaisa returned to Boston to see the friends she had made a year earlier. While she was happy to be back, albeit not officially, it was frustrating to be so close to Christopher and not have a way to connect with him. She had not spoken to him since he had called her at work in September, which only made her obsess over him more.

Watching the Regatta along the Charles River with Jill, Mindy, Deborah, and her on-again, off-again friend, Joseph, Kaisa leaned back on the blanket, picked up her 7-UP can, and resumed sipping her strategically disguised beer. She turned to Jill, "I hate that I can't see Christopher while I'm in Bos- "

"Could we not talk about him today?" Jill said tersely, cutting her off.

"Sorry," she said, placing her hand on Jill's forearm. "I know you don't like it when I bring him up. Maybe it's the beer talking." Kaisa's tolerance for alcohol had not changed from her lightweight status, even after a year of parties. But the beer WAS talking to some degree, and it was telling her to find a bathroom QUICK!

The few nearby porta-potties smelled disgusting or were not in working order. Last year Jill and Kaisa navigated the bathroom situation nicely by casually walking into a nearby Marriott. This year finding a civilized place to relieve herself was a loftier challenge. The mass crowd of drinkers also meant fewer establishments willing to offer public restrooms. Each hotel, bar, or store she tried to access had one or more employees managing the door, and they weren't making any exceptions.

There was only one alternative left - find as private of a place as possible. *Men have it so easy*, she griped. She kept walking and walking, looking for a secluded spot. The liquid was pressing down hard on her bladder and was verging on painful. Pretty soon, her pants were going to be that spot.

She approached a fence lined with male students, all with their backs facing her, no doubt answering nature's call. Near that fence was some greenery that seemed like a viable option. She unzipped her pants and was about to crouch down when she heard a familiar voice

"Kaisa?"

Well, this is awkward. "Oh, hi, Benjamin," she said, quickly zipping them back up.

"What brings you and every other student from the greater New England area here?" he asked.

"Same reason as you, probably. It seems like the same 'crew' from last year," she joked, making air quotes.

"Good one. Who are you here with?"

"Jill, Mindy, Deborah, and her sometimes boyfriend, Joseph."

Benjamin hesitated. "So, Deborah IS here with someone? I noticed a guy sitting with you all, but I didn't know whom he belonged to. How about you? Are you back in school now?"

"No, I'm just visiting. I'm on a six-month co-op working at an advertising agency in New York," she proudly announced.

"That's cool," he remarked.

"What's going on with you?"

"I'm supposed to be on co-op, but I'm working at the

American Bar and Grill waiting tables. There are not many openings for a philosophy major."

"I'll bet," she agreed.

"How long are you here for?"

"Oh, just through the weekend, I leave tomorrow."

Benjamin paused for a moment. She sensed the wheels spinning in his head. "Hey, I took tonight off, in case I overindulged. Do you want to stop by my place and hang out?"

Kaisa thought about his offer for a second. There was a time when she would have jumped on it. As much as she wished it was genuine, it was Benjamin, and there had to be an ulterior motive. Plus, she was not Deborah's stand-in and didn't want her sloppy seconds. To that point, maybe there were still some dirty STDs lurking in his genitals. Whichever one it was, it probably wasn't a good idea. "Thanks, but I'm going to have to pass. I'm only here for a short time, and I promised to visit some other friends," she stated, her bladder about to burst.

"You sure you don't want to come over? I still have your R.E.M. tape."

"No, thanks, and no biggie. I got another one. You can keep it," she said, wishing he would go, so she could.

When he finally left, she felt relieved in more ways than one.

Back home, Kaisa resumed her mundane routine: work, sleep, repeat – seven days a week. All her friends had returned to school, so she spent most of her free time alone or with her parents.

Around Thanksgiving, Kaisa was lying late one night in her bed, thinking about making one more trip to Boston. Jill had called to say she was planning a holiday party, and Kaisa did not want to miss it.

As Kaisa was drifting off to sleep around 11 p.m., the phone rang. Maybe it was Jill calling her back from Boston. She turned on the light and scrambled to pick it up, but her mother beat her to it, as usual.

"Collect from (click) hiss." Kaisa was a little disoriented at first, hearing multiple voices between the operator, her mother mumbling, and the mystery caller.

"Collect from Chris," the operator enunciated. "Will you accept?"

Right place. Wrong identity. "Yeah, yeah," Kaisa said emphatically. "Mom, it's for me." She held on, not saying a word until she heard the click of the receiver.

"Am I interrupting anything?" he asked.

"No, I'm in bed."

"Were you sleeping?"

"Almost," she groaned. "So, what happened to you. I haven't heard from you since September?"

Christopher explained he had spent the last six weeks traveling and visiting his sister in Florida.

"How did you get down there?" she asked, considering he was always broke and said he was living in a monastery.

"I thumbed."

"You hitchhiked? You're lying to me."

"No, I'm serious, I thumbed my way down, and my sister gave me money for my trip back. I thought a change of scenery might help me finish those papers. I went to the Library of Congress in Washington, DC, for some inspiration, but still didn't finish them. On my way back, I stopped in New York."

Kaisa shrugged her shoulders and contorted her face in exasperation. "Wait, you were in New York? Why didn't you call me?" she complained.

"I was super busy. There wasn't going to be a chance for us to get together."

She shook her head. They had not seen each other in months, he had her number in Manhattan, and he couldn't find a few moments to drop by?

"By the way, I'm a little mad at you," he said.

"You're mad at ME? WHY?"

"You told me that the fare from New York to Boston was 25 dollars."

"I told you I wasn't sure," she insisted.

"Well, I'll have you know the price went up! When I went to buy the ticket, they told me it was 35 dollars. I had to go around the station and beg for the additional ten bucks to get me home."

She could not believe his lack of preparedness. *Who only leaves themselves $25 when they travel? How stupid is that? And he did not have $10 in a bank account that he could* *have retrieved from an ATM? Oh well, he deserved it for not taking the time to call me when he was in town.* Kaisa rubbed her sleepy eyes. "So, to what do I owe this pleasure?" she sighed.

"I just wanted to see how you were doing." His answer was an improvement from his usual: 'I'm horny as hell.'

"I went to a Suzanne Vega concert otherwise nothing much new is happening."

"Did you go with anyone else?" he asked.

"No. I went alone. It was at Radio City Music Hall across the street from my job. She sings this song that reminds me of you. It's called 'Gypsy.'"

"I'm hardly a gypsy," he countered.

"Taking off at a moment's notice, bumming rides with people, begging for cash, not having a real address, sure sounds like a gypsy to me!"

Christopher responded with silence, which usually meant she had made a valid point.

"You know this popping up in and out of nowhere, it's kind of pissing me off," she said, knowing the language would irk him.

"Do you have to use those terms?" he scolded.

"Yes, you say you're going to call me, then you don't, and I think I'm not going to hear from you anymore, and then you call out of the blue, weeks or months later."

"That's life," Christopher said. "Do you want me to stop calling you?"

Sometimes she wished she had ended it a long time

ago and let him slowly fade into oblivion. Seriously, who was she kidding when she would do anything to keep him interested. How could she give up at this point when it was almost time to return to school?

"I'm coming up to Boston the second week of December if you will be around and would like to meet."

"Is that definite? It would be nice to see you," he said. "Are you coming up to stay permanently?" he inquired

"No, just for a long weekend. I'm staying with Jill and Deborah, my old roommates. Remember you met them when we all visited that time."

"You're staying with the VD girl?"

"Yes, the one you wanted a ménage a tois with."

"Let me guess. You told her that."

"Yeah."

"You can't shut up, can you?"

"Why do you care? I didn't think you would ever see her again."

"Anyway, Deborah and Jill are having a Christmas party in their new off-campus apartment on Columbus Avenue. Deborah helped get me an interview at Rizzoli bookstore. I'm going there as well and hopefully will get a job for when I'm back at school."

"Oh, that's great. Maybe you can help me replace some of my books. Are you going to live with them when you get back?"

"No, I'll be in a campus apartment."

"You should get your own place." For a minute there, it sounded like he was suggesting he move in with her.

"By the way, the girls don't have their new phone number yet, so call me here the day before I leave so I can give you their number, and we can meet up somewhere. Hey," Kaisa whispered, turning toward the wall and pressing the phone against her mouth so her mother wouldn't hear, "Do you want me to suck your cock?"

"Please, Kaisa, don't start with that when you are not around. You know you make me so hot."

"I just wanted to give you a little incentive, so you make sure to call me," she said, happy that she hadn't lost her effect on him.

Christopher apologized for calling collect and promised to have some cash on hand next time.

"See you soon, I hope," she said before reluctantly severing the call.

Hanging up the phone with Christopher was like throwing a needle back into the haystack. The click of the receiver meant he was out of reach unless he decided to pop back into her life. She couldn't give up now, especially since he was making it a point to stay in her life.

Kaisa turned off the light. Out of nowhere, her legs started shaking. She could feel her thighs reverberating in rapid sync. The sensation spread up her torso and crawled up her face until her teeth were chattering uncontrollably. Her stomach filled with lead butterflies involuntary trembling consumed her body.

It was part of the ride at his emotional amusement

park, worth the high, even if the dizzying thrill made her sick once in a while. Kaisa lay in her bed in temporary misery, as she waited for the attack to pass. She would just have to power through the dizzying thrill until it subsided. It wasn't the first time and it definitely wouldn't be the last.

CHAPTER 18
The Arranger of Disorder

C hristopher called as promised the day before Kaisa left for Boston to confirm his desire to meet. But because he did not have a place of his own, his visit was predicated upon whether she could isolate some alone time.

"Really?" she said, "I have to ask my friends to leave their own apartment?"

"Yes. I wouldn't be comfortable even if they were in another room."

"I'm not sure what their plans are, but I'll try to figure it out," she said. "Call me tomorrow when I get there."

"I'm not sure I can. I might be back late. I will try. We'll talk by Saturday," he said before hanging up.

Around 5 p.m. on Saturday, Kaisa hadn't heard from him and was starting to doubt any rendezvous would happen. She avoided telling Jill and Deborah of her intended plans. There was no point in starting trouble if he wasn't going to follow through. Ironically, as luck would have it, both Jill and Deborah were scheduled to work that night at Narcissus. Given that Kaisa could have had the place to herself this evening, felt like an enormous lost opportunity.

By dinner time, she had about given up and was considering tagging along with Deborah and Jill to find another "meaningful relationship." But her energy was low after a long week at the agency. She was tired and anxious about upcoming deadlines at work, not to mention fatigued by Christopher's emotional rollercoaster. Maybe taking it easy was a better idea.

Kaisa took a nice hot shower, put on her long red flannel plaid LL Bean nightshirt, and settled in for the evening. She called Mindy to ask if she was available to come over while the girls finished dinner.

"You seem to be breaking up," Kaisa said during their conversation, "I can't hear you." Kaisa was speaking so loudly she didn't realize she was talking over the call-waiting click. "Hold on, Mindy," she said before switching to the other line. "Hello?"

"Kaisa?"

Instantaneously, a surge of something punched her in the gut, and brought Kaisa to her knees.

Jill was seated across from Kaisa. "Look how her eyes

widened like that," she said, pointing, clearly stunned by Kaisa's physical reaction.

Kaisa gripped the phone. "I thought I wasn't going to hear from you!" she said, trying to release the words from her closing throat.

"I said I would call you Saturday. So, what are you up to?"

Kaisa took a deep breath. "Would you believe Deborah and Jill will be out tonight?" she exhaled.

"Really?" he replied with a lift in his tone.

"They work as cocktail waitresses at Narcissus."

"How amusing. So, you're going to be alone?"

Kaisa's insides were full of knots. It was taking every ounce of effort to sound composed when she wasn't even close. Like an addict dying for her fix, she couldn't stop squirming. Deborah joined Jill to witness Kaisa's reaction to his voice as Kaisa lay on the floor, punching Deborah's large duffle bag of laundry, trying to release her jitters. "Yeah. You could come over here, maybe, if it's okay with my friends," Kaisa offered, looking up at Deborah and Jill in desperation.

"Are we letting him come over here?" Jill remarked in a loud whisper to Deborah and Joseph, who was visiting again.

Kaisa shifted the receiver away from her mouth and covered it with a trembling hand. She knew it was a great imposition but hoped her friends wouldn't embarrass her and approve of the invitation knowing they hadn't seen each other since summer. "Could Christopher come over here, pleeeeease?" she mouthed, gritting her teeth.

"She's begging," Jill said, shaking her head.

Kaisa waited on their blessing as Jill and Deborah consulted with each other raising their arms and her doubt that they would give in.

Jill gave Kaisa a reluctant nod. Excited by the thought of seeing him again, Kaisa began rattling off directions to the apartment in her geographically challenged way.

"Kaisa," Christopher exclaimed abruptly, "I know Boston very well. The address is enough. I will see you in about an hour."

Kaisa hung up the phone. *Oh crap. I forgot about Mindy on the other line.* But she was too wound up to call her back now. She needed to pull herself together first. Still feeling on edge, Kaisa got up and paced around the apartment, trying to calm down. Jill and Deborah did not look happy. Hopefully, they weren't regretting giving their permission for her impending visitor.

"You know, we're not thrilled that he is coming over here," Jill said. "I'm not sure if this is a good idea."

"I know, but I promise to be careful with everything. I won't let you down." She begged the girls again for confirmation that it was okay for him to come. Not that she could call him back and cancel. While it was evident they did not trust Christopher, they could trust Kaisa to respect their wishes.

"Fine, he can come over," Jill said, "but you have to stay here in the living room and don't even think about going into the bedroom. We already had one accident and don't want another."

"Yes, the laundry you were pounding on is clean," Deborah asserted.

A half-hour later, Jill and Deborah left for work. Kaisa thought Joseph was departing with them, but he hung out a little while longer as if the girls asked him to babysit.

"Look, I know it's not my business, but Jill and Deborah are worried about you. What do you know about this guy? You don't know where he lives anymore or how many women he's been with. Instead of making you feel good, it's pretty obvious that he makes you feel like garbage. Your whole relationship, or whatever the hell it is, is not healthy!"

Indeed, Kaisa was curious about Christopher's social life in her absence. She was also aware their friendship wasn't healthy, but like any addiction, knowing something isn't good for you doesn't always stop you from doing it or giving it up. He was her vice, regardless of the ambiguity and withdrawal symptoms.

"Yeah, I know," she merely replied, not seeing the benefit of starting an argument with Deborah's sort-of boyfriend. *Who the hell is Joseph to tell me about unhealthy relationships anyway? He is just one in Deborah's rotation until she gets bored with him. So why is he getting on my case? He's not my friend.*

"I'm going to Mindy's place, so I won't be far away."

"Tell her I'm sorry I left her hanging on the phone earlier."

"I will. Call if you need me," he said before walking out the door.

Now that she had the place to herself, it was time to set the mood, which she had been carefully planning for a while. Still feeling a little jittery, she neatened up the apartment to burn off some energy then dimmed the track lighting. Kaisa retrieved a special mixtape that she created in case their meeting ever came to fruition that would serve as a soundtrack. She inserted the tape into Jill's stereo in preparation for his arrival.

She changed into her Suzanne Vega concert shirt and the black pants she bought with her employee discount at The Limited. She brushed her hair, put it up in a ponytail with a tortoiseshell barrette, and then dabbed on some makeup.

Kaisa was zoning out watching TV when the downstairs buzzer screeched with its ear-piercing blare. *He's here!* She checked her hair and makeup one more time, then pressed play on the stereo, but the wrong side was playing. "I hate upside down cassette players," she grunted aloud as she ejected the tape and fumbled the cassette with her shaking hands before placing it back in,

The buzzer sounded again. *Somebody is antsy.* "I'll be right there," she said, pressing down on the intercom button.

At the top of the last flight, her eyes panned down to the bottom of the steep staircase, eager for a long-awaited glimpse. Below was a blurred male silhouette behind the etched glass. Taking one last deep breath and shaking her wrists, she let out a silent sigh and focused on her cream-colored scrunchy socked feet as she descended the remaining blue carpeted steps. The socks belonged to Deborah, but she had left them on from earlier, figuring there was less of a chance of them getting soiled.

"Well, look who's here!" she said as she opened the door.

"Hi," he breathed, giving her a haphazard hug. He looked different, with stringy hair that hung far below his chin. He was wearing an oversized, padded denim jacket that didn't appear warm enough for Boston's December weather and, of course, had his signature backpack in tow. The jacket had rips and tears all over, with burgundy flannel liner peeking through the holes.

"Come on," she said, waving him inside.

"Are you alone?"

"Yes, I am, like you asked."

"Good, because if someone else is up there, I'm leaving."

"You don't have to worry," Kaisa assured him. "Let's go. Their place is on the third floor."

"This is nice," he commented, nodding his head after entering the apartment.

"Yeah, it is. I wish I lived here." Kaisa embraced him, but he ignored her sign of affection, seemingly too preoccupied with the new surroundings.

Do you know how much they pay a month?"

"I'm not sure."

He took off his shoes and roamed around as if he was inspecting the place. The sparsely furnished living room area had an enormous throne-shaped wicker chair covered in a sheepskin throw and lots of jumbo pillows on the floor. He immediately pointed to the bedroom. "Why don't we go in there?"

"Sorry, but we're not allowed."

He looked at her incredulously, raising an eyebrow. "Why won't your friends let us into the bedroom?"

"Do you remember when I went to your apartment dressed in the kilt skirt?" she asked.

He nodded.

Sure, that he remembers. "Well, we weren't too careful because you left evidence of our activity on the skirt which belongs to Deborah."

The blood drained from his face. "If I knew that, I wouldn't have invited your friends over that time and especially wouldn't have come upstairs tonight if they were home."

"Forget about it," she said, "I had it dry cleaned. Come on, we can use these pillows, and we'll be comfortable here."

Christopher opted for the big chair while Kaisa sat on the floor to have him in perfect view. She brought him up to speed about her lackluster home life and her two jobs. As usual, Christopher talked about current events but not much about his day-to-day-activities beyond his mounting academic assignments. In the light, his appearance had noticeably changed since the summer. He looked a bit haggard, thinner, and much older than 27 years. But he was still beautiful, in his charcoal wool cardigan, pinstripe blue, white shirt, gray pants, and rag wool socks. His fair hair gently framed his face resting on either side of his strong jaw.

She wanted to lunge forward and wrap her arms around him. "I haven't seen you in months, and I'm sitting this far away from you," she whined.

"No, this is nice. I'm enjoying our conversation. Hey, I thought you might like to know that I've been working," he said, puffing up his chest.

"On what, more papers?" she said with a sardonic smile.

"No, I'm a teaching assistant," he remarked. "You are so sarcastic."

Kaisa was impressed. "Is that so? What do you teach?"

"Sex education," he teased.

"That would be your specialty," Kaisa mused.

"No, I actually work with one of the professors."

"So, that means you have an income?"

"Yes," he affirmed quietly, but not so confidently.

"But not enough to have a place of your own."

"No, not yet," he said.

"Yay, you finally got a job!" she shouted. "It's about time."

"Did I deserve that?" Christopher asked.

Kaisa didn't have an answer. "So, where are you living now—not still in the monastery?"

"Not so much anymore. I live in Back Bay and sometimes in Cambridge. I stay from time to time with friends."

Kaisa didn't know what kind of friends. She had yet to meet anyone in his social circle. "It would be nice if you could get settled in one place again," she said, thinking about their shared past at 293 Marlborough Street.

"What are you playing on the stereo?"

"I call it my Chris-mix. It's a bunch of songs that remind me of our friendship. I made an extra copy for you as a Christmas present. It's a little Suzanne Vega heavy. I think her music is cool because it doesn't use all the same easy rhymes and clichés. Not many artists have songs with 'fancy poultry' in their lyrics."

"I didn't know we would be exchanging gifts. I'm sorry I didn't bring anything for you. Thank you for thinking of me, but I don't have a place to keep this right now."

"That's okay. I can hold onto it for you," she offered. "I was thinking we don't have a song, so maybe you can pick one from this."

"Sure, we do," he said with a devious smile. "What's that one we heard one night? Something like Boom, Boom, Boom, Let's Go Back to My Room," he snickered.

"Ha, Ha. You're funny."

I want you to hear the song that reminds me of you." Kaisa said.

"What's that?"

"Gypsy. The one I told you about." She was happily surprised that Christopher didn't give her one of his 'oh pleases' and was willing to listen. After several fast forwards and a few rewinds in search of the right track, she landed on the last verse of the previous song.

"Can we be seen?" he asked, turning to the window.

His question came out of nowhere, and she was surprised he asked since the exhibition at Marlborough Street never seemed to bother him. Who was he hiding from? "Yeah, this apartment isn't as high as the Hotel Hemenway, but there is less of a chance if you come down here on the floor with me," Kaisa suggested.

He arose from his wicker throne and sat next to her. She aligned two pillows so they both would be comfortable. Christopher gently lowered his head onto one of the cushions. She curled up alongside and placed her chin on his shoulder, so elated that she was finally holding her Gypsy. It had been such a long time.

They laid together as the music played. He was still for most of the song, but toward the end, she could tell his attention was waning when he started tickling her sides.

"You're not listening," she said.

"I'm listening," he assured. "What did you think of the song?" she asked when it ended.

"It's very poetic, but honestly, I kept getting distracted thinking about you."

He lifted his head and locked his ice-blue eyes on her gaze. Slowly, he leaned in and kissed her lightly, then more deeply with unsatiated hunger parting her lips with his tongue. Kaisa delighted in the weight and warmth of his body as it melted into hers. With increasing intensity, they bumped, grinded, romped, and stomped in a synchronized cadence. She could feel his erection growing harder until it was piercing her inner thigh.

"I am delighted you are back. I forgot how much I like you. Take off your pants," he said.

"No, I want you to do it."

Christopher attempted to undress her but fumbled for some time with the closures on her pants. Kaisa giggled under her breath, as she suspected it would be quite a project for him. Undoing this pair required opening a hook, several buttons, a zipper, and a little strap that went around a loop that was secured by another smaller button. It was like one of those dolls meant for toddlers to help build motor skills. All her pants were missing was a snap and some Velcro, and she would have had every clothes securing mechanism covered. But nothing could stop him or even slow him down. He released the last button effortlessly and shoved his hand into her underwear, touching her and igniting her senses.

"I'd love it if you'd talk dirty to me," he said.

"Why? I don't want to."

"Oh, come on," he pleaded. "You know what I want to hear."

Her cheeks grew warm. She looked away, then uttered in a low sensual whisper. "I want you to lick my pussy."

He smiled in affirmation.

"You want me to lick your pussy?" he teased.

"Mm-hmm," she murmured.

"Will you spread your legs as wide as you can for me?"

"Yes," she exhaled.

He crawled between her legs to do what he did best, knowing that part of her intimately by now, including the pressure points that made her wriggle in pleasure. His technique was enhanced with unexpected thrusts of his fingers that made her body convulse and contract. It wasn't long before his rapidly flickering tongue sent a burst of euphoria that washed over her. She let out a satisfied cry. *Heaven.* He continued to gently stimulate her clitoris in its heightened state of sensitivity as Kaisa sighed and moaned in blissful agony.

Next, he edged his straddle across her chest, toying and teasing her by tapping his penis on her face and gliding it over her closed lips. "How I've been thinking about you, imagining your mouth on me."

"Well, you can keep imagining," she said, turning her face in the other direction.

Kaisa felt obligated to reciprocate but was hesitant. 'Who else has he been with while you've been apart,' echoed a voice in her head. *Damn you, Joseph!*

"You know Chris, I want to pleasure you, but I'm not sure where you've been or with who." Considering she had a sexually charged up man on top of her, it was probably not the best time to address this topic.

"I haven't been with anyone. I've only had erotic thoughts of you," he insisted, no doubt trying to dismiss her concerns.

So much of her wanted to believe him. "I can't tonight. There are too many unknowns."

"I haven't seen you in months. We finally have this precious time to ourselves, and you're bowing out now?"

"You always say, I'm the one who expects something in return, now the shoe is on the other foot, isn't it?"

"Please, Kaisa, it has been ages, and I've so been looking forward to being with you. If you don't want to swallow, you don't have to."

Kaisa pondered for a moment as she wrestled with her decision. She had to follow through. She had invited him here, and it wouldn't be fair not to reciprocate. Besides, since she had known him, he never gave her any sexually transmitted diseases.

"I think that room is the safest and would be the easiest to clean up." God knows she didn't want to leave any traces on the sheepskin rug. Kaisa got up from her horizontal position and crawled over to the bathroom as not to expose her naked butt to the neighbors. She took him into her mouth and pleasured Christopher until what sounded like his heart's content.

"That was fun. Thank you, sweetheart. Hey, I'm

starving. Have you guys got anything to eat?" he asked, making his way to the kitchen.

"I'm not sure what's in there," she said. "None of it is mine."

He found some eggnog and helped himself. Kaisa hoped the girls wouldn't mind, or hopefully not notice. After finishing his drink, he placed the empty glass on the counter and walked toward Deborah and Jill's room.

"Remember, we are not allowed in there!" she said.

He ignored her request, saying they were done with sex for the evening, and the girls would never know. He claimed Deborah's futon and pulled a book of poetry from her milk crate bookcase. "Come here and sit next to me," he requested. He paged through until he found a romantic passage and read a few verses aloud while Kaisa pretended the words were his and were meant for her. Christopher placed the book on his lap. "It's getting late. I should be getting back."

To where she still had no idea. "How can I reach you?" she asked.

"Give me your number."

"I won't be back until the third of January, and I won't know my new number until after then."

She gave him every possible point of contact, writing down names, and 40 digits worth of phone numbers, including work, which was good until the end of the year, Deborah and Jill's apartment, Mindy's place, and her home number. She hoped he would call one of them eventually when she returned for the semester.

"Let me walk you out," she said. Kaisa led Christopher downstairs, wishing she could vanish so she could follow him to wherever he was going. "I do hope to hear from you soon. I would be hurt if you didn't get in touch."

He held her by the shoulders as she met his gaze. "I hope you know I would never do anything to hurt you."

Did any of the emotional torment over the last year count? He warned her about getting too involved or attached. Granted, she did deserve a man that treated her better, but it didn't lessen how deeply she felt for him.

"It was good to see you, sweetheart," he said, as he leaned in to give her a quick peck goodbye.

"Did you have fun?" Deborah asked when she and Jill returned around midnight.

Kaisa looked away from the television. "It was great to see him," she said with a wide smile. "Thanks so much!"

"Listen," Jill said, pulling up a chair next to Kaisa, "we're just going to cut to the chase. We're really worried about you and this whole thing with Christopher."

She wasn't surprised. There was no way the girls, especially Jill, were going to let this evening go without putting in their two cents, even though she followed their rules.

"Thanks, I appreciate your concern, but I can handle it. I've got it under control."

"I wouldn't call what I saw earlier tonight under control," Jill retorted. "This thing you have with

Christopher is beyond messed up at this point. We think you should talk to a counselor when you get back to school, or we can't remain friends. You can get services for free from Northeastern graduate students."

Kaisa digested their unexpected ultimatum. Was this some sort of intervention? Tough love? Love these days was tough enough as it is. "Are you serious?"

"We mean it, Kaisa. We're not kidding."

All in all, it seemed like a reasonable request, and it wasn't the worst idea. "Okay, I'll check it out when I get back," she said, keeping the peace. *After all, they let him come over tonight.*

Perhaps talking to someone with an objective opinion would help put things into perspective. It couldn't hurt. Whether it would do any good or help her quit the Marlborough Man was another story.

CHAPTER 19
Somewhere. Out There

Winter 1988

I n January, Kaisa began settling into her new on-campus apartment. This year, her roommate was Deborah's antithesis, a quiet, reserved, heavy-set, masculine girl. While she and her other two roommates were pleasant, none stood out or even compared to the cast of characters from the year before.

So much had changed. Jill and Deborah were off campus. Mindy was a senior and an R.A. at another building. Heather dropped out or transferred. Kaisa wasn't sure which.

She followed through on her promise to set up a few sessions with a counselor. Her friends were her lifeline and support system, and she didn't want to lose them, so what choice did she have? Jill was right. Northeastern graduate students studying for their master's in psychology offered their services for free. She had to agree that she was struggling with the mystery and complexity of their friendship. Admittedly, he probably wasn't the best thing for her.

Despite that, now that she was back and he was within reach, she could not stop thinking about him or where he could be. Her time away only solidified how much he meant to her, or at least the effect he had.

Kaisa started her new part-time job at Rizzoli Bookstore, an upscale, impeccably designed, independent shop tucked behind a three-story waterfall in the center of Copley Place. The job was not exactly the right fit for a non-bookworm like herself. But Rizzoli's was far too sophisticated for the average bookworm. Most of its clientele were hard-core bibliophiles.

Unlike giant chain bookstores that offered every genre under the sun, Rizzoli's inventory primarily focused on four categories: Art, Photography, Architecture, and Fashion. There were small sections for Bestselling Fiction and Non-Fiction, Film, Music, and one case of children's books. Most of the tall mahogany shelves had beautiful hard-cover coffee table books that were works of art in themselves. Books on the top shelf could only be accessed using a ladder and were undoubtedly placed up high to keep them in pristine condition and taunt aspiring readers.

Her new boss, Lisa, was friendly and welcoming. She had short spiky hair, wore no makeup, and had a similar masculine appearance as Kaisa's new roommate. On her first day, Lisa helped Kaisa fill out her paperwork, showed her the schedule, and introduced her to the other staff.

There was Tim. He was tall, thin, with curly blond hair that hung in tendrils and bounced when he walked, much like him. Terrence was adorable, with kind eyes and a warm smile. After speaking to him for a few minutes and listening to the way he enunciated his words, Kaisa got a sense that, unfortunately for her, he probably wasn't interested in women. Bobby looked like the lead singer from Madness and was a student at Boston University. Bobby was sweet and cute and didn't have the mannerisms of Terrence or Tim. Kaisa had an inkling he might be straight until his boyfriend came to meet him for lunch. *Maybe that's why Deborah quit.*

Finally, Lisa introduced Kaisa to Adam. She asked him to show Kaisa around and help familiarize her with the store and the procedures. He was about 5' 11", kind of nerdy, with chestnut brown hair styled into what could be best described as a bowl cut.

Adam carefully explained the procedures but otherwise didn't say much about himself.

"Do you go to school in Boston?" Kaisa asked.

"Yes, I'm a theater major at Emerson College."

"So, how long have you been working here?"

"About six months now. I'm just killing time until the fall when I start film school at USC."

"USC?"

"University of Southern California."

"That's so cool. I have an aunt that lives in California. Do you like it here?" she continued.

"I do. It's peaceful and quiet, and I like that. I don't do well with drama."

"And yet you're a theater major."

Adam cracked a smile. "I guess one kind of drama is enough."

Kaisa couldn't have agreed more, although she had plenty.

"You want to come to Copley Place with us?" Jill asked when calling Kaisa a few days later. "Deborah, Mindy, and I are going shopping."

Kaisa waivered on her tempting invitation. "I'd like to, but I promised myself I would go to aerobics today. I've missed the last two classes," she said. The aerobics class was supposed to be another step in a positive direction, figuring she could better spend her time burning off tension, steam, and calories.

"Come by our place tonight at seven then. We're going to order pizza."

Later, with her post-workout-high, revved metabolism, and a caloric deficit, Kaisa was ready to gorge. Mindy was at the apartment too, so it was almost a Suite 401 reunion. She was thrilled to be hanging out with her old friends, hearing their stories, anecdotes, and love prospects. Kaisa remained silent through most of the dinner, wary of chiming in with her Christopher-filled thoughts. It was nearing the end of January, and he still hadn't called, despite knowing every conceivable way to reach her. He had truly become the Gypsy. Was he in Boston, Cambridge, or did he go back to Nashville, DC, or maybe elsewhere?

"I miss this," Kaisa said, sipping her second beer. "You know Christopher is the only person I haven't seen or heard from since I've been back. But every time I think I won't see him again, he reappears in one way or another."

"Like a hemorrhoid?" Jill said with a deadpan look on her face.

Kaisa curled her face. "I'm hopeful I'll hear from him soon."

The group went quiet. Jill glanced at Deborah and back at Mindy, who gave an affirmative nod as if they were signaling in secret code.

"What's going on?" Kaisa asked.

"Well, we didn't want to tell you, but it's funny you say that about Christopher," Jill said cryptically.

"What do you mean?"

"Today, when we were entering through the Westin, I spotted him getting on the escalator in front of us."

"Of all times, I chose not to go to aerobics!" Kaisa screeched, her eyes wide as saucers. "Are you kidding me?"

"I'm not. Just to be sure, I leaned over to Deborah while casually pointing him out. He must have overheard me say his name and turned around. I think he recognized who I was because he flew up the escalator and ducked into a nearby flower shop. I wasn't sure if I should follow him or whether it was wrong of me to interfere, but we all agreed to go for it. So, I confronted him.

I confirmed he was Christopher Morton, reminding him that we met him last year. Then I asked him what was new. He said he was still in school, leaning over to show us his ratty blue backpack.

He asked if we were still living on Hemenway Street? And I was like, 'NO, we have an apartment on Columbus Avenue.' At this point, I wanted to say, 'you lying bastard, you were just there last month.' He stuttered something like 'it was nice to see you,' then literally ran off going back down the same escalator he just rode up with us. Then he crossed the street, turning one way, then another, wandering aimlessly toward the library like he was on drugs."

"He didn't look well at all, physically," Mindy added. "He was kind of unclean and unkempt."

"You gave him my new phone number, right?" Kaisa asked desperately.

Jill's jaw dropped. "No, I didn't," she fumed. "Did you listen to anything I just said? He didn't even ask about you."

"You probably freaked him out. I haven't seen him since we met up at your apartment, and I have no way of contacting him. You guys know that! You all know how I feel about him and how much I've been dying to see him," she cried.

"That's the point. You are dying to see him and waiting for his call, even though you don't know a freaking thing about him or where the hell he is!" Jill shouted.

"So why did you tell me you ran into him, to torture me?"

"I resent that. After thinking about it, I thought you should know. He looked really messed up."

Kaisa looked around as all the girls nodded in agreement.

"If he calls here looking for you, I'm not giving him your information. He is not good for you, and eventually, he will hurt you badly, I am sure of it."

"Ultimately, it's for me to decide when it's over, not you," she screamed, throwing her empty beer bottle against the tile floor, breaking it into pieces.

"That's it, we're tired of your soap opera," Jill said.

"Don't worry. You won't have to hear any more about it. You pawned me off to that counselor because you don't want to listen to me, not that she's been much help."

Kaisa stormed out of their apartment. *Where's the loyalty? How could they blindside me like that? They probably felt they were doing me a favor. But they know how much he means to me. Whether he should or not is my decision.*

At least that incident answered a few questions in Kaisa's mind: 1) My friends aren't on my side; 2) He's in town, but Jill probably scared him off; 3) I'm pretty sure we don't have the synchronized timing to meet again.

It was a dark and cold walk back to Northeastern, but

she was numb from either the remaining endorphins, the adrenaline, or the beer, so she barely noticed. Kaisa's only desire was to scour Copley Place to see if she could have the same luck as the girls. But they saw him hours ago. He had to be long gone by now. She could only hope by working at Rizzoli, the odds of seeing him again would be in her favor.

Kaisa's fuse was still raging when she arrived at her apartment. Her other roommate had a couple of beers in the fridge, and after Kaisa gave her the abridged version of the story, she was more than happy to gift them to her.

She felt betrayed by all of them but more by Jill, especially after she had abided by her request to see the counselor. How could she expect her to quit him cold turkey? Against her clouded judgment, Kaisa left Jill a nasty drunken message around 11 p.m., relaying these thoughts and slamming the phone. Afterward, she realized it probably wasn't the best idea.

At work the next day, Kaisa wasn't her usual chipper self.

"What's up with you today?" Adam asked, waving his palm in front of her face." You seem distracted."

"My old roommates saw a ghost yesterday. Now I'm looking for it," she replied, standing at the cash register, carefully monitoring the activity outside of the store.

"What?" he asked, wrinkling his face.

"I'm sorry for being so vague. I'm a bit preoccupied."

"That's okay. Sorry for the cliché, but you know a watched pot never boils."

"Tell me about it," she agreed.

"Everything okay? if you don't mind me asking."

"I am a little out of sorts. Maybe you can distract me today."

"I'll do whatever I can," he said, laying a hand on her shoulder. Hey, I have an extra ticket to the upcoming animation festival at the Somerville Theatre. Do you want to go?"

"Sure. Does this mean I have to go with you?" she teased.

"Unfortunately, yes, the ticket and I are a package deal."

"Yeah sure, that would be great," she said, cracking a smile. "I saw something for that in the Phoenix. You know, I'm a sucker for Bugs Bunny."

"I know. I remember you telling me that."

Kaisa grinned. At least someone was listening to her.

By February, Kaisa still hadn't seen her ghost. It was becoming more unlikely that her phantom would show. Kaisa's stomach sunk.

Her social circle had also shrunk significantly since Deborah, Jill, and Mindy were no longer speaking to her. Kaisa had apologized for throwing the beer bottle and leaving a nasty message, but Jill wouldn't accept it.

"We've tried to be tolerant of your behavior, but none of us can deal with you right now. We need a break for an indefinite while," was what she said the last time they spoke.

Wow. Wasn't Jill the one who would make all of us crank our boomboxes and blast "Lean on Me" freshman year? I guess that sentiment no longer applies. Kaisa could have done without Deborah and Mindy, but the thought of not having Jill in her life hurt. Jill had not only become like a surrogate sister, but she was a far more insightful, smarter, and available friend than Gina ever was. If Christopher did eventually show up, she had no idea how she would ever navigate this thing by herself.

Following Deborah's philosophy of the best way to get over someone is to get under someone else, Kaisa was introduced to one of her roommate's friends who lived in the same building. He was hot, and there definitely was chemistry. Maybe he could help fill the void and divert her attention. Stan had recently broken up with his girlfriend. Perhaps they could console each other and have some fun as well. Although it was unclear if he was looking for something meaningful or just fun? The truth was Kaisa still longed for both.

After a marathon study fest one night, Kaisa was vegetating in front of the television. She could hear her phone ringing in the other room. *Who could be calling after 10 o'clock?* Too tired to get up, she contemplated letting it go. But since it was late, maybe it was important. She trudged over to her room, catching the phone on its sixth and likely final ring. "Hello?"

"Kaisa?"

Her heart jumped. She knew that voice, the one she believed she would never hear again.

"Where are you?" Kaisa asked.

"I'm at a payphone. I need to see you."

"How did you get this number?"

"I tried your old roommates a couple of times but only got their answering machine. Then I called your home phone. Your mother was nice enough to give it to me."

Thanks, Mom. You are the only one who has never let me down.

"Are you alone?" he asked.

"No, I have three other roommates here."

"Can I come by later when everyone is asleep?"

"Well, um, most of them go to bed around midnight," she replied. As much as she wanted to see him, Kaisa was unsure about having a guest that late. But she had no idea when or if he might call again if she turned him away. She agreed and relayed her new address.

"I'll see you around 1 a.m.," he stated.

"I don't want you to wake my roommates with the buzzer, so I'll watch for you. My apartment is on the top floor in front of the building. Look for me. Once I see you, I'll come downstairs to let you in."

Kaisa took a power nap and woke up just before 1 a.m. She approached the living room window and sat on the flat wooden arm of the worn college-supplied loveseat. This year, her apartment was on the 10th floor with a coveted view of the Boston skyline and that memorable Prudential building front and center. She scouted the brightly lit outdoor pathway, anticipating his arrival for about twenty minutes, like a tortured Juliet awaiting her mysterious Romeo. In the distance, a tall, scraggly silhouette was nearing the giant streetlight. She opened the window and leaned out into the frigid air, straining her arm until she got his attention.

She found Christopher scrunched in a dark corner just inside the vestibule and waved to him to come inside.

Kaisa presented her ID to the proctor and picked up the clipboard. "Just sign in here," she said, handing Christopher a pen as he emerged into the light. You have to put your name and signature.

He scribbled a name that wasn't his and handed it back to the sleepy proctor at the security desk. "Let's go," he said.

She ushered him to the elevator while Christopher kept his head down. As the elevator scaled to the top floor, she examined him under the unflattering fluorescent light. His hair was even longer than the last time they met. It looked stringy and greasy, like the girls said. He was wearing the same clothes as their meeting in December, and his flannel-lined denim jacket had a few more holes.

She invited him into the shared living area. The room was dim, with only the kitchen light casting a shadow on the distressed wood dining table. This apartment was quite a change from their last meeting place with its drab, overused, uncomfortable furniture, gray tiled floor, and a stained maroon carpet.

"Northeastern housing is nothing special," he commented.

"It's a campus apartment. What do you expect?" she said.

Kaisa asked how he was and if anything had changed since they last saw each other. He was still spending nights at the monastery and wasn't teaching anymore.

"I got that job at Rizzoli Bookstore," she said, hoping it might give him a reason to visit her whenever he frequented the area.

"That's nice."

"Hey. You want me to help you get a job there? It would be perfect for you with your knowledge of books and authors."

He snapped back, "I'm too busy with school."

Kaisa rolled her eyes. *Really? So am I.*

"Hey, I brought something to set the mood," he said, as he walked toward the window and pulled a joint from his jacket pocket.

"I'll pass. It's not my thing," she said, putting up her hands.

"I've seen you smoke."

"Tobacco cigarettes. Not weed!"

"You must have tried it before?"

"Yes, three times, and I could never do it right, so I

don't bother anymore. Where did you get that anyway?"

"It was a gift from a friend."

"Sure, nice friend."

Christopher put the joint in his mouth and pulled out a packet of matches.

"You can't light up in here! It's an on-campus apartment. My roommates will smell it. For God's sake, I have an R.A. across the hall!"

"Oh, come on, we can blow the smoke out the window; no one will know."

Kaisa wasn't going to compromise in this case. "Sorry, that's not an option. If you want to smoke that, you are going to have to go outside."

Christopher sulked while he reluctantly put the joint back into his pocket. "Okay, why don't you come over here and sit with me," he said, crooking his finger.

Kaisa joined Christopher on Northeastern's sorry-excuse-for-a-loveseat. She laid her head on his shoulder to rest her eyes, then felt his hand cup her breast.

"I'd love to play around with you a little," he whispered.

Aside from being close to 2 a.m., Kaisa didn't want any part of that. Mindy was right. He looked unclean and didn't smell like he had showered recently. "I'm not in the mood now. Maybe next time."

"Really, sweetheart, we haven't seen each other in two months. I've been thinking of no one but you."

"It's late, I'm tired, and I have class tomorrow."

"You are as stubborn as always," he complained. "Why do you have to be that way?"

"Because this time, it's my apartment, so you have to play by my rules! Plus, any one of my three roommates could come out to go to the bathroom or something and see us."

"Do you mind if I crash here for the rest of the night?" he asked. "I promise to leave early."

"I wouldn't mind, but as you can see, the furniture out here doesn't lend itself well to overnight guests," she said, pointing to another short, uncomfortable sofa with wooden arms. "My single dorm bed is a joke. Besides, I don't know my roommates that well. They might freak out if they woke up and found a man sleeping here in the morning or the middle of the night."

"I see you are still ruled by what your roommates think."

"I think you should go now," Kaisa said sternly. "I have an early morning class."

"Maybe I should stop bothering you altogether."

Kaisa paused and rubbed her eyes. "No, it's fine. It's just really late, and I'm beat. You know you can always call me if you need a friend."

He rose from the loveseat and squeezed her hand. "I hope to see you soon."

Kaisa waited by the window until she could see his now lanky frame drifting among the shadows. A puff of smoke billowed above his head, possibly a combination of his cold breath and the recreational cigarette from his pocket. She followed his figure as he strolled across the courtyard then vanished once again into the night.

Christopher visited Kaisa's apartment a few more times over the following weeks. He would only come late at night, as to not interact with any of her roommates. Each time he wore a shabbier version of the same outfit and was either stoned or looking to achieve that state by asking Kaisa if she had any pot.

This newfangled friendship was pushing her limits. Besides having no idea where he was or how to reach him, Kaisa wasn't fond of this version of Christopher and found herself craving the "normalcy" of 293 Marlborough Street. But she couldn't deny feeling honored that while he could have left their friendship behind and reached out to anyone else, he kept choosing her.

"I saw this book I like at Rizzoli's," he said one evening.

"When were you at Rizzoli's?"

"The other night, I don't remember."

"It would be great if you could stop by during one of my shifts. I'd love to see you."

"I'll keep that in mind. You think you can get that book for me?"

"Which one?"

"The coffee table book on Austrian Expressionism. I had to sell mine that time to pay rent."

"Chris, I can't afford that," she said.

"Who says you have to buy it?"

"I can't steal it. There are cameras everywhere, even in the back room, and it's a large book, so even if I could elude the cameras for a second, I could hardly put it in my coat. I could get you 20% off."

"Never mind, you don't seem to want to do any favors for me anymore."

She knew what he meant. Kaisa couldn't bring herself to be with him sexually, as much as he persisted in trying to persuade her. At this point, there were too many unknown variables for her to justify or rationalize their intimate encounters. Besides, Oprah Winfrey had a show about women whose boyfriends walk all over them. Not that he was her boyfriend, but it seemed to fit her situation. The expert advised the women to put the sexual aspect of their relationship on hold for a while and see if things changed or didn't. Thank God for Oprah. This was the type of advice she was hoping to get from her counselor: an exit strategy or even a two-way dialogue, especially with the void Jill left.

The counselor personified the phrase "you get what you pay for." Kaisa spent her counseling sessions rambling about her situation while watching the counselor's vacant expression as she nodded her head, likely thinking of what she was doing for lunch or how many minutes were left. Whenever Kaisa asked for advice, the counselor would deflect from answering and ask Kaisa what she thought she should do. Kaisa knew the answer she was driving at each time, which was to stop seeing him, but that didn't mean she had the ability or the tools to follow through.

"Do you know the difference between being lonely and being alone?" her counselor asked.

"I don't know. They both suck?" Kaisa responded.

"No, Kaisa," she said, clearly unappreciative of her sarcasm. "Unreturned feelings can make someone feel lonely. Someone can feel lonely even if they're with someone. But being alone is feeling content with yourself."

"If I were fine without him, I wouldn't need to be here. I can't help how strongly I feel, despite everything. What can I do to stop feeling this way?"

The counselor dismissed her plea and recited more of the same mantra: 'This person is unstable, and you don't have a healthy relationship. You should break up with him.'

Gee, I wish I thought of that.

CHAPTER 20
I Give In, Again and Again

One slow day, when there were very few customers, Adam and Kaisa were stocking some new arrivals at the store. With her friends taking a break from her, a useless counselor, and not being able to make much of a connection with her new roommates, it was nice to have Adam. He was easy to talk to and seemed to enjoy her company. Despite knowing each other for a relatively short time, Kaisa felt like she had known him forever.

"Do you have a boyfriend?" she asked.

"Excuse me?" he protested. "What makes you think I would have a BOY friend?"

She didn't want to state the obvious but felt the need. "Haven't you noticed a pattern in the employees here?"

"No. What?"

"Like, everyone who works here is gay."

"That's a big assumption," he stated.

"Well, everyone else is. I thought Bobby was straight, but he threw me for a loop when his boyfriend came to visit. He said not all gay guys act like Tim or Terence. Many feel more comfortable blending in. I thought maybe you were like Bobby and flying under the gaydar. Plus, you're a theater major, and you played show tunes the last time we closed the store."

"Because you told me you like musicals. I also like classic muscle cars, so where does that leave me in your stereotype?"

Kaisa shrugged her shoulders. "Look, I come from a conservative town. I am not used to people who are out so openly. Besides the people who work here, I don't know anyone else who is gay or at least admits to it. The other day Bobby asked me for a sip of my soda. He wasn't sick or anything, but I felt weird about giving it to him with this whole scary AIDS thing."

"I think it takes more than sharing a soda to get AIDS," Adam retorted.

"I don't know. I've heard it's transmitted through bodily fluids." Kaisa paused for a moment. "Never mind, so, I guess you don't have a boyfriend," she said, trying to lighten the mood.

"How about you? Do you have a boyfriend?"

"To be completely honest, I don't have a boyfriend. But I see someone from time to time. It's complicated," she said, answering the question while deliberately avoiding details.

"Okay. Just wondering," he replied. "Hey, the box is empty. I'll go to the back and get another."

While straightening some books that were not standing at attention, Kaisa glanced at the store entrance. Her face lit up. Just outside the doorway was Christopher. *How thoughtful, he finally came to visit me at work.*

He looked hot. His hair was cut short, and he had changed from his usual denim uniform to a navy overcoat. Kaisa didn't want to seem overly eager. She restrained her enthusiasm as she waited for him to come inside.

Minutes passed, and he was still outside of the store. *What's taking him so long?* She stretched her neck to take another peek. It looked like he was talking to someone. At that moment, a young female with honey-blonde hair entered the store, with Christopher following close behind.

Kaisa tucked herself behind a bookcase. Despite being out of earshot, it was evident from his facial expressions and body language that he was flirting. Kaisa weaved through the store to get within an audible distance without being seen. Little by little, she homed in on their conversation, which was littered with words and phrases like coffee, talk, and join me. Kaisa was dumbfounded, her face twisted with emotion. She couldn't decide if his actions were rooted in stupidity, oblivion, or audacity. *He knows this is where I work, and he chose to come here, of all places, to chase another girl?*

That was enough. It was time to move in on his action. He was her man, after all. Right? She casually approached from behind. "Can I help you find something?" she called out. Christopher acted as if he didn't hear or recognized her voice. Kaisa tapped him on the shoulder then pounced in front. "Do you need any help?" she asserted.

He seemed only slightly startled by her presence and casually responded as if she was an average store clerk. "No, thanks, we're just browsing," he said, shifting his focus back to his original pursuit. The girl gave a wry smile and strolled deeper into the store, either sensing the tension or trying to dismiss Christopher's advances. But he continued to follow her.

Kaisa seethed at his blatant disrespect and complete lack of consideration for her feelings. "Are you trying to get her to suck your cock?" she said in a whisper loud enough to communicate her rage but not loud enough to attract the attention of her co-workers or her boss.

Christopher grabbed Kaisa by the arm and pulled her aside. "Look, leave me alone and stop harassing me," he said coldly.

"Harassing you? I'm not the one calling at all hours of the night!"

"You and I are not a couple," he said.

It was the harsh reality, but it didn't make his statement hurt any less. In her heart, she knew that this relationship was far from exclusive, but he must have developed some feelings to continue contacting her while she was away and seek her out again after living away from Boston for six months.

"Leave me alone, or I will never call you again," he

threatened. "Besides, we don't have much of a thing going anyway anymore since you don't have a place of your own."

"What are you insinuating? The fact that there is not much between us anymore is MY FAULT!" Kaisa shoved Christopher aside and rushed toward the ladies room.

A few minutes later, after she pulled herself together, she peered around the store, her eyes red and raccoon-like from her "waterproof" mascara. Adam was back at the bookshelf stocking the remaining inventory, but Christopher and the girl he was following were gone. Kaisa casually strolled over to their station with her head hanging low.

"Something wrong?" Adam asked. "You look like you were crying."

"Don't worry about it," Kaisa replied. She didn't want to tell Adam that her world just collapsed, although he probably sensed something terrible happened.

"I'd give you a hug, but I'm sure our boss would frown upon employee fraternization."

Kaisa smiled.

"When is your shift over today?" he asked.

"Four," she said.

"Me too. Do you want to get coffee after work?"

"I think I'm done with coffee," she said sadly, "as of about 10 minutes ago."

"Oh," he said. "How about ice cream then, upstairs?"

When it came to brightening her mood, ice cream

always did the trick. "That sounds great. I'll buy," she said.

"It's my treat," Adam offered, patting her on the shoulder.

At four, Adam and Kaisa grabbed their coats, punched out, and went upstairs to Frusen Gladje, the Haagen-Dazs knock-off. Kaisa ordered a strawberry milkshake, and Adam ordered the Banana Cream Pie flavor in a cone.

"And you wondered why I thought you were gay?" she mused, poking a finger in his ribs.

"Yeah, maybe I should have picked chocolate chip. Why don't we go sit over there?" he said, pointing to the white metal bench.

"This hits the spot," Kaisa said, sipping on her milkshake. "I feel better already."

"I hope you don't mind me asking but, who was that guy in the store today? Is he the 'complicated relationship?'"

"You saw that?"

"It doesn't take that long to get a box of books."

Kaisa sighed. "Indeed, he is, and it probably should have ended a long time ago."

"How long has that been going on?"

"Since last year. It's a big mess. I've been trying to move on, but he's like a vortex on my heart."

"He seems like kind of an asshole."

"Gee tell me what you really think," she said in wry amusement.

"I think you deserve a lot better than someone who chases other women in front of you. A gorgeous and smart girl like you shouldn't have any problem finding someone nicer than that."

If he only knew. "Thank you for the compliment. You'd be surprised. Are we still going to the Animation Festival?" she asked.

"Yes, I've been looking forward to it."

"Me too. You have no idea how happy I am to have you as a friend," Kaisa added.

Adam nodded and replied half-heartedly, "Yeah, ditto."

Kaisa canceled her next appointment with her counselor. Adam was a good listener, provided much better insight and advice, and for the same price. And tonight, Bugs Bunny cartoons would also serve as therapy.

"You must be excited about going to film school in the fall," asked Kaisa as they exited the theater. "I couldn't imagine living 3000 miles away from my parents."

Adam nodded unconvincingly. "My mom and her new family are moving to Florida anyway, so it's not like there would be a home to go back to." Adam went on to say things were not the best at home and how much it sucked living there full time as he also wasn't a fan of his stepfather. His six-year-old half-sister was the only family member whom he said he would miss. "My mom had me when she was young. I've always felt she resented me for showing up too soon, so our relationship has never been the best. Can we talk about something else?"

"Sure, like what?" asked Kaisa.

"Anything to get off the topic of family."

"What's your guilty pleasure?"

"You're going to laugh," he said.

"No. I won't. I promise," she said, crossing her heart.

"I love children's books," he admitted.

"That's odd at your age."

"Says someone who just spent three hours watching Bugs Bunny."

"Hey, Bugs Bunny is a classic and was originally intended for adults."

"Well, I find children's books are simply written but can be very deep. Sometimes when I'm feeling a little off, reading them helps me calm down and put things in perspective."

"So, you and your sister like the same books?"

"You're funny," he said, wrapping his arm around her neck and putting her in a playful chokehold.

Kaisa twisted around until they were chest to chest as he held her in his grasp. She gazed upon his sweet, genuine face as his eyes met hers, and for an extended moment, they lingered in each other's arms. She felt safe, warm, and at ease. "I had fun tonight, but I should be getting back," she uttered.

"Yeah, I'll take you home," he said as he released her.

"Huh?" Kaisa said.

"See you back to your apartment," he confirmed, "unless you want to come back to my place for a beer or two or three."

"No, I'm not in the mood to drink tonight, plus beer makes me horny," she said through a giggle.

"You sure you don't want to come back? My mom's away for the weekend," he said with a nudge.

"It's late, and your place is in the complete opposite direction. You can see me off at Park Street, and I can make it the rest of the way."

The T-ride was bumpy and standing room only. Kaisa fell into Adam a few times as the train swerved on the tracks, which he didn't seem to mind, and surprisingly, neither did she. When the train pulled into the Park Street stop, Kaisa kissed Adam on the cheek and thanked him for the evening. She pushed through the crowd and jumped onto her connecting train.

Kaisa was trying to keep her grade point average from plummeting. Sadly, she had performed poorly on recent tests in two of her far too left-brain classes: Statistics and Quantitative Models. She barely understood what the latter class was about, much less the concepts associated with the course. Ninety minutes straight of intense calculations per class made her feel like her brain was going to explode.

Tonight would be devoted to studying. She set up her desk with the required books and notes and placed her phone in the other room to avoid distractions. Nothing or nobody was going to get in her way. The second she opened her book to begin, there was a knock on her bedroom door.

"It's for you," her roommate said, handing her the phone.

"Kaisa?" Christopher said, his voice quivering.

He has a lot of nerve calling me. Without saying a word, she immediately hung up.

"Who was that?" her roommate asked.

"Nobody."

A minute later, the phone was ringing again.

"Do you mind answering?" Kaisa asked.

"Nobody is on the phone again. Do you want to just take it?"

Kaisa reluctantly put the phone to her ear. "What?"

"You probably don't want to talk to me right now."

"How perceptive of you. What was your first clue?"

"Kaisa, please, I need to see you. I feel very strange tonight."

"Yeah, well, too much pot can do that to a person," she scoffed.

"That has nothing to do with it. Kaisa, I'm serious. I

feel like I'm at my wit's end. You said I could call you if I needed a friend."

"If you need a friend, call that girl from Rizzoli? Bye!"

Kaisa went back to studying and was quite productive. After putting in a solid two hours, she needed a break and a snack, but nothing in the refrigerator was turning her on. She grabbed her coat and some money and set out to the local convenience store.

"Perfect timing," said a voice as she was crossing the courtyard. "It's good to see you, sweetheart. I was just about to buzz your room."

Kaisa stepped back to avoid Christopher's clutch, then turned around toward the building.

Christopher followed close behind. "I needed to see you."

"Now who's harassing who?" she snapped.

"Kaisa, I'm in a real bad state," he said, his voice shaking. "Can we please just talk?"

"You can't come inside."

"Can we sit here?" he said, inviting her to one of the benches in the courtyard.

Kaisa put on her game face and sat down.

"I feel like I'm going crazy and didn't know who else to turn to. I am so fucked. I have all these outstanding assignments for school, and these professors will not give me a break. They don't understand what I'm going through. I'm sorry to burden you with all of this, but you are the only person I have always been able to rely on. I can't believe I pushed you away. Having you in my life is the only thing that's keeping me from jumping in front of a T."

Kaisa was concerned but skeptical. Was he trying to manipulate her again? Christopher's mood was uncharacteristically somber. At first, his words reminded her of his self-centered diatribe at the Booksellers Café a year earlier. But she had never seen him act like this, his words dripping with despair and sadness. He needed someone right now.

She pushed her emotions aside. "Don't say stuff like that," she cooed, putting her arm around his shoulders. "I want to be there if you need me. But if you are seriously depressed, maybe you need more help than I can give?"

"What do you mean?" he asked.

"Maybe you should talk to someone more qualified than me."

"Like a shrink? No, I wouldn't waste money on that. Plus, my life is not anyone's business."

"Some universities offer counseling for free. I've had a few sessions with a Northeastern graduate student. While I wouldn't recommend her, in theory, it's not a bad idea."

"Why have you been talking to a counselor? There's nothing wrong with you."

"Because my friends asked me to with you coming in and out of my life. I would have abandoned it after the second session if they were currently speaking to me."

"I told you many times before not to share what happens between us with your roommates. See what happened. They cut you off because you made choices about your own life with which they disagreed. Nice friends."

Kaisa was beginning to wonder if her choices regarding their friendship were entirely her decision, even though she was the one who technically made the final calls.

"Do you have any pot?" Christopher asked, quickly changing the subject.

"You know I don't, and I don't think you should have any either."

Christopher sat quietly for a moment, then sprung from his seat. "I didn't have any dinner tonight. I'm going to Store 24 to get something. I'll be right back. Do you want me to get anything for you?" he exclaimed.

"Yeah, I was just about to get a pint of Ben and Jerry's."

His pants jingled as he scoured his pockets. "Do you have any money on you? I may not have enough."

"I only have a 20," Kaisa said as she pulled the bill out of her purse. "I'll go with you."

"No need. I'll bring you back the change," he said before he swiped the money out of her hand and ran off.

Kaisa waited upstairs for Christopher and her ice cream. Store 24 was only two blocks away, but after nearly four hours, he still hadn't returned. She couldn't imagine where he went or what might have happened. Given his erratic behavior earlier, she hoped he was okay.

It was 12:30 a.m., and she was exhausted. *He's not coming back.* It was time to give up and get ready for bed. Kaisa brushed her teeth, put on her pajamas, and slipped quietly under her cozy comforter to not disturb her sleeping roommate.

"BZZZZZZZZZ," blared the intercom from the living room. She jumped out of bed and dashed to the front door to answer it as fast as possible, hoping the jarring noise didn't wake anyone.

"Who is it?" she asked softly.

"It's Chris. I know it's late."

"Hold on. I'll be down in a few minutes. I have to change." Kaisa fumbled in her dark room for something to throw over her pajama top, assisted by only a sliver of light from the kitchen. She reclaimed the sweatshirt she had worn earlier from her desk chair and proceeded downstairs.

"Where the hell did you go?" Kaisa huffed when she found him downstairs.

"I got sidetracked. Can I stay here with you tonight?"

It seemed Christopher had more than dinner. He smelled of marijuana and was high as a kite. His special friend must have given him another "gift."

"I can't invite you up. You know there's no place for you to sleep. Besides, these girls still haven't met you."

"I'm sorry for coming back so late. I didn't want you to worry about me. I'll either go to the monastery or the MIT Library, which is open all night. I'm not sure yet. I hope to see you in a few days." he said before dissipating into the shadows.

Kaisa returned to her room and pulled out her old journal. She hadn't written any entries about their encounters since the beginning of the year. She began chronicling this latest exchange then threw it aside after one paragraph, tired of the absurdity of it all.

I have been trying so hard to get my life back in gear, and it's not working. Christopher is so contradictory and hypocritical. He pushes me away then reels me back in. Pick a philosophy or get a life. I don't know how much longer I can take this version of him. God, if he were anybody else, I would have given up on him a long time ago.

If he did call or return in a few days, she would not be there as Spring Break was on the horizon. A chance to escape this unwelcome reality and figure things out. Her destination was nowhere warm or exotic, but back to the comfort of home. It couldn't come at a better time.

CHAPTER 21
Things Can Only Get Better

"Hey. Is anybody home?" Kaisa bellowed as she walked into her campus apartment after Spring Break.

Her greeting was met with silence. Kaisa looked in each room to see if anyone was around. No one was back, but her new answering machine was flashing with several messages. Kaisa threw her small suitcase and backpack on her bed and sat down to listen:

"Kaisa, I have been thinking a lot about you. I know things are weird right now. You mean a lot to me and I screwed up big time. Please, I hope you will find it in your heart to forgive my behavior. I sincerely want to make it up to you. I will try you again in a couple of days."

The tape was filled with one apologetic message after another, each a variation of the previous one. There may have been more, but the tape ran out. Using every ounce of willpower, she deleted all his pleas from the cassette. *Jill would be proud.* Finally, there was an advantage to not having his number. She couldn't be tempted to call him if she felt weak.

Kaisa decided to go downstairs and check her mail. Just as she was about to leave, her phone began ringing.

"Hello."

"Kaisa?"

"Yes," she silently confirmed.

"I see you're back."

"Yeah."

"Did you get my messages?"

"I just listened to them."

Christopher let out a strong exhale. "I meant everything I said. Please hear me out. I know you've always wanted for us to go out somewhere. As you know, I barely have any money right now, but I was hoping we could start by spending some time together out in the open. I can't promise anything fancy. Would you like that?"

"Um, yeah, that would be nice," Kaisa replied. Even though things were stranger than ever, how could she turn down what she had been waiting for all along? "I have one condition."

"Name it."

"You can't come around here stoned out of your mind

at all hours of the night. I can't take it any longer."

"Don't worry, you won't have to." He solemnly promised to clean up his act and asked if she could give things a little more time to get back to "normal."

Kaisa agreed to give him one more chance but swore it would be the last time.

From that point, Kaisa and Christopher's relationship took a turn for the better. Christopher called almost daily. They saw each other more often, once a total of six times in just a week and a half—a record. They met more and more outside of her apartment at places like Copley Place, the Museum of Fine Arts, or just walked together through the streets of Back Bay. Perhaps he was showing his appreciation because everyone else cast him aside, and she was the only one who didn't turn him away. Or could it be he was finally falling in love with her?

"Do you still type papers for other people?" he asked on one of their walks.

"Not so much anymore. Business has been slow. But I can still type 65 words per minute," Kaisa assured him.

"Good. I could really use your help. As you know, my professors are pressuring me to finish my incompletes from the previous year. They've said they have waited long enough and aren't interested in any more excuses."

"Sure, just let me know when."

A couple of days later, Christopher called Kaisa at 10

o'clock at night. "Could I come over? I'd like to get a jump on those papers."

"I have a test tomorrow," Kaisa replied. "I can't be banging on typewriter keys when my roommates are trying to sleep. Call me tomorrow afternoon. I'll be at work most of the day."

Without fail, Christopher called Kaisa at work, twice in fact, and arranged to meet her that night at her apartment. But then he called her later at home to cancel their paper-typing date. "How about tomorrow?" Christopher suggested. "If I call you in the morning, can you skip a class?"

"Listen, Chris, I can't sit around and wait to see whether or not you're going to call, much less miss classes for you."

"Yeah, I'm sorry, I'm not being very considerate."

"I'll tell you what, if you call me by 9 a.m. tomorrow, I'm willing to miss Psychology if it's the only time you can make it."

"Okay, if I don't call you in the morning, then we'll get together tomorrow at four."

Kaisa ended up in Psychology class after another full night of insomnia. She was distracted and unmotivated and should have probably skipped it. Most of this class seemed like common sense anyway, and the professor's monotone drone was sleep-inducing. Kaisa chose a spot at the back of the large lecture hall, out of the professor's line of sight. She extracted her notebook from her backpack, slumped down in her seat, and briefly shut her eyes just as class was about to begin.

"Today, we're going to continue our discussion on personality disorders, beginning with the sociopath. This disorder is one of the most difficult to recognize. Sociopaths are mostly charismatic and friendly because they know it will help them get what they want. They are expert con artists and always have a secret agenda. People are amazed when they find out that someone is a sociopath because they're so effective at drawing people in. But in reality, they are emotional vampires. You expect more, get less, and in the end, get taken."

Kaisa was so tired and lost in another world; she only heard bits and pieces. She was too busy, practicing her future signature — writing Kaisa Morton over and over in her notebook.

The next time Christopher and Kaisa were able to coordinate their schedules was that Sunday. Again, Christopher wanted to make sure the coast was clear and refused to come over unless Kaisa was going to be alone. She assured him all her roommates were out for one reason or another, and she wasn't expecting them to return until early evening. It was one of those beautiful Spring days that make you feel guilty for being inside. She went downstairs to wait for him in the crisp April air hoping his papers wouldn't take all day so she could enjoy some of it later.

Christopher arrived shortly thereafter and waved to her from across the courtyard. As they entered the vestibule, Kaisa flashed her student ID while Christopher tried to casually slip past the proctor without signing in.

"Your friend has to sign the guest book, or I won't let him in," the proctor demanded.

"Don't put my real name down, make one up," Christopher muttered into her ear, "I feel odd enough being here during the day."

"Why so secretive?" she asked.

"You know how I feel about the dorm scene," he whispered. "If you put another name, I can pretend I was never here."

"Whatever," Kaisa said and wrote, 'Phil Collins.'

Christopher walked with his head down through the deserted hall. "Nice T-shirt," he said as they rode the empty elevator up to the 10th floor.

"It's one of my favorites." It was apropos of their pseudo-relationship, based on the quote, "If you love something, let it go free. If it doesn't come back, it was never yours." For the most part, Christopher had returned when he was out of reach. However, the quote on Kaisa's shirt was slightly modified: 'If you love something, let it go free. If it doesn't come back, hunt it down and kill it.'

"That doesn't seem like you," he said.

"You'd be surprised," she answered.

"Would I?"

"I mean, I wouldn't go so far as to kill someone, but I'm good at hunting people down. Some of my friends say I'd make a great detective. I'm very resourceful."

"I'm sure you are. Well, here you go," Christopher said, handing Kaisa a tall stack of handwritten papers.

"Wow, there are a lot more pages here than I expected, and your writing is awfully small."

"Um, can I use your phone?" he asked.

"Who do you want to call?"

"Just my mom. I usually talk to her on Sundays, and it will keep me from distracting you. I don't want to bother you while you're busy."

Kaisa checked the clock. It was about 1 p.m. She knew his mother wasn't local, and even though it was Sunday, an out of state call would cost a lot, especially since it wasn't after 6 p.m. "I'd rather you not call long distance on my phone," she said.

Christopher's face soured. She almost expected him to stamp his feet. "I can third-party bill it to my phone if it is a money issue. I've done it in the past."

"Fair enough. My phone is in the common area now."

"Thanks," he said.

He went into the living area and dialed. As soon as it appeared he had reached his party, his voice dropped to an inaudible decibel. Kaisa heard him walk into the other bedroom and shut the door. She put on the radio and started typing:

'This paradox incorporates any materialist model where any particular configuration of matter, or ultimate substance, maps to or results in consciousness.' *Wow, this might take longer than I thought.*

"One 12-page term paper down," she said, her head

spinning. Kaisa went to the kitchen to reward herself with a snack and check where Christopher was. But he was still in her other roommates' bedroom with the door closed. She looked at her watch. *He's been on the phone for almost an hour and a half. That's one expensive call. I wonder if he lost track of time.*

Part of her wanted to interrupt and say 'hi' to his mom. She had known her son for over a year, yet she knew next to nothing about either of his parents and doubted they knew anything about her. Kaisa walked over, lightly tapped on the door with her knuckle, then slowly opened it a crack. "Do you want anything?" she asked.

He shook his head and made a face, then lifted his index finger to his lips and shooed her away.

About 10 minutes later, Christopher returned to Kaisa's room. "My mom can go on and on sometimes," he said. "How are things going here?"

"I finished one paper already," she announced, "and I'm working on the second one."

He thanked Kaisa and gave her a brief hug. "Do you mind if I use your shower?"

Kaisa shrugged. "Sure." She resumed typing but kept her ears perked, waiting for a loud thud, the sound of flowing water, and the metallic scrape of the shower curtain. A heavy institutional door separated the shower and toilet from a large mirror, counter, and makeup prep area. Kaisa got up from her desk to check things out. As luck would have it, he had left his clothes in the prep area.

How could she not jump on a chance to put her detective skills to work?

First, she picked up his sweater and inhaled his masculine scent. Kaisa thought it might be funny to prank Christopher by hiding his clothes and leaving him stranded. He deserved some sort of retribution for his past behavior. But it would probably cause even more trouble, so she swiftly abandoned the idea. Instead, she slid her arms into its oversized sleeves and put it on. Underneath the sweater, his wallet was protruding from the back pocket of his jeans.

True to form, his wallet had only a few items. There were two fives, a student discount pass, a Boston Public Library card, but not one credit card or driver's license. One item looked back at her from behind one of the sleeves: a laminated photo ID from some unknown bank. She eagerly pulled it out. Wow, not only a picture but a social security number to boot! This was going to be hers.

Thoroughly enjoying this rare opportunity for discovery, she moved on to his backpack, stuffed with papers and schoolbooks, and pulled out a handful of contents. Wedged between the papers was a pocket English to French dictionary. What is this for? He never mentioned he was studying French. Maybe he needs a language credit?

Kaisa heard the water stop. She shoved the papers and the dictionary back into the bag, ran to the typewriter, and threw the ID into her desk drawer.

Her new favorite song was playing on the radio. "Oh, I love this song," Kaisa said, turning up the volume. Every time she heard it, she hoped that Christopher would one day share its sentiment.

Christopher emerged in her doorway smelling of Ivory soap and strawberry scented shampoo. "That was refreshing. Thanks for that."

"No problem," she said, her eyes focused on the task at hand, rapidly banging on the keys.

"Have you seen my sweater? Aah, you're wearing it."

Oh crap, I forgot to put the sweater back. She hoped he wouldn't mind her helping herself to it. Kaisa would have preferred being wrapped in his arms, but the sleeves of his sweater were an acceptable alternative. "I like it because it smells of you."

"It looks nice on you. Why don't you keep it?"

"Thanks," she said. *What a 'boyfriendly' thing to do.*

"I'm thinking about you," Christopher said.

Really? Was he in tune with the lyrics? 'The next time I fall in love, it will be with you.'

Kaisa smiled and turned in anticipation. He was sitting on her bed with his freshly washed penis dangling in his hand.

"Maybe later," Kaisa said sadly. "This is taking longer than I thought."

Typing his papers ate up the entire beautiful afternoon. By early evening, Kaisa was past the verge of frustration.

Christopher was also getting anxious and worrying about her roommates coming home. "How close are you to being finished?" he asked. "I'd rather not meet any new roommates. God only knows what you've said about me."

"I didn't think it would be like 50 pages. You can't expect me to interpret your scribble, type, proof, and turn around four 12-page papers in two seconds," she grumbled. "Plus, your papers read like a thesaurus threw up. They wouldn't have taken so long if you refrained from all the circumlocution."

"That's a big word. Where did you learn that? From your word-of-the-day calendar?"

"Yeah... so. That's what it's there for. It's a perfect definition. You use an excessive number of unnecessary words in your papers, which make your points vague and evasive," she said, pointing out a long run-on sentence. "Kind of describes you at times."

"You're such a comedian," he scoffed.

"I am finally done," she said. "I'm assuming you are going to compensate me for my time and effort."

"I'll show you my gratification when we meet next," he said.

"No, I don't mean in that way. I mean actual money."

"I thought you were doing this as a favor to me," Christopher said indignantly.

"I said I would help you. I never offered to do it for free, especially if I knew it was 50 pages. You have a lot of nerve expecting that. You know I type papers for money, and I'm paying college tuition myself."

"I never agreed to pay you. Otherwise, I would not have asked for your help."

"Like you had any other choice. I can't believe you are not willing to offer me anything. Normally I would charge someone $100 for this. To be fair, you don't have to pay all of it now. But I would appreciate something for wasting my afternoon."

"How am I supposed to pay you when you know I don't have any money to my name. I can't even afford a place of my own right now."

"Oh sure, but you somehow have the funds to buy pot then and again," she remarked.

"I told you it's from a friend!"

"What kind of 'friend' hands out pot for free all the time?"

Christopher stewed in silence, his nostrils flaring.

"Besides, you still owe me 20 bucks from when you swiped my money and didn't return with the ice cream or change!" Kaisa fought back.

"When was that? Anyway, I don't have it right now. Just finish up these last pages. I need these by tomorrow, and I have to go."

"What is this word?" she asked, pointing to his multi-syllable scrawl.

"Unfathomable."

"Yes, exactly."

"Why does everything have to be quid pro quo with you?"

"What does that mean?" she asked.

"Since we're focusing on new vocabulary words, it means like a contract. You shouldn't expect something in return for everything nice you do," he shouted. "I should have known YOU would; you always do!"

"So, do you! I honestly didn't think it would take this long or that I would be typing War and Peace," she snapped. "God forbid I should expect much of anything from you. I should throw these papers out the window and have you collect them in the courtyard," she taunted, dangling a handful of pages near an open window.

"Don't even think about that." He lunged for the papers, scooping them out of her hand. "Thanks for the shower and the papers. Enjoy my sweater. I'm literally giving you the clothes off my back," said Christopher as he rushed out of the apartment, slamming the door.

Kaisa sat at her desk, staring out the window, analyzing what went wrong. It had been weeks since Christopher came by or called. The more time passed the less likely she felt that Christopher would ever resurface.

Even though she hadn't heard from Jill, Kaisa called her anyway but could not get past her answering machine. "I am so upset. I wish I could talk to you," she wept. "Christopher fucking used me, and now he's gone. We had a fight, and I haven't heard from him since. I thought I meant something to him. I finally asserted myself, and I guess he didn't like that. I am afraid I will never see him again. I can't believe how much this hurts," she whimpered through heaving sobs, trying to catch her breath. "I'm sorry for rambling. Please call me. I miss you and all the girls."

With no one in the picture, Kaisa got under Stan to numb the pain. But it wasn't long before he took advantage of her vulnerable state and became her fourth time after a few rounds of strip poker, which she was sure he intentionally lost. The sex was mechanical and robotic, as if he were working toward a purpose. He didn't look into her eyes the entire time. Perhaps it made it easier for him to envision who he genuinely wanted there. She might as well have been invisible.

Later that night, he woke her at 3 a.m. to confess that he was going back to his girlfriend.

"What about us?" Kaisa asked.

"I thought I made it clear that we were just hooking up?" he said. "My girlfriend and I just needed some space."

"That wasn't my impression. You should be careful who you mess with," she stated.

"What do you mean?" he asked.

"You'll see."

The next morning Kaisa cut the silhouette of an anatomically correct male out of a large shopping bag, ripped off the dick, and shoved the body under his door.

She found out later from one of her roommates, the gesture freaked him out so much, especially since Fatal Attraction was a box office smash, that he avoided Kaisa at all costs. Any time he saw her in the courtyard, he sped up his stride. Kaisa gave him devilish smirks as she watched him run away. She had no intention of doing anything else but enjoyed the fact that he thought she might. *Oh well, maybe next time he'll think twice before doing what he did to me to someone else.*

CHAPTER 22
Please Let Me Get What I Want

E ver since Christopher disappeared, being at work was incredibly hard. Kaisa was constantly distracted, hoping he would just show up. When she walked the streets of Boston, she retraced their steps around Copley Square, Saks Fifth Avenue, Back Bay, and of course Marlborough Street, praying she might find him at one turn to officially say goodbye or, more likely, fuck you. But of all the faces she passed, none belonged to him.

Today was her final day at Rizzoli. The last day she could look out for Christopher while getting paid. It was also the last time she would probably see Adam. He had been so good to her. Kaisa carefully selected a compact children's book that she had seen Adam pick up a couple of times. It had a collection of creative and inspirational sayings meant to lift a child's spirit during life's unpleasant twists and turns. Kaisa paged through the book taking in its simple advice. "If the sky falls, have clouds for breakfast," and "if there's no happy ending, make one out of cookie dough." *If only it were that easy.*

She selected two books and ran over to the cash register to buy them before Adam showed up for his shift. "Terence, can you check me out?"

"Sorry, honey, you're not my type."

"Ha-ha, I mean ring these up for me?"

"These are cute. Who are they for?"

"One is for Adam, and one is for me. He likes children's books. Don't tell him I told you. It's a going-away present because today's my last day, and he's leaving for California soon."

"It is? It was nice working with you. Thanks for letting me know. I hope he has something for you?"

"Why?" questioned Kaisa, wrinkling her nose.

"You know he likes you, right? Talk about checking someone out; you should see how he looks at you," he said, slipping the books into a bag and handing Kaisa her change. "You didn't hear that from me."

With the few minutes left on her break, she hid the bag under her jacket in the back room then went outside to make one last wish at the central waterfall. While scrounging in her purse for a penny, she felt a tap on her shoulder. Kaisa jumped then eagerly spun around.

"I'm sorry, I didn't mean to startle you," Adam said. "Are you looking for your ghost again?"

"It's okay. I haven't heard from him in like two months."

"Have you tried calling or going to his place?" he asked.

Kaisa hesitated. "I can't."

"Why not?"

She paused and looked away. "I don't have any of that information," Kaisa confessed.

"You don't?"

"I haven't had it since September of last year."

"You know how crazy that sounds?" Adam said.

"Yes, I know it sounds pathetic. I'm an idiot. Please don't remind me," she bitched.

"Come here for a second," he said, tugging on her sleeve and pulling her aside. "I didn't mean anything by that; it's just odd. I didn't know you were such a wild child," he joked. "Hey, it's your last day, right? Do you want to hang out after work? I'm here until close."

"So am I," she said.

"Yeah, I kind of hoped we'd be on the same schedule," he jested.

By 7:30 p.m., the last few customers finished their purchases and left the store while Adam locked the door behind them.

"What's on the playlist tonight?" she asked.

"I don't know. What do you want to hear?"

"I'd like to hear something new."

"I have something from my collection. It's not new, but it's a classic." Adam came back with his backpack and pulled out a cassette.

"Great choice. The Stones. You can't always get what you want," she sang.

"I have something else to celebrate our last night," he said, pulling out a bottle of tequila.

"Another great selection, but we're going to get in trouble," Kaisa said cautiously.

"Chill out. Lisa's not coming back tonight. She had a date, so she asked me to finish up and give her the keys tomorrow." He sat down, took a swig from the bottle, and handed it to Kaisa.

Kaisa joined him on the floor. "I can't have more than two shots of this."

"Oh, live on the edge, have three."

Kaisa and Adam reclined on the carpeted steps leaning back on their elbows while they alternated taking shots from the bottle.

"I have something for you. I almost forgot," Kaisa said, reaching for her Rizzoli bag and handing a book to Adam. "I thought you might like this. I wanted to thank you for putting up with me and bringing some sanity into the chaos that is my life right now."

Adam reached over and gave her an extended hug. He looked at her, smiled, and kissed her on the cheek. From what she could tell, his eyes were communicating more than thanks. Kaisa returned his gaze offering acknowledgment and permission at the same time. He slowly leaned in and rested his forehead on hers. She closed her eyes as his lips met hers.

"I love you," he said through his faint breath

Her insides fluttered. "What did you say?" The reality was she heard. She just wanted to hear it again.

"Oh my God, did I just say that out loud?"

"Yes. Did you mean that Adam?"

"Of course, I did. I've felt something for you for a while. I didn't see the point in telling you because I'm leaving, but I guess the alcohol pulled it out of me."

Kaisa wasn't sure what to say. She wanted to feel more and reciprocate in some way because it took courage for him to put his heart on the line. She had to admit it felt wonderful to hear those words from someone she cared about. "I feel a little something for you. I just don't know what. But I'm glad you told me how you feel. Maybe we just needed more time. Love at first sight always seems to end badly. At least for me, it does."

"I guess it's best we didn't go any further because I know I wouldn't be able to stop thinking of you," Adam admitted."

It was comforting that Adam was wired the same way as she was. There was hope that she wasn't the only one. "I think we're a lot alike. I tend to get anxious and can be overly sensitive sometimes."

"There's nothing wrong with having strong feelings. It just means you have passion."

"That's exactly what I say," Kaisa said, agreeing wholeheartedly.

"I guess this is goodbye forever?" he asked.

"It doesn't have to be. I wouldn't mind hearing from you. I want to visit you at your Malibu mansion someday when you become rich and famous."

"I think we better lock up now," Adam said.

He walked Kaisa to the door. They exchanged a long bear hug, and Adam kissed her on the forehead. Kaisa walked home in solitude. *Maybe now is as good a time as any to be alone and work on me for a while.*

As they say, be careful what you wish for. As Kaisa packed up her dorm room, she took a mental tally of her Boston friends. All former members of Suite 401 were leaving Northeastern, or so she had heard. Jill and Deborah were transferring to schools out west. Mindy was graduating and moving back to Pennsylvania. Adam was off to California. And Christopher was nowhere to be found. All she had left was his sweater, ID, and a deep cut carved into her heart.

A couple of weeks later, Kaisa was back in New York, working for the same advertising agency. One evening, she came home to an envelope from the Boston phone company on her bed. *What is this? I shut off my phone and paid the last bill before I left.* Kaisa opened the envelope and read the contents. *This has to be a mistake!*

She immediately picked up the phone to call customer

service before the office closed. "Hi, I believe I was mistakenly billed. I got a letter saying there is an outstanding charge on my account for $80 for an 83-minute call to Paris, France."

"Let me transfer you. Another department handles disputes," the operator replied.

Kaisa bounced around to several agents until she reached to an investigator.

"I'm sorry," the investigator said, "but this call was third-party billed to a couple who claimed the costs were fraudulent. Since the call originated from your phone number, the charges are being rebilled to you."

"This number was disconnected about a month ago. When was this called made?" she inquired.

"Sunday, April 12 from 1:09 to 2:32 p.m."

Kaisa caught her breath. *He said he was calling his mother! He didn't tell me she was in Paris.* "I believe I know who made that call, but I have no way of contacting him. I don't have that kind of money. That's like a third of my week's pay." Through a tearful vibrato, Kaisa told the investigator a little more history than she probably wanted to hear.

"I understand your situation, and I'm sorry you are in this position. I'll give you the number in Paris. Maybe you can get in touch with him and get this matter resolved."

A few hours later, Kaisa got up the nerve to call. Completely overlooking the time difference, she picked up the phone and dialed the number.

"Hello?" said a groggy young female American voice.

"I'm looking for Christopher Morton. Is he there?"

"It's 2 a.m. Who is this?"

"I'm a friend of his from Boston. He called this number three months ago from my apartment without my knowledge. Do you know him? He owes me 80 bucks."

"Yes," she snarled, sounding underwhelmed, "I met him, and I'm not surprised. He was seeing my old roommate Rebecca. She no longer lives here. I don't know where they went, nor do I care. I'm sorry, I can't help you."

Kaisa's jaw plummeted to the floor. She was confident Rebecca wasn't his mother. "Sorry to wake you. Thanks anyway. Good night."

Her temperature rose as her body consumed with rage. *Bad enough, he stiffed me with an expensive phone bill, but he made that call to another woman while I was doing him a favor?* Kaisa couldn't sit still. She got in her dad's car and drove to the beach, running nearly every light and stop sign while yelling at herself along the way for being such an idiot.

As she trudged across the rough New England sand, she pulled out her lighter and lit the paper with the phone number and threw it against the shoreline. She wanted to watch it turn to ash, burning any memory of Christopher out of her brain. But after several attempts, the wind kept blowing out the flame. *Is this a sign that he's always going to haunt me?* She picked up the partially singed, crumpled mess and felt guilty for littering. What remained, she threw in the garbage.

Absorbed in her thoughts, she dragged her feet in the wet sand, kicking the seaweed that had washed up at high tide. *Happiness makes up in height what it lacks in length. I don't buy it. I think Robert Frost got that wrong. The high of joy doesn't even come close to the mental, physical, and emotional anguish I feel now. It's my fault. I had my chance to escape earlier before I got in too deep. My sense of adventure pushed me to take this further. No one forced me into this. Nobody held a gun to my head. I could have always said no. But I never did. At times I felt violated and disgusted with myself like I do now. And yet, every time he called, I went back.*

The next morning. Kaisa's mind was on turbo, plotting her next move. *How can I let this slide? Why should he get away with this?* "I'm trying to locate a graduate of yours," she said, calling the Harvard alumni office. Once again, she explained her sad, pathetic situation about the phone charges to, fortunately, another sympathetic employee.

Less than an hour later, Kaisa received a reply. "Unfortunately, I don't have much beyond a forwarding address in Paris on record, where he asked to send his diploma. I can fax it to you."

But the address wasn't of any use. There was no other name and, at the bottom, was the same phone number as the groggy American girl.

Kaisa curled her fists and gritted her teeth. *What am I going to do now? Jump on a plane to France? Wander the streets of Paris? Then what? I don't speak French.* It wasn't like she knew where to find him to deliver any retribution for how he treated her. Neither she nor her parents could afford it anyway, nor did she want to waste any more time or money on him. Kaisa's only option was to try to put the emotional wreckage behind her if she wanted to retain any sense of dignity.

She wondered if she was destined to ever find closure or a happy ending, or would she have to make it out of cookie dough?

CHAPTER 23
Building a Mystery

Winter 2003

T wo more minutes, and Kaisa's batch of homemade cookies would be ready. It was the last detail in preparation for her son Michael's playdate with his new friend Dixon. The oven's warmth mixed with a caramelized scent added a special touch to the frosty January day. Being new in town, Kaisa wanted everything to be perfect. She had precisely weighed each ingredient before baking her Mrs. Fields-like chocolate chip cookies for two six-year-olds who would have, more than likely, been happy with the store-bought variety. Kaisa hadn't met Dixon's mother, although they had spoken on the phone. She had invited her to come as well so they could get to know each other. But last night, when Kaisa came home after a long work week, there was a message on the machine:

"Hi Kaisa, I'm so sorry I won't be able to come over

tomorrow. I flaked and forgot it was my ex's weekend. Not to worry, Dixon wants to come and play with Michael, so I arranged with my ex to bring him. I hope you don't mind."

She immediately called Dixon's mom back to let her know it would be fine. Kaisa didn't care as long as the playdate was still on. Michael would have been crushed.

Her thought was rudely interrupted by the oven's annoying 'beeeep.' She pulled out the tray of cookies and inhaled their sweet aroma. After placing the tray on the cooling rack, she rummaged through her utensil drawer, searching for an offset spatula to scoop up a warm cookie for herself.

There goes the doorbell. She wiped her hands on her apron before taking it off and throwing it on a chair. Through the sheer white curtain, she could see a little boy accompanied by a tall, graying, balding man. She stood for a moment, scrutinizing this vaguely familiar silhouette as if she were witnessing an apparition.

"Hi, Dixon's here for his playdate," he said with a hint of sarcasm in his voice.

Dixon darted immediately toward Michael, who was peeking around the corner. They both sped off in the direction of the den.

Dixon's dad stretched out his hand. "Hi, I'm John Sklarz."

"Please come in," Kaisa offered as she more closely examined his face. John wiped his feet on the mat and stepped inside.

"I can hang up your coat if you like," she said, not being able to take her eyes off him.

"That's not necessary. I'm just dropping Dixon off. I was planning to go to the mall in the meantime. It doesn't make sense to drive back home 45 miles for a two-hour playdate."

"You're welcome to stay here for a while," she suggested, trying to ease his crankiness. "Would you like some coffee? I just baked some cookies."

"That's nice of you. But I much prefer tea if you have it."

"Sure," she said. Kaisa led him toward the kitchen. John unbuttoned his coat and hung it on the back of a chair.

"You mentioned you lived 45 miles away?"

"Yes, I used to live here in town when my ex-wife and I were married, but now I work at a private school in Westchester and live in faculty housing."

"Oh, what do you do there? Kaisa inquired.

"I'm a history teacher."

Kaisa served the tea and placed a plate of cookies in front of him.

"These are pretty good," he said after taking a bite.

"Thank you. I love to bake, and it makes the house smell so warm and cozy," she added. "Why don't you sit down for a moment." She wanted to learn more about this man, facts that she could latch on to, but he wasn't very forthcoming. Long awkward pauses punctuated their conversation in between her questions. She kept studying John's face, watching him check his watch several times and listening to his breathy soft-spoken voice.

"I think the kids have another hour and a half or so. I'm going to run a couple of errands. Do you have a writing utensil and paper?" he asked.

Kaisa pulled out a small notepad and pen from a junk drawer and gave them to him.

"Here is my mobile phone," he said, handing her a slip of paper. "Call me if Dixon wants to leave early. Otherwise, I will be back at four," he said as he put on his coat.

"Thanks. It was nice seeing–I mean, meeting you."

Kaisa couldn't get over how much John resembled Christopher. Who was this guy who showed up at her door? The one who was wildly identical to the man he could be today. He looked and acted so much like him, just an older version of what she could remember but with glasses, and this time, without a backpack. Then she realized the date; it was January 9th. It's like he keeps giving me reasons not to forget him. She had to verify his identity to be sure.

But first, she had to check on the boys, who seemed to be getting along nicely. "Would you like me to put on a movie?" she asked. "We have all kinds." Kaisa opened a box with an extensive collection, primarily supplied by her mother. After the boys chose one, she popped a cassette into their VHS player.

With the kids occupied, Kaisa headed to the basement

and turned on her computer. She had developed a love/hate relationship with this thing called cyberspace. The ability to find someone had grown exponentially since the internet-less eighties. So much had changed except that indelible scar he had left on her heart. Since the dawn of the internet, her chances of eventually locating Christopher and finding the closure she felt she never got became more probable. Despite all the years of reflection and perspective, Christopher's departure and betrayal still stung.

When in full detective mode, she had been able to uncover details or track down just about everyone she was curious about, except him. The fact that he had a common name didn't help. The closest link she ever found was an opinion page from 1991 proudly authored by Christopher Nicholas Morton, Paris, France. She recognized his long, drawn out sentence structure before she even read the byline with superfluous words and words like superfluous, that he chose to make him sound more intellectual or possibly to meet a word count or a minimum page requirement. The same pretentious, verbose language that spewed from his mouth onto those term papers.

She entered 'John Sklarz' into the search bar. His information required some digging, but she was able to verify most of what he said with facts and photos from their limited conversation, like where he worked, where he went to school and his current address. That satisfied her curiosity and proved while he looked and acted so much like Christopher, he wasn't the same person, just a facsimile.

"Are you stalking people again?" her husband asked, walking into the room.

"No, I'm doing research," she replied.

"On whom?"

"Dixon's dad. He reminded me of that Christopher Morton guy I told you about. Do you mind that I still wonder about what happened to him?"

"You haven't seen or heard from him in years. Why should I feel threatened by a ghost?"

"I hate that it still bothers me," she said. "But until it's resolved in some way, I don't know if I can ever let it go."

"We all have a past, and, ironically, both of ours relate to Boston. Remember when we were first dating, and my drunk ex-girlfriend broke the screen door to my apartment or the time she got pulled over by the cops, and she gave them my address. You were there both times, and you trusted and believed me that it was over when you could have run."

"Yeah, those were the days," she sneered. "At least you were able to say goodbye."

"I hope if you do ever find him, you'll want to stay with me," he said, kissing the top of her head.

"Don't be stupid. I love you."

"I love you too. Do you want to get naked later? I'll do that thing you like," he winked.

"I'll see how I feel after Michael goes to bed. It's been a long week."

Derek and Kaisa had been married for about seven years. Their relationship was not love at first sight. It took a little time for Derek to grow on her. He was a great father, husband, and equal partner, but highly predictable. Her life had become very routine. The only adventure as of late was juggling a growing career, children, and other obligations, which were extremely tiring. Kaisa barely had enough energy or desire to do more than watch television at the end of the day. Though she did crave a little mystery once in a while.

While driving to work the following Monday morning, Kaisa was testing out the sound system in her new Mercedes. As she listened to the radio, her mind zigzagged from one memory to another until it worked its way back to college. Sarah McLachlan was crooning about a 'beautiful fucked-up man' who not only evaporated but punctuated his disappearance with a metaphorical knife in her back. REM reminded her when she was 'a simple prop that occupied his time.' Despite being in a healthy relationship, on occasion, something, like a song, would trigger Christopher's memory and bring him to the forefront of her mind. Kaisa couldn't help to think that part of her was still broken. Not broken up that she and Christopher were no longer together, but that there were pieces of her that, up until now, she hadn't been able to reclaim or reconstruct.

After her hour-long commute on the congested

highway, Kaisa arrived at her window office. It was early, and no one was there, not even her demanding boss. She could ease into the workweek, check her personal email, and surf the net for a little while.

Just as she opened her browser, a tempting banner ad for a People Search site popped up at the top of the page as if the computer was reading her mind. The site claimed to have an extensive database compiled from statements and billing records and cited several testimonials from people who found long-lost relatives with next to no data. How could she resist this opportunity to possibly locate Christopher and tell him what he robbed from her besides her time and about $200? Perhaps this could finally give her peace of mind. But, considering he left for France so long ago, he could be anywhere in the world by now.

Using what few fragments of information she could recollect, Kaisa did the initial search and found a list of Christopher Mortons in Boston several pages long. Each one had an estimated age to help narrow down the search. Based on her calculations, he would be 41 or 42. But no one matched that age. She scrolled through the names again. There was a Christopher Morton with only one address: 293 Marlborough Street. But he was... 51? That can't be, right? "He told me he was eight years older than me, not 18!" she shouted before catching herself and throwing her hand over her mouth. *Oh my God, he was twice my age when we first met! Here I thought his thinning hair was premature aging, not actual aging.* Their age discrepancy raised questions in her mind about the many lost years in-between. What was he doing before he went to graduate school for 12 or so years? Now there was a lot more to find out.

Kaisa selected that Christopher Morton on the site. After watching a green bar load from 0 to 100% appearing to scan all sorts of records, it said: 'We've found THAT Christopher Morton. Get a full report for $19.99.' What was another 20 bucks? It was worth the gamble if it revealed something new or provided a lead. She entered her credit card number and waited for her results. But the report she eventually received was sparse with nothing more than that old address in Boston.

"That's bullshit! I paid $20 for nothing?" She called customer service to dig a little deeper and hopefully get more for her money.

"I'm sorry. I checked again. I have no record of any address in the U.S. for this man after 293 Marlborough Street," the agent said.

Christopher had not only disappeared from her life but off the search engine database.

Sadly, the one critical piece of evidence she once had – his social security number – on that ID card had been misplaced or more than likely thrown away by an insecure ex-boyfriend. She recalled scouring every last inch of that apartment before she moved out. Digging deep into the crawl space and checking every crevice, praying it got wedged in a drawer or the fold of a cardboard box or was in a corner she had overlooked. Kaisa had poured through her old notebooks, flipping through each page, but the ID was nowhere to be found. She had to accept that, like Christopher, it was gone.

Kaisa racked her brain, determined to unearth something new. What else could she remember to help cobble together this cold trail? Of the few facts he revealed, she knew his birth date. The little framed certificate from Harvard that hung on his apartment wall came to mind, which confirmed his middle name, graduate school, and major. Harvard's back-office staff had been so forthcoming years before; maybe she could get lucky again. Perhaps she could get a transcript. Her university transcript had vital information, like her social security number and home address. Maybe his would as well. She opened another tab. Kaisa looked up how to order a transcript online and was directed to a primitive portal.

Enter your first, middle, and last name:

Christopher Nicholas Morton

Which school did you attend: **Harvard Divinity**

Which year did you graduate: **1988**

Enter your date of birth: **3/20/52**

With the new information about his actual age, she had to be close.

INVALID shone in deep red letters.

Since it was January, his birthday wouldn't have occurred yet. She tried again:

Enter your date of birth: **3/20/51**

That was it? She was in. Requesting someone else's transcript was that simple. For all its sophistication and the brilliant minds it churned out, it was ironic and a little disappointing that Harvard had such a rudimentary self-service portal that was so easy to crack. At that moment, a small comfort came over her. There was some truth to what he revealed about himself, or at least kept his facts consistent with his alias.

The office was filling up with people, and it was time to get back to work. Before logging off, she requested a copy of the transcript to his attention in care of her work address.

The transcript arrived a week later, but unfortunately, it didn't have the critical information as she had hoped. The document showed his curriculum, grades, and that he passed a French language examination. There was one new fact. He graduated from Vanderbilt University in 1973. The same year she started kindergarten. It dawned on her how awkward and creepy it must have been for other students to see a sophomore escorting a 36-year-old man into her campus apartment. *I guess that's why he wasn't into the dorm scene and said he would be uncomfortable around a bunch of kids.*

CHAPTER 24
One Way or Another

Summer 2017

B efore long, another decade and a half slipped away. Kaisa thought about Christopher less and less, but every so often, something would trigger her desire to seek him out. The worldwide web had expanded its net, becoming progressively more sophisticated, opening new opportunities to help her investigate where he might be and what he might be up to. Unfortunately, the time, effort, and money she had put toward online finder services didn't yield anything more than that Boston address she already knew. No matter the search engine, from the most primitive, like WebCrawler and AltaVista, to Yahoo and Google, before it became a verb, Christopher had eluded them all.

What I could have done with a Google search 30 years ago. If only this tool were available when he disappeared, I might have been able to move on by now. If she were to begin a search at this point, where would she start? His trail was cold, along with her chances of locating him. She was sure whatever remained of that trail was covered in ice.

From time to time, Kaisa referred to her old journal, trying to make sense of his cryptic past. Over the years, the disks and devices on which she stored some of her deepest thoughts faded into obsolescence. Along with the other remnants she had acquired along the way, Kaisa invested in a 1973 Vanderbilt Yearbook from eBay in hopes of validating the transcript and remembering his face. When she received it, there was no picture of Christopher Morton, but one of a William Morton, in his place and a photo that looked like it could have been him. That just added to the complexity of the puzzle. As far as she recalled, William was his younger brother, not a twin. *Did he avoid that photo session too?*

The only bait left was her proclamation on Facebook, which she published under the "Seeking Closure" moniker four years earlier. It was probably time to take that down too. After posting her page, she checked it every day, hoping for some nugget of information. But all she got were suggested friend requests and useless notifications. She continued to sign in, albeit less frequently, until she chalked it up to yet another failed attempt and stopped monitoring it completely.

While streaming eighties music one boring morning at work, Kaisa was inspired to check in on the people that were a part of her life back then. She hadn't seen them in years but had rekindled most of her friendships, albeit only on Facebook.

One missing Facebook friend was Adam. Kaisa hadn't connected with Adam in a while. But there was no reason she couldn't check in from afar. As she recalled, his last correspondence was an answer to the email she wrote shortly after moving to her new home. Thankfully, Adam's last name wasn't that common.

Google yielded a smattering of images and results. She recognized those gentle eyes with a sweet smile peering through a heavily bearded face. She continued clicking on the search results, getting to know him all over again, or the person he had become. LinkedIn was sparse, IMDB had two credits: one as a photographer and one for a producer on a cable comedy series.

Kaisa signed into her Seeking Closure Facebook page and found his profile. There were pictures from a couple of scenic road trips to the mountains and some old photos of him and friends, but no girlfriend, wife, or family, except for one picture of his sister with her dog. It didn't look from his recent posts or status that he had anyone special in his life. Kaisa dug into his friends list. She found an old picture of Adam on his sister's page with them both standing on a dock at sunset and smiling. Sincere expressions of sympathy and condolences lined the right-side column. The date of the post was only a month earlier. Kaisa smacked her hand across her gaping jaw. *Nooooo!*

Determined to learn more, Kaisa continued surfing and searching until she landed on a link to a coroner's report. His death was attributed to blunt trauma and chronic alcoholism. Kaisa sat back in her chair and thought about him as tears welled up in her eyes. He was only 49 years old.

Through the watery blur, she noticed a red one in the message area on her dusty community page from someone named Frida, whose profile picture was an illustration of an avocado with a hand caressing the pit. *It must be someone playing a joke. This ought to be good.*

05/01/2017 1:09 PM

Hi.

I wanted to write you a message. Sorry, my English is not best. I met Christopher Nicolas Morton in Paris in July 2016. It was very hot weather, unusual for Paris. I were looking for some fresh air and possibly peace of mind, reading a book in the Tuileries gardens near the Louvre. This tall, blond, blue-eyed man in is 60's approached me to ask some direction (How can I go at the Vincennes's Park, is that really far or can I go by walk?) I explained him that no, it was too far for walk. I don't remember how, but we started to chat about living in Paris, the attacks of Charlie Hebdo and Bataclan, Donald Trump (He'll never make it, said the monsieur, we laughed about it.) We spend about two hours talking about ancient Greece (I studied ancient Greek and Latin in high school), the Peloponnese War, and Italy (I am Italian). I were a little bit sad and then that man out the blue was dragging me in a conversation so brilliant and so interesting. I forgot my sadness and we exchanged email addresses. I discovered he lived in my neighborhood though I had never met him before. We met each others several times, always having long and eclectic conversations about history, trips, Alain de Botton, Russian orthodox religion, Oprah, and drinking the horrible French coffee.

I don't asked him much about his life. He lived in a hotel, paying for storage for his books. He told me he were from

Springfield, Tennessee. I made a joke about the Simpsons. He said that he stopped watching TV before the show was on air. He loved books, had parents involved in teaching or library (I'm a librarian too). He seemed a passionate reader. We weren't dating, not in a romantic way, but I appreciate him very much. He seemed a little bit weird sometimes because he said he's been living in Paris for years and still not speaking French. (I were glad I had to improve my English). He never mentioned a job. But I didn't care and don't do now. The last I met him, it was winter, a few days before Christmas. We spent time walking in the Buttes Chaumont Park and had a coffee. He offered me a book in Italian. I were very touched and at the same time, ashamed because I hadn't nothing for him.

I didn't wrote him for months. I wrote him an email in March, but he never answered. I think he's gone. I googled him and found your page. I don't know if you can get closure now. I guess I'm trying to get closure too. I miss him sometimes. I wish I could know him better because he were one of the strangest and very interesting people I ever met. I hope I were helpful somehow, and I hope he is fine wherever he is.

Kaisa's hands were shaking. The description was Christopher personified. Every word of her broken English was a building block to a fractured past, as Christopher slowly came back to life. While she hoped what she was reading was true, she couldn't help feeling skeptical.

She closed the message and re-read the description on her community page. There were details in Frida's passage that couldn't have been extrapolated from the brief recap, like that he had tons of books or how he initiated a conversation by asking directions. Christopher even capitalized on the semester he spent at Harvard learning about Ancient Greece and the Peloponnesian War, according to his transcript. Kaisa wasn't surprised he did not have a phone number, a permanent address, or a job. He was just as transient as before. His behavior hadn't changed in 30 years.

It was then, Kaisa believed wholeheartedly that the woman who reached out to her had to be real. She knew too much for how little Kaisa put out. She envied how Frida was able to carry on long conversations on so many esoteric subjects and not in her first language.

I must write back immediately. Then she noted the date of the message. It was three months old. Maybe she had missed her window again for closure. But she had to try. Kaisa spent most of her day penning a response. That night, after a bit more editing, she sent her reply:

08/01/2017 7:38 PM

Hi Frida – You have NO idea how pleasantly surprised I was to read your post this morning. This is a separate page than my real account, so I don't check it much, and after so many years, I had just about given up. At first, what you wrote seemed a little hard to believe. But the way you described this person, like how he introduced himself to you by asking for directions, was the same way he approached me 30 years ago. I checked back to see what details I put in my page descriptor because you must understand that I was a bit skeptical in this Catfish day and age.

Everything else you explained about when you were friends brought back a flood of memories and described him to perfection. Would you still happen to have that email address? If I could connect to even what might not be an active email anymore, I think it will help me finally close this chapter. Thanks again so much for taking the time to write. I hope to hear from you. By the way, did you ever get a photo of him with your phone? Back when I knew him in the '80s, I only had a camera. When I tried to take a picture once, he got furious and made me throw out the film. - Thanks, K.

She hit send, then eagerly waited for a response, hoping she wasn't too late. Kaisa checked the Facebook page several times a day until three days later, she received a new message:

08/04/2017 3:37 PM

Hi K - or "Seeking Closure" if you prefer so. I'm very surprised to read you. I didn't think to have any answer. It is very touching your struggling to seeking closure for 30 years. I'm very curious about your story. I believe very much in serendipity. I don't have any picture, I'm sorry, we weren't that close. His reaction to you taking pictures of him were very weird! Is that guy a vampire? Is he on the run? Anyway, I will be glad to hear more details of your history. Here the email adress (I never wrote him again): cnmorton78@yahoo.com. So, good luck!

08/04/2017 7:58 PM

Dear Frida - Thank you for the email address. I don't know if he will ever respond, but it is the closest I've come to contact information in 30 years, and I appreciate it. It seems he still doesn't have a place since you said he was living in a hotel. So, it may not be as easy for him to get to a computer, and my guess is he didn't have a phone either. I'll let you know what happens. Thanks again. K

Kaisa finally had what she had been searching for – current contact information or more current than she'd been able to access in decades. It was totally plausible that this could be his email because it was one of the older providers like AOL or Hotmail.

For a second, she contemplated if she should even bother reaching out. *Would he even remember me? Here I go again, back to questioning and continually contradicting myself. How can I give up now that I'm this close?* She would contact him but give herself a day or so to write a response. No way she was going to send this long-awaited message with poorly crafted sentences and bad grammar.

That Saturday evening, she opened her Christopher Morton Gmail account. It didn't seem wise to use her personal email address and risk exposing her full name and her computer to potential viruses or hackers:

New Message

TO: cnmorton78@yahoo.com

RE: Could it actually be you?

Hello Christopher –

I set up this email account to receive responses from a Facebook page I created some years ago. I tracked your email down via someone who posted about their experience with you. I am reaching out to see if you might actually be who I think you are. We knew each other in Boston and met 30 years ago on a winter afternoon in Copley Place. I was a freshman at Northeastern. From then on, we had several steamy encounters for about a year and a half. You took off to Paris in April 1988 after Harvard Divinity School, and I never heard from you again. It's been a long time, and I am almost positive that you can't wrap your head around who I am. But I couldn't resist sending a note. If it's you, I'd appreciate a reply. Either way, it's been cathartic. By the way, the brownstone where your studio apartment was on Marlborough Street is now a refurbished single-family townhouse that sold in 2013 for $4.9 million.

Three days later, on the ninth of the month, much like the day she met him, she got an email in the form of a garbled mess. It looked like spam, with no message, just a bunch of odd characters and links and a weird email address: 'thank..you@m0.me.com.'

After some digging, she found Gmail rejects or blocks

emails that are not encrypted or come from unsecured networks. If he was living in a hotel, he was probably using a public computer. With some further online research, Kaisa figured out how to check the email's origin by its IP address. Indeed, the message originated from a server in France. It might have been Christopher, but technically she still got nothing.

TO: cnmorton78@yahoo.com

RE; RE: Could it actually be you?

Christopher - I'm not sure if you tried to contact me or I'm being scammed. I received a weird spam-like message in reply. But I wanted to give you the benefit of the doubt. I have emails on other servers, but they provide my full name, and I'm not comfortable giving that out if this isn't really you. Gmail says to send the person a link to authenticate the email, but it is way over my head and didn't seem to make much sense unless you're a developer or immersed in the digital landscape.

I have another idea. I'd appreciate it if you would contact me through Facebook. I have a profile called Seeking Closure. Mine is the one with a picture of 293 Marlborough Street. It requires a Facebook account, but it's free, and you can create one easily with fake info if you like and message me here. http://www.facebook.com/seeking.closure. You can paste the above in the browser to get to the page. Hope to hear from you soon.

Kaisa launched her email into cyberspace and waited. In the meantime, she invested one last $20 in a verification site to input her newly found data. She never heard of Springfield, Tennessee, nor had he ever mentioned it. This search service offered an outdated Springfield, Tennessee address connected to William Morton and his relative Christopher Morton, formerly of Marlborough Street in Boston. But no other relatives were mentioned.

08/09/2017 8:25 PM

Hi Frida – If you have time, I would love to hear more about your meetings. I have some questions if you don't mind answering. Did you and Christopher only contact each other via email and meet up that way? I sent him a note to the address you gave me and got some weird looking spam message in return because Google's servers blocked it. It's funny it seems even Google is telling me this is not worth reading and to let him go. - Thanks, Kai

<u>08/11/2017 11:25 AM</u>

Hi Kai, I'm sorry about that. I think he want to disappear. After all this time (8 months since I last met him), I barely think he was real. I'm glad you met him, thou, so I'm not crazy. I hope he didn't break your heart. He was a strange, charming person, but I let him go. This is life in Paris: you meet people and you loose people all the time. You know, I kind of knew that he didn't have much money. I didn't wanted him to invite me anywhere and preferred to walk in the Park. One time we went out for lunch and forgot to eat. Another time we met in a Russian Orthodox church during the Sunday mass, and then he buy me a coffee after. I hadn't any expectation. It was just to practice English with a well-educated person. I think I'll never see him again. I hope that I didn't re-opened an old wound. It is difficolt to let things go when you don't understand, mostly if you were in love.

<u>08/13/2017 9:01 PM</u>

Hi Frida-I find your story about your lunch funny, mainly because you both didn't eat, so he didn't have to pay for anything. I remember he took me to a cafe the second time we met, and he made me pay for my coffee. Almost every time I would see him, he would ask me for money. My friends told me I was nuts to keep it going. I find it interesting in 30 years that his behavior hasn't changed. You told me he lived in a hotel and still doesn't have a place of his own. Can you tell me how old you are? My guess is young because that's what he likes. But I'm sure since he was in his 60's you weren't interested in a relationship with him. For me, I was 18/19, and he was like 35 or 36 and lied that he was in his twenties, so it was a different story. I was young, foolish, and hopeful. - Thanks, Kai.

08/15/2017 9:52 AM

Hi Kai, I am so sorry to hear that he broke your heart. Did your relationship with Chris last a long time? Because it is not easy to be in a relationship, and he never pays anithing!

Having my heart broken right now (not by him), I know what it does, and I am a grown woman. I am 35 and as naïve as a stupid little girl, a magnet for weirdos. Maybe I am the closure you are seeking. Maybe it's just me, telling you through so many years it doesn't matter, he doesn't worth it. I enjoy practice my English, so thank you for your patience for reading me!

08/15/2017 9:59 PM

Hi Frida – Your English is way better than my Italian or French (I don't speak either). I enjoy reading your messages. I am sorry to hear that someone else is breaking your heart now because you seem like a nice person. I have had my share of men that were jerks too. He wasn't the only one. Now I am married for over 20 years and have two nearly grown children. A good man is out there for you.

The email address you gave me is the closest I got to contacting him since 1988. I'm glad he finally paid for someone's coffee. You are not opening an old wound. You finally gave me a way to close it. Just hearing your stories has been very helpful. Thanks - Kai

08/16/2017 1:49 PM

Kai - I'm glad to hear it. My wound is closing too. I'm spending a week in Sicily with an ex-lover, trying to see him as a friend when everybody treat us as a couple. Weird situations are definetly my cup of tea. I'm glad I helped you. You seem a sweet girl too.

Weeks later, Kaisa found herself, once again, sitting at her desk, with no reply from Christopher. She thought he might try to contact her this time since she was sure that

he had exhausted every human resource by taking advantage of so many people by now. If he recalled that innocent and trusting girl, maybe she could be enticed again to do him some favors. She was in a far better financial position than she was back then.

Kaisa brainstormed other ways to verify if she had indeed tracked him down like hacking his email. Just being able to take a peek into his private thoughts would be satisfying in some regard. Most techniques she found on YouTube looked too risky or seemed like a scam. Those she did try didn't work with the way his account was set up. There was no option to add an alternate recovery email or cell phone to gain access. The only way to get in was through his security questions:

1) Who is your favorite uncle?
   He never mentioned an uncle, so forget that.
2) Who is your favorite author?
   Good luck with that one as well.

Based on the questions alone, it was likely the email address belonged to him, but these subjects never came up in their banter. There was no way she was going to crack this code either.

Kaisa anxiously waited a few more days, hoping every time she opened her inbox, there would be that long-awaited confirmation that she was able to hunt him down. But that once-promising email address was another dead end.

It was apparent, he didn't have the balls to come back or the decency to show any remorse for his actions. *It's not true. Time does not heal all wounds, and sometimes it's not so easy to "just get over it."*

But thirty years was enough. Her physical desire for the Marlborough Man was long gone, but not her determination to end it on her terms. The unresolved fury from this age-old betrayal quickly rose to the surface. She typed fervently for 45 minutes, deleting and rephrasing until she constructed her own grand finale. This was the only way she was ever going to be able to communicate how much he hurt her and the closest thing to closure she would ever get.

TO: cnmorton78@yahoo.com

RE; RE; RE: Could it actually be you?

Christopher -

I asked myself, why did I write a friendly email to you? I figured, at first, I was more apt to get a response this way. Get more flies with honey than vinegar. But Gmail rejected your supposed response because it came from somewhere unsecure. Even Google had the insight to notify me that you're a dick who is no good for me, and what you had to say wasn't worth reading. Instead of taking a hint, I gave you a simple alternative to message me via Facebook. I even sent you a link to my page. I should know better by now that you wouldn't be bothered to figure out who I am or go out of your way so that you could apologize to me after three decades.

You're an asshole. I know that firsthand. Not only did you hurt me by disappearing to Paris so many years ago like a coward, but you decided to amplify my pain by jabbing and twisting a jagged knife into my back by leaving me with an $80 phone bill for a call to your girlfriend Rebecca in Paris when you told me you were calling your mother. All while I was helping you by typing your papers. (By the way, AT&T felt bad for me and didn't make me pay, and I'm sure this chick long since wised-up and dumped your ass). But you stole so much more from me than that. I cared so deeply for you, and you just exploited and manipulated me in so many ways.

I had a couple of message exchanges with one of your intended victims. She was smart, unlike me. But I'm sure she wasn't interested in anything sexual because YOU'RE REALLY OLD NOW!! She described you to a T. Your opening line and how you can carefully pull someone into a dialogue, lift their spirits only to destroy them later. You eluded her too, big surprise. It's fucking sad that your pathetic behavior hasn't changed in 30 years. You still are a lazy, entitled, pretentious piece of crap with no job who is a leech on society.

But I'm sure it's not so easy for you to lure your victims anymore. Beauty fades, and that is all you had, except for your endless supply of bullshit. You are practically invisible now. It must suck that you are pushing 70 with a flaccid shriveled cock. No young girl wants to suck on that like I did unless you pay them, and we've already established you're a freeloader without a pot to piss in. Yes, I found out your real age or at least the age of the alias you are pretending to be (3/20/51). One of the many lies you told me. Is/was William your brother, or is that really you? Because I could only find a William Morton in the Vanderbilt Commodore Class of 73, who resembles a younger version of what I remember of you. Did you fake that information too? At least that's where you told Harvard Divinity you went to school and graduated. Are you a sex offender? Is that why you made absolutely sure I was 18 at the time. Did you have an encounter with someone underage? Was that the court case you were involved in, and why you wouldn't let me take your picture? Who knows what was lies, and what was the truth? But it doesn't matter now. Yes. It's incredible what I have been able to uncover after all this time – God Bless the Internet.

Or maybe I'm catching you a little too late because you are so old, and you are finally dead and rotting in hell. Good. You deserve to die alone with no one to give a rat's ass that you are gone. The world is finally rid of a non-contributing lowlife like yourself, preying on the innocence and kindness of others.

This message was a long time coming, and this was far more cathartic.

Kaisa

She scrolled and scanned through it one last time after reading it over again and again. It was the nastiest of nastygrams that she had ever authored. With a satisfied grin, she pressed send. While it made her feel good to release all the pent-up anger and frustration, down deep, she couldn't deny that all she ever wanted was some sort of acknowledgment of her pain and an apology. But that was never going to happen.

Several weeks went by, and she received nothing in return. *He will never grow up or own up to what he did. I was just a tiny part of his journey. At least I got the chance to speak my truth finally, and hopefully, he read it.*

Kaisa signed into Facebook and deleted her community page. This was probably the opportune time to purge the remaining remnants of his existence. Kaisa retrieved a box from her basement marked "Anything Northeastern." She carefully sorted through each item. Among the pile of papers, photos, and notebooks was a printout of the last email she had received from Adam stuck in her copy of the children's book she gave to him that last night at Rizzoli's.

TO: kblaz1968@hotmail.com

FR: caliadamxyz@aol.com

RE: How's it going

You have reached me, which is why I haven't changed my screen name or internet provider since 1995. I am not so sure about the rise to stardom, but other parts of my life are good. I am currently living in Hermosa Beach but am looking for a new place with the love of my life in West Hollywood. She works for a local talent agency. We've been going out for about a year now, and it is as special as when we first met. Time flies when we are together.

Congratulations on your new home. I'm glad you enjoyed reminiscing while packing boxes for your move. It's fun to focus on the past, but you can't lose sight of what is ahead. Regarding your old journals and keepsakes, if memory serves me correctly, I did try to get you to use your brain instead of hormones when dealing with Christopher, but you were head over heels in lust. I would like to believe that anyone who has treated us poorly will get theirs times 10. You were a lot smarter and wiser than you give yourself credit for back then. You just got caught up with an asshole that knew how to manipulate a young girl who was infatuated. It was one of those times when emotions, feelings, and heart rule over the brain. However, certain people stick with us for better or worse, no matter how hard we try to shake them. Just know, you are stronger and wiser for having been through it. You handled the situation to the best of your ability based on your life experience, which was not as much as it is now. It is like comparing a 1996 Mustang's

performance to a 2001 Mustang. No contest.

Take care,

Adam

Kaisa carefully folded the letter and placed it back into the book. She hoped Adam was in a peaceful place, forever enjoying clouds for breakfast.

CHAPTER 25
No Reason to Even Remember You Now

Fall 2017

K aisa was on the shuttle headed toward the train station after work when she received a text:

Are you coming into the station at the usual time? I'm making chicken for dinner tonight.

It was her husband. Derek dropped her off and picked her up from the train station on the days she didn't drive, which due to traffic, was every day lately. *Hooray, chicken again.*

Kaisa grabbed her bags as she got off the shuttle. No sooner had she replied and put her phone back into her purse, it sounded with its 80's retro ring tone. "Who Can It Be Now?" She didn't recognize the number. It was probably another spam call, but Kaisa had sent out some resumes not that long ago. "Hello?"

"Kaisa?" said a voice she could barely hear over the cacophony of commuters.

"I'm sorry. Who is this?"

"It appears you haven't lost your potty mouth." The voice was vaguely familiar but with an older gravel-like rasp.

The hairs on her body stood on end. *No, it couldn't be.* Her insides twisted and tingled, and her heart skipped several beats. "Oh my God, Christopher? How did you get this number?"

"I Googled you. I feel weird just saying that."

"How is that possible? I don't think I included my last name in the email. And I didn't send it from one of my personal accounts?"

"I figured it out, remember I went to Harvard," he snickered. "Actually, it wasn't that hard. Your email said you were a freshman at Northeastern, and I only knew one Kaisa."

"But I don't understand how you got this number?" she asked.

"One of the links I clicked on had it. I just Googled your first name and your alma mater and received several sites in the search results, including pictures as a confirmation."

He must have found her online portfolio that had her resume and contact information. How frustrating that he only had to type a few words, and BOOM he found her. Unlike all those times, she searched his common name at various intervals over the years and produced not one digital trail. Kaisa had enough of an online presence that made her easily traceable. Having a unique name probably helped.

"Where are you calling from?" she asked.

"I'm in Boston, staying at one of those Air BNB's in the North End. The owners aren't home now. I swear they are one of the few people left with a landline."

"So, you're not in France anymore?"

"I couldn't wait to come back to the Trump Republic," he sneered. "It took me all those years to save up enough to fly back. My sister helped me with the rest."

"I'm not in Boston anymore. I haven't been for years," she said tersely.

"Oh, the number I called had a 617 area code."

"Well, I'm in Connecticut waiting for my commuter train home, right now."

"Why don't you take a train here instead. I'll wait for you. I'd love to see you," he said.

Kaisa looked up at the lighted sign announcing the incoming arrivals and departures. Her train was scheduled to arrive at 5:46 p.m. but was slightly delayed. The train just below on the marquis, bound in the same direction and departing on the same track, was no less than a 5:51 Amtrak headed to Boston's South Station. Those long, suppressed thoughts, scenarios, and rationalizations ricocheted through her brain. It was like he knew. It was fate or serendipity, like Frida said. "Would you believe there is a train leaving for Boston in just a few minutes?" she confirmed.

"Get on it."

"That's ridiculous. I have no change of clothes, and I'm on my way home."

"I see you haven't changed. When's the last time you did something spontaneous? You know it's still warm out. Maybe I could find a way to access another rooftop."

"Where am I supposed to find you?" she asked, shouting over screeching brakes and the rattle of incoming trains.

"When does it get in?"

"I'm not sure. I'm going to have to book a hotel room. Can I call you at this number?"

"Yes. I'll meet you at Back Bay Station, and we can go from there."

He still had his uncanny ability to diffuse her emotions and influence her decisions. *What if I got on that Boston train? It would be another adventure. I haven't had one of those in years, and I could see what he looks like now? It might be kind of cool.* She walked to the corner of the platform away from the crowd and cupped her hand over her mouth. "You know, I've wanted to fuck you for a long time," she said. "You would like that, wouldn't you?"

"Very much so, and I don't have to worry about taking away your virginity anymore."

"Yeah, that's long gone," she flirted. "Are you getting aroused?"

"It seems you haven't lost your touch on me."

Just then, a train pulled into the station. As the doors

parted open, Kaisa thought about it for a split-second and got on. As she rode, she looked out the window, thinking about her decision. When was the last time she did something on a whim and totally irresponsible? It had been a while since she had visited her favorite place in the world where she used to walk for miles without even noticing; from Northeastern down Huntington Avenue, through Copley Plaza along Back Bay's alphabetical cross streets: Arlington, Berkley, Clarendon, Dartmouth, Exeter, Fairfield, Gloucester, and Hereford. Just thinking of that journey now made her tired. She checked the Amtrak schedule on her phone. The train was expected to arrive in Boston around 8:47 p.m. She texted Chris the information.

The train pulled into the station. Kaisa got up from her seat and proceeded down the stairs to the street level. There he was, waiting to pick her up, as always.

"How was work? Anything interesting happen today?" her husband asked.

"Oh, would you believe, after a million years, I finally heard from that guy I knew in Boston? The one I told you about? He reached me on my cell phone no less."

"Wow? What did you do?"

"I told him I would meet him at Back Bay Station tonight," she chuckled.

"Are you going?"

"Ha, Ha. No, I told him I was getting on the Amtrak to Boston."

"I know you and your curiosity. You weren't even tempted to go?"

"Maybe for two seconds. I'd like to think I'm not that stupid anymore."

"What if he calls you when you don't show up."

"He won't. He'll just move on to someone else. Don't worry about it. Besides, I already deleted the number."

"You mean blocked the number."

"No, the number he found was the one I use online from that burner app."

"What's a burner app?"

"It's new. You can create a fake number using any area code that goes through to your regular phone, in case you don't want to give out your real number. I had it on my resume in my online portfolio. It's better than plastering your real cell phone all over the internet."

"It figures you would be up to speed with spy tools, being the detective you are."

"God, sometimes I do love today's technology," Kaisa smiled. "So, what did you do today?"

He told her of his work travels, that their younger teenage son was at a friend's house, and that Michael was coming home tonight from college. Yes, her husband, Derek, was the antithesis of Christopher, and that was wonderful. For one, he worked hard for everything he earned. He provided for his family and was loyal to a fault. What she had with him was not worth jeopardizing. Their love wasn't transactional but reciprocal and unconditional. There was no need to escape from this reality or second-guess herself. She had a healthy, stable, and admittedly sometimes boring life, which she discovered was a hell of a lot more satisfying than uncertainty and adventure.

Just as they turned onto their street, "Fields of Gold" came on the radio. She leaned in and turned up the volume.

"Our song is playing," he said as he pulled into the driveway.

"Let's just sit here and listen to it," she said, eyeing her love.

"That sounds good to me," he said.

"Do you think we have enough time to have a little fun before the kids come home?" she asked. "I'll go take a quick shower."

"Sure. That sounds even better."

ABOUT THE AUTHOR

Milda Leonard has been writing for years as a part of her day jobs. In 2017, she turned her passion for words into a full-time profession and now writes for a living, but mostly about less sexy subjects like automation software. Her prose have appeared in Time Magazine, multiple consumer and trade publications, and numerous corporate websites. She is a two-time Connecticut Press Club winner. Milda lives in New England with three pets, one of her two grown children, and one husband. Marlborough Man is Milda Leonard's debut novel and Boston is still her favorite place in the world. Follow Milda on Twitter @mildasmusings or contact her at mildasmusings.com

instagram
#marlboroughmantour2021

Made in United States
North Haven, CT
19 October 2021

10425748R00225